17, MORRIS ROAD

Parul Sharma grew up in small towns of India, places of unhurried pace, dusty streets and quirky people. She never stopped thinking about those places and the people, and it reflects in her work, which often uses geographic settings as quiet characters. Parul deeply admires classical writers and remains committed to sharp humour and beautiful language as her primary tools of storytelling.

Parul's other novels are *Bringing Up Vasu: That First Year*, *By the Water Cooler* and *Tuki's Grand Salon Chase*. She is an alumna of MICA (Mudra Institute of Communications, Ahmedabad) and continues to work in the research and insights space. She currently lives with her family in Singapore.

17, MORRIS ROAD

PARUL SHARMA

hachette INDIA

First published in 2024 by Hachette India
(Registered name: Hachette Book Publishing India Pvt. Ltd)
An Hachette UK company
www.hachetteindia.com

1

This is a work of fiction. Any resemblance to real persons, living or dead, or actual events or locales is purely coincidental. Certain place names have been used to retain the historicity and/or character traits in the text as far as possible.

Subsequent edition/reprint specifications may be subject to change, including but not limited to cover or inside finishes, paper, text colour, and/or colour sections.

ISBN 978-93-5731-329-2

Hachette Book Publishing India Pvt. Ltd
4th & 5th Floors, Corporate Centre,
Plot No. 94, Sector 44, Gurugram 122003, India

Typeset in Embury Text 10/14.5
by R. Ajith Kumar, New Delhi

FSC www.fsc.org MIX Paper | Supporting responsible forestry FSC® C010615

Printed and bound in India
by Thomson Press India Ltd.

Dedicated to
all of us 80s kids

A poignant tale of love and nostalgia,
written with heart.

SHAZAF FATIMA HAIDER, author of
How It Happened and *A Firefly in the Dark*

Contents

Mumbai, 2016

1

The Birthday Party

We are having a party. I dread parties. Sanjay is making his way to me, tall and lanky and bespectacled, hair falling in waves on his forehead, looking absent-minded. This is the way I must have appeared to the world all my life, as if not quite sure whether my last turn was in the right direction.

'Mum, where is the controller for the PlayStation?'

'Eh, yes, very good.'

'Mum, you are not listening.'

'I am trying to remember where I have kept the ice cream. Check the oven, won't you, darling.'

'Mum!'

'Oh, all right, okay. The controller is wedged between the sofa cushions where you last hid it from Bulbul.'

He looks at me and smiles and walks away. There has to be a mistake, see. This bundle just fell out of my uterus three seconds ago. And yes, the years felt like decades, aeons, *yug* and *yugantar* in Mummy's words, when we were living through them, but they did rush by, and now you tell me he is eighteen. Worse, you tell me he's off to live on his own in a land far, far away, where there will be drugs and guns and he will, no doubt, try to dodge them by eating pizza all the bloody time, washed down by gallons and gallons of cola.

'He will be fine,' I hear his father telling me. I would take him seriously, but he is wearing a pink birthday hat – *Happy 18th Sanjay! It's all downhill from here!* – over his now nearly all-grey mass of curls and holding a pink gin cocktail with a jolly-looking umbrella sticking out.

'What would you know?' I claim of this gangly man, who was once a gangly youth much like the one now in the throes of merriment with other young devotees of some obscure video game. This is my husband, Adil. Adil looks like a professor – he always has. Professors and cops – you can pick them out of a line-up.

'What would I know, she asks,' he grumbles but looks happy. He begins to serve the ice cream, soft dollops tumbling expertly into glass bowls. The house is too full; I can feel the walls bulging outwards. The pink gin cocktails have taken the edge off most conversations, and people are leaning against the bookshelves and sitting on our various quilted chairs, eating the mango ice cream sourced from the Parsi dairy in the neighbourhood. Bulbul, in charge of the party décor as she always is, has draped fairy lights everywhere. Popcorn has been spilt. I look at the crushed pieces on the carpets, and a lump threatens to erupt in sudden, sentimental tears again. It's been quite the theme, this spilt popcorn, right from the parties where toddlers would scream their heads off and I would slip the hassled, grateful mothers wine in paper cups and the middle-school years, where no matter how much we cooked, the food would just never be enough, and then most recently, when the high schoolers would zap the popcorn in the microwave and eat it straight from the greasy packets while I muttered helplessly in the background about how terrible this must be for their collective health. Someone brushes against me, and I come out of my reverie and look around sheepishly.

Sanjay and the other gangloids have decided to go out after this party. The *real* party, he winks at me. Bulbul is arguing with him to be taken along. I can see he is resisting half-heartedly; he wants her to come. Adil is being pushed for a later curfew. He is acting quite the disciplinarian, looking sideways at me for approval, and quite drunk now, holding his hands up in defence. Some of the parents are calling it a day, joking about old bones and heading out of our apartment now. Only a few remain. I suddenly find myself with nothing to do, and the emptiness of my hands is unbearable. I pour myself a drink and sit down, sighing like my grandmother used to, the one bad knee calling out for attention like it always does on long days like this one. I am only forty-five, I keep reminding myself.

It's the kids that age you, Gaya. Sukh's voice is in my head like it's been all these years. He didn't get to age though. Frozen in time at the ripe old age of twenty-eight. Bulbul was only one when he went, and Jo, well, she never quite recovered. None of us did, but it got better when Jo and Bulbul moved to be close to us. Sukhbir was that quintessential – *what a self-conscious word that is* – army man; his defined biceps and aviators were as real as they were an act. A *Top Gun* hangover that never quite faded, I would tell him. He didn't stick around long enough for me to tease him about a middle-aged gut and all of, well, everything that was supposed to have come along with these advancing years.

Jo is here now. She looks the same, wispy and frail, though she's strong as a horse. Sharp, too. Her latest documentary about *tadgola* – ice apple – sellers in Mumbai has been picked for a film festival in Berlin; she wants to take Bulbul along. Jo was the kind of mother who made working with a child look so smooth. She used to nurse Bulbul under her sari *pallu* while she gave talks to film students at her old institute, holding everyone in thrall. She's talking animatedly now to one of Adil's professor friends, her words trying to keep up with the speed of her thoughts, her too-big *ikat* dress billowing now and then with the gusts of wind flowing in from the open windows. Mumbai is almost bearable today.

'Jo, the plates,' Adil is calling out to her. She picks up the plates but doesn't stop talking. She needs words to make sense of the world. Every thought must be verbalized and shared. Sometimes, in the days after Sukh's death, she would call me at four in the morning, having spent the night with a sleeping Bulbul, the words collected overnight threatening to spill out of her. She talked through her grief, and we listened to her, Adil and I. That's all we did, listened and listened as she talked and put together another world for herself and Bulbul.

But we have been through that, I tell myself. That part of our life, our collective lives, is over. Bulbul is now almost seventeen, and she is confident in a way that breaks your heart, in a way that makes you want to protect her and set her free all at once. Jo's words have splashed all over her, all her life, and she has become quiet as a result, a discerning, incisive listener.

This, right here, is my world.

Sanjay and the others are headed out now. Bulbul has applied lip gloss, I notice. Even so, how much like Sukh she sometimes looks, tall and stately, strong-legged and athletic. She already towers over Jo, who is now wearing a determined expression and looking for me.

'I'll help clean up,' she offers. We smile at each other. We know she is no good at this. Her home is a tumbling mess of books and carpets and lamps. Bulbul is the one who creates order. Adil overhears and laughs, too. Jo leaves, and soon, there is only the aftermath of the gathering.

Adil and I begin a half-hearted attempt at cleaning up, stopping often to talk about the guests, complaining about what they said and what they wore and how they treated us – old, comfortable habits and patterns of much-married people.

'Will you stay up for Sanjay?' Adil asks. He has already changed into his striped shorts and his Hustle Hard T-shirt, holding a book and looking ready to collapse.

'I will.' Of course, I will. I always have. The boy has been the only stable success I have had in an obvious sort of way. All my other attempts at a career – and there has been a whole series of them – were always mild and short-lived, like a delicate houseplant that I couldn't quite grow. I tried my hand at baking, but the old ladies of Bandra are old hands at that game, and honestly, the lemon drizzle cake was just not cutting it. I tried supplying organic laundry detergent (100 per cent vegan), too, sourced from a freethinking plant-based company. I thought the hipster crowd would be all over it but turns out, even hipsters like squeaky-clean laundry that we couldn't quite deliver. Plant oils had to bow out to the commercial giants. The 'Detergent Days', as we now call them, were quite, quite depressing for me, and even now, the aroma of lemon and lavender brings on waves of nausea. I had to stay quiet and lie low for some time to recover from that. Till Rama Aunty's Original Rice Flakes Namkeen came along, but let me not get into that now.

All this to say that mothering Sanjay is pretty much all I have done by way of a job well done. I found it relatively easy to tune into that instinct that guides parents with not too many false steps along the way. He is secure in a manner that belies his age. Even Bulbul, not given to idolizing anyone except her dead father maybe, looks up to him.

It's been a while since the young people stepped out. I look at the time; only forty-five minutes have passed.

Now the phone will ring, I am sure of it. It will be the police, informing me of the accident. *They were speeding, madam ji, too many drinks.*

I shake my head and try to focus on the book I have

picked up, but anxiety is a tougher nut than that. Adil dying, Sanjay dying, my mother dying – these are the currents of fear I have learnt to live with. I try to blame Sukh, of course, dying as he did, suddenly and heroically, but I know that it runs even deeper than that.

I must have dozed off in the chair but wake up when the key turns in the lock. Sanjay is asking Bulbul to be soft as she heads to her apartment. Bulbul and Jo live on the same floor as us, separated only by six terracotta planters in the hallway. I smile at Sanjay drowsily and head to the bedroom to sleep till the milkman rings the bell at six the next morning.

2

The Phone Call

The next morning, I called Jigna *ben*, supplier of *theplas* to youth headed to foreign lands since time immemorial. Or the past twenty years, at any rate. Jigna *ben* comes highly recommended by mothers more knowledgeable in the rites and rituals of sending offspring abroad than I, a mere rookie at the game.

'Gayatri *ben*, *shu tame Gujarati bolo chho*?'

I understand enough of the language to understand that I am being quizzed on my Gujarati proficiency.

'Oh, no,' I reply, a little ashamed.

'*Koi nahin*, never mind,' she consoles me, but her disappointment is evident. I decide to quickly march to matters of business.

'So, Jigna *ben*, will five hundred *theplas* be enough for one semester? He will come back in the winter,' I ask.

Someone is on call waiting. I pause the conversation with Jigna *ben* for a moment to look at the unfamiliar number. The phone intelligently informs me it's from someone in Dehradun. The place still has a visceral pull on me, I rue to myself as Jigna *ben* drones on about her expertise at dehydrating *bhindi* and *lauki* and even *parwal*, for god's sake.

'Jigna *ben*, someone is at the door. Let me call you back?' I try to get a word in.

'... this is a busy season, I have several clients sending *bachhas* to Purdue, to Yale, to Columbia...' Jigna *ben*, Dehydrator Extraordinaire, is more conversant with American universities than the average career counsellor.

I hang up and call the number. A woman's sweet voice answers almost immediately.

'Didi, *pehchaana*?' I am immediately annoyed at this. How would I know who this is? I need a cup of coffee.

'Uh, um, no.'

'It's me, didi, Shaili!'

Shaili? From all those years ago. I find myself unable to answer, immediately at a loss for words.

'How are you, didi, how is everything? I got your number from Facebook. I saw Sanjay's pictures also. How much like you he looks!'

My number is visible on Facebook? I realize I never changed the settings after my Rama Aunty's Original Rice Flakes Namkeen phase, when I was actively soliciting namkeen-eaters on the internet. And now here is Shaili. I have a vision of her at sixteen, long-haired, ribboned braids falling below her slim waist, rake-thin body clad in hand-me-down salwar-kameez. Flowery prints on the dupatta tied around her waist. Working, always working. Tending to the dogs. Serving tea. Rubbing oil into Amma ji's arthritic legs.

'All well, Shaili, I... I can't believe it's you.'

'Khee khee khee, didi, you forgot us all after you left, *na*. My dadi died, didi.'

Her grandmother, Mauna, the gardening woman. She had been one of the fixtures at 17, Morris Road. The old woman was pushing a hundred even then, or at least it had appeared so to my youthful eyes, so it was no surprise really that she had passed through the veil.

'I am, uh, sorry to hear that, Shaili.' I truly am sorry but only a little.

'Oh no, she was fine, was working in the litchi *baag* right till the end. *Bas*, we found her dead in the morning, right under the tree. Best way to go for her.'

I would think so. She loved the trees more than life itself and had a corresponding dislike for all humankind. She had threatened to break my bones when she suspected me of picking the *mogra* flowers off the dwarf bushes, right outside the same litchi *baag* where she finally met her maker. Easy tears had flooded my eyes at her sharp words, the effortless self-pity of my years gushing through.

'Best way indeed.' I finally broke the awkward pause. I don't know how to ask her why she is calling me. I think of Jo and how she would have prattled easily through this conversation.

'Didi, the thing is, Shivendra Saab is in town. He asked about you.'

Now I really am speechless, the words stuck like marbles in my throat. I don't want to hear any of this. She has no business barging into my life like this, calling me. I am forty-five now, and I want none of this.

'He will be moving soon.'

'Where to?' I am curious despite myself.

'To Canada. To be with Bubbles didi. He is not that well now.'

'What happened to him?' Sanjay will be back soon. I should get going with my day. I really have no time for these ghosts from the past. And yet, part of me has already regressed to sixteen again.

'*Wohi*, same thing that happens to everyone in this family. They are cursed.'

I make a weak scoffing sound.

'He is going to go live with Bubbles didi in Toronto. She also lives alone. She got divorced.'

I am silent once again, hearing Shaili leak out all the inner tales of the Rawat family to me, a veritable stranger now, a ghost myself.

'Will you come to see him, didi? Koko... I mean Shivendra Saab would really like to meet you. He said so.'

'What nonsense is this, Shaili? Why would I come to meet Koko now? I am busy. You know I... I have a son. He is going to America next month. I am just very busy.'

'He doesn't know I have called you, didi, but I know he wants to see you. It would be very good for him.'

'I need to go now, Shaili.' I hang up and catch sight of myself in the Bombay Blackwood glass cabinet holding our wine glasses. I look wistful but quite attractive, I decide, straightening up a little, ironing out the easy slouch that has come in unawares. *How annoying to hear from that silly little Shaili. Always poking her nose where she shouldn't. How would I just get up and leave to see Koko? That doesn't happen, you know. Hmmm, Toronto. Roommates with his sister after all this time. Can't be easy. Also, she said he is unwell. Poor Koko.*

I instruct Sangam, the cook, on the lunch menu, expertly putting the party leftovers to use, not even having to think about it too much.

Imagine the audacity though. As if I have nothing better to do with my time. I have a lot of things to take care of, if you must know, Koko. I am busy, very busy. Swamped.

Sanjay comes home looking perturbed, raking his hands through his hair. I make a mental note to ask him about this at the right time, namely once he is fed. He hasn't changed much since he was a toddler if you ask me, the same temper when he skips meals. Oh lord, how will he cope in Georgetown? I trace the line in my mind from Mumbai to Georgetown, the miles stretching endlessly.

And also, Koko, I don't think I am brave enough to go back in time.

Adil comes home. Jo drops in for a while. We sit and talk about Bulbul's school and all that it is doing wrong. She stays back for dinner, and everyone complains copiously about Sangam's cooking while tucking in with great enthusiasm.

This is my life now, these domestic conversations, this food, this planning of the next meal. I have no time for you.

My capacity for inner dialogue is apparently endless.

'You've been so preoccupied, Gaya,' Adil finally points out after dinner. Jo and Bulbul have left, and we are watching an absurd show. I put down the coaster I've been fiddling with and realize I know nothing of the show and the story that is being quickly done away with to make way for some action.

'I know. It's that idiot Shaili, calling me out of the blue.'

'Shaili... Shaili... oh, from Dehradun.' Adil has heard all the stories. Well, not all.

'She was asking me to visit.' I look at Adil. He leans back and smiles at me, his clear eyes unblinking behind his glasses.

'Do you want to?'

'I... no, of course not. I have so much to do. Sanjay will need so much done before he leaves.'

'All right then.' His voice is gentle, and he turns to the screen immediately. How he loves these mindless action shows.

I feel a headache coming on. I hardly ever get headaches. I decide to go to bed. Sanjay is still up. I knock at his door and go in. He is sitting at his desk and has his headphones on but takes them off when he sees me.

'Come in, Mum.'

'Are you planning to stay up late again, Sanjay? You know it's so bad for your nerves.' He has had a minor nerve disorder since childhood. It was as if the world had come crashing down when we had first found out about it. The doctor had advised against surgery. Even that seems like yesterday.

'God, Mum, stop worrying so much.'

'I am sorry, but that's an occupational hazard.'

He is now fidgeting with his Rubik's cube.

'What is it, Sanjay? What's bothering you?'

'Mum,' he looks up from the cube, 'here's the thing. Do you think we can fly out from Delhi? You know, I could look up Quasi, and then we can take off. I know we have booked the tickets and all but still. She'd like that.'

I am silent for a moment. This is one of those big parenting moments that one is supposed to be prepared for. Sanjay and Quasi. I didn't see that one coming.

'It's an additional flight from here to Delhi then, Sanj.'

His face immediately shutters.

'Yeah, okay, all good. Thanks.'

I feel unsure. This needs Adil.

'I am going to check with Dad, okay? Let me see if we can change the flights. Is Qasima... Quasi... has she decided on DU as her final choice?'

'Well, she did have a perfect score, so she will get any college.' The pride in his voice is unmistakable.

'All right, Sanj, I am going to check with Dad. We will try and change the flights. Should be okay.'

I go back to the living room and ask Adil. He is quite unsurprised and unfazed.

'Ah, yes, okay. I will change the flights tomorrow.'

'Adil, do you think it's serious? This thing with Quasi.'

'To him, it might be.'

'What does that mean?'

Adil laughs as he turns off the light.

'It means that we have no control over it. Good night, Gaya.'

See how much turmoil and change there is, Koko? Do you see it? Asking me to come visit. As if.

3

The Long Flight Away

Adil Karachiwala hates goodbyes. That's just how it is. This means that I am entrusted with the task of heading to Delhi with Sanjay and setting him on his journey into the world. To be fair, it is not too much to ask for. He has handled the torturous process of helping Sanjay apply to the schools, the essays, the online seminars, the calls to alumni... Adil has done it all. But now, he is spent. And temporarily depressed. And uncharacteristically unshaven.

'Do you remember the time you went to see him off at playschool, Adil?' I ask him as I pack some last bits and pieces. Adil is comatose in bed. It would be quite funny if it weren't so heartbreaking. I have to be brave enough for both of us.

'You have never let me forget. In my defence, I was not the only dad who cried that day. Dr Hemnani wailed much louder.'

I laugh and choke a little at that memory.

'Gaya, we should take a vacation after all this,' he says, rubbing his eyes. 'It's been a lot. And we should lift our spirits a bit, right before we become empty nesters.'

Empty nesters.

'I told you we should have a fuller nest.'

He smiles and says nothing. I cannot bear to be serious about this now.

'Jigna *ben* came through with the five hundred *theplas* and whatnot. I think Sanjay's curried origins will be smelt a long way off.'

'He might sell them for spending money.'

I sit down heavily on the bed.

'It will be okay, it will.' Adil is talking to himself.

'Yes, and then I can look forward to menopause in peace.'

Adil laughs.

'You are a loon. Is it time yet to leave?'

'Yes, I want to head out now. Do you want to say bye?'

'I did. Last night.'

Adil stays up while the rest of us troop down. It is not too tearful, the farewell. Bulbul keeps boxing Sanjay's arm and finally cries when he envelops her in an awkward side hug. Sher Khan, the most beautiful cat on this earth, deigns to come down to the parking lot, too, and twirls around Sanjay's legs twice before taking off without a glance. Jo gives Sanjay a scarf with *karmanyevadhikaraste* embroidered in tiny letters at one end. It's quite spectacular, like most of Jo's gifts are.

'A belated birthday present,' says Jo with a wave and turns away to hide the droop of her mouth.

'Man, I will miss all this,' says Sanjay as we get into the Innova. I wince at this. It starts to rain, like it has almost all days of that week. *Quite fitting,* I think as I watch the droplets splash on the car. We drive to the airport listening to The Smashing Pumpkins, the one band we have listened to all these years, this boy and I. We talk a little about this and how this will be the first time in his life that he will miss Ganesh Chaturthi. He has always loved the festival, like a boy born to Mumbai must. Unlike me, who has turned away from it.

Pooran Chand takes out the suitcases at T2 and stands to attention, clearly overcome by emotion. Sanjay fist bumps him and offers a 'Later, PC, my man.'

We read through the flight. I catch sight of our joint reflection in the window as it becomes dark outside, and yes, they are right. He really does look like me, especially now, with his glasses perched on his nose as he reads.

It's late evening by the time we get out of the airport in Delhi. His flight to New York is scheduled for the next morning.

He has perked up, though. Quasi has come to the airport, glowing in the way only the very young can, not needing effort greater than her black leggings and white trainers. She seems to have grown taller, too, I notice as she bounds up to Sanjay, his grin mirrored in her eyes, her long curls bouncing around her face.

It is quite touching how happy and shy they are. I need to look away for a bit to catch my breath.

'Mum, is it okay if Quasi and I take off for a bit?' Sanjay runs to the car and asks me as I am getting our overnight luggage loaded into the boot of Suggi's car.

'Will she drop you to Suggi Masi's place?'

'Yes, she has a car. I'll be back after dinner.'

'Well then, you have my blessings, critter. Remember you have a flight to your future tomorrow.'

He grins and disappears with a quick hug.

Suggi is predictably upset when the nephew doesn't appear for her elaborate dinner.

'Hey Bhagwan, Suggi, this is too much, even for you.' I try to distract her as I take in the array of gravy and pulao and naans. Suggi is still thumping around, giving instructions to her cook in the kitchen, very much the lady and mistress of her vast Malcha Marg mansion. Her dogs are lolling about at my feet as I nurse a cocktail, waiting for dinner to finally be done and served.

'Bhai, *dekho*, we can't do the Mumbai-style vada-pav nonsense. Good food takes time.' Her words are sharper than usual. Her displacement by the young Miss Firdausi hasn't gone down very well. Suggi has to win, always and at all costs.

The food is delicious, and once Suggi has eaten, her mood also mellows.

'Young love, Gaya, young love,' she informs me over her post-dinner whisky and cigar. 'If only my life had turned out differently, I would have pursued it myself.'

I narrow my eyes at her. Suggi had never had any time for love. She had excelled right through school and had gone to law college, only to be made the youngest partner at Mehta, Mehta and Trivedi at thirty, where she still held roost many years later, lording over all and sundry like only Suggi could.

'Suggi, listen, I got a call from Shaili.' I hesitate to tell even her. 'You remember her? From Morris Road.'

'Shaili? Well, that's a name I didn't expect to hear again. What does she want?' What people want is the first question Suggi always asks, right after she has finished asking what she wants.

'She said Koko is unwell. He is planning to move to Canada.'

'Oh, good! There is nothing left in that ruddy old town anymore.'

'Wasn't Arbour House lovely? Don't pretend you didn't care about it.'

'Not with the same passion that you did! I liked it, that's true, but it was a long time ago, *yaar*. Did Koko ask Shaili to call you?'

I don't answer, but she is my sister. Her radar is in fine working form.

'I knew it! Old flame and all, *haan*?' She laughs till she splutters. Who could say that this woman could make grown men cry in court?

Finally, she settles down.

'So, what does he want, old Koko?'

'He wanted to meet me.'

'Oh, wow, check this out! Man's still got moves! So, will you go?'

I am saved by the bell as Sanjay makes an appearance, looking quite happy.

'Suggi Masi!'

'Uff, this boy, so handsome! Listen, pretty, did you eat, or will love keep us alive? You missed your favourite paneer butter masala today.'

'We were in Defence Colony market, Masi, of course, I ate.'

'Come, I will feed you halwa anyway.'

Suggi spent the rest of the evening fawning over Sanjay, so I wasn't subjected to any further interrogation on the motives and motivations of Shivendra Kumar Rawat aka Koko. I was feeling my bones ache and was permitted by the two to be let off early. I could hear them talking and laughing out in the garden late into the night. I smiled and thought of the first time Suggi had held Sanjay, right after his birth. That's pretty much the only time I saw her fall completely and blindly in love. Sanjay has received some fairly definitive luxury gifts from her, including, against my wishes, a motorcycle, but her decoding of my son goes far beyond just spoiling. She gets him in ways that Adil and I cannot, free of expectation and judgement. If it hadn't been for Suggi's insistent generosity and Sanjay's scholarship, it would have been near impossible to make the funds for this impending American education. I stare at the blank ceiling of Suggi's guest room till, finally, my eyelids start drooping.

Suggi leaves for Panipat early the next morning for a meeting with some sugar baron, and Sanjay goes to meet Quasi yet again. I eat a solitary breakfast of toast and tea and then call Adil.

'All good with the shipment?'

'Yes, we need to leave for the airport soon. He should be here any moment now. Are you all right?'

He sighs dramatically and laughs but doesn't reply.

'Poor, poor Daddy. Here is Sanj now, speak to him.' Sanjay comes in, looking a bit flustered, and unexpectedly, Quasi follows. Apparently, the young person had decided to wave off Sanjay herself. I feel half a surge of resentment and quickly quash it. It really is time to cut the cord and let him loose.

As it turns out, it was a good decision. Under Quasi's quietly watchful eye, I am able to hold myself in check at the airport and behave quite admirably given the circumstances, moistening my eyes in an appealing manner rather than throwing myself on the airport floor and beating my chest. Sanjay ambles off quite confidently, headphones around his neck, grey sweatshirt hanging loosely off his lean frame and turns around once to give us a wave. The West has got my boy.

'He's going to be fine, Aunty,' says Quasi, rocking on her toes and heels, hands in pockets. We are once again standing outside the airport, waiting for the cars. I nod at her wisdom.

'What are your plans now?' she asks.

'My plans?'

'I mean, Sanjay says you were a stay-at-home mom. That's pretty cool. What's next for you?'

'I… uh, I don't know.'

'There's no hurry. My mum runs an NGO; they work with tribal artisans. I could hook you up with her. Oh, here comes my ride. Bye for now, Aunty.'

'Bye.' I wave weakly.

What are my plans? What am I going to do next?

I am quite stumped. Am I to work with tribal artisans? How are they different from non-tribal artisans?

My phone rings. Dehradun again? Oh, good lord, how terribly infuriating is this Shaili?

'Yes?' I answer, virtually exploding with self-righteous indignation.

'Hey there, Gayatri.' I hear a voice, followed by a small laugh.

It's Koko.

4

Koko, Now

'Koko! I thought it's Shaili. How are you? Where are you? How is your health?' Words are tumbling out of my mouth in a rush. Decidedly inelegant. This is not how I ever imagined myself in the event of running into him again. In my mind, we reunite at a dimly lit café in Prague, where I happen to be because I am uber successful and am being felicitated for my immense success. In these imagined reunion scenarios, Koko looks at me with a deep sense of loss, admiring my classic beauty, untouched by time, and beseeches my forgiveness for all wrongs – imagined and real – done to me. Of course, I am graceful in the face of his apologies, looking even prettier as I forgive him.

'Oh, you know. Age and this and that. I am full of aches and pains these days.' He laughs a little. Tall, lanky, brown-haired Koko, the one who turned all the eyes. Self-effacing, charming Koko in his school blazer, the shiny badge proclaiming 'Sports Captain'. Koko who spoke such anglicized Hindi, couldn't say *akhada* and *kevda* and *dahi-bada* without softening the harsher syllables.

'But let's not get into that, Gayatri. Shaili says you refuse to come here.'

'Uh, that is not what I said exactly.'

Classic Koko. Straight to the point and completely oblivious to my life, built carefully and painstakingly. Speaking to me as if we had spoken every day these thirty years. We had spoken. He had called me after Sanjay was born. And, oh, before that, hadn't he called me at the time of my wedding, too, the idiot? And he had visited Suggi once in her early years in Delhi, where they had got riotously drunk and evaded all meaningful conversation so that Suggi's only response to all my quizzing had been – *I really can't remember*.

'I can't come right now, Koko. I have a lot of commitments here.'

'Oh? Like what? Come now, you can tell me.'

'Um, I just sent my son abroad. Like fifteen minutes ago. I am still standing outside Delhi airport.'

'But he has left safely, yes?'

'Yes.'

'That's good. So, what will you do next?'

'I don't know. Why does everyone keep asking me that?'

'I wish I could see you one last time, that's all.'

'Don't be dramatic,' I say, but a sudden thought strikes me. 'What exactly is wrong with your health, Koko?'

'Oh, it's this autoimmune thing. It's affecting my kidneys and liver and so on. I am not dying. Not right away, anyway.'

It takes me a moment to comprehend. Jo's aunt had

had cirrhosis after a lifetime of starting her day with a large vodka and tonic. She had met a rather premature end. Her family has been full of these characters.

'Shit, Koko, I am sorry to hear that.'

'Sorry enough to come visit? Ask your husband.'

I bristle immediately at that, exactly like he intended me to.

'I don't need to ask anyone.' He laughs.

'Then come. It will be great. We will go to Ellora's for pastries and drive to FRI.'

'Do people still do that?'

'We can find out. It would be nice to catch up before I leave Doon once and for all. My intentions are honourable, madam.'

'Shut up; let me think. I will call you back.'

I hang up and look around. Cars everywhere. People seeing off people. So much movement.

Technically speaking, I really have no commitments. Sanjay has gone off to college. Adil had merely mentioned a holiday. I have no pets, not since Beavis. I shake my head. I am not being rational. What good will it do to visit a childhood memory anyway? Nostalgia is overrated, and in any case, it will only be heartbreaking to see the crumbling remains of what was once beautiful. Doon would be depleted, a shadowy ghost.

I sigh. Who am I fooling? Of course, I want to go back in time. Not for Koko. Not for Shaili. Not for the person I was while I was there.

Just for Arbour House.

17, Morris Road.

It did have a piece of my heart, that colonial

bungalow with its columns on the façade holding up the roof, built by some nameless craftsmen of the past, their spirits still lurking in its corners. Lush with fruit trees – litchi, mango, jackfruit. Home to the birds of the hills – the *bulbuls*, quarrelsome parrots and the orioles. Flowering shrubs everywhere.

Adil calls just as I turn into Suggi's driveway. He is still at work and wants to know if our firstborn has been packed off to distant lands in a timely fashion. I tell him about Koko's call.

'Oh, is it?' he says. 'And how is my buddy Suggi doing?'

'Adil, I am telling you of another man taking undue interest in your wife. You could show some emotion.' I am quite annoyed at how benign Adil thinks this is. I could be planning to take off with Koko, elope to Canada and start a maple syrup business.

'Oh, god, Gaya, please. I will not react to some youthful romance that happened decades ago. Do you think you could get me *ghevar* from Haldiram's. 'Tis the season.'

'*Ghevar*?'

'Yes, get *mathri* also. And get the pickle that I like.'

Well, this is infuriating. Elvis has barely left the building before I am being written off for the retirement home, emerging only to do the *mithai* shop run. I ask the driver to turn the car around and head to Haldiram's at the nearest mall. I am anyway loath to mope about in the empty house that speaks of Suggi's solitary, if opulent, inhabitation at every turn.

Haldiram's is noisy and crowded and soothing to

my frazzled self. I look around at the happy people so focused on food that their whole existence seems to have truncated to their plates of *kulfi falooda*. I, too, order *chole bhature* to settle the world order and to join this freakishly happy cult. To be sure, by the time I settle in at a corner booth and on my fifth bite, I am in the throes of some intensive self-therapy. I jot down some critical points on my phone.

What has upset me?

It is a combination of

1. My son leaving the shores and therefore feeling at odds.
2. The appearance of Qasima Firdausi: indicating my son is growing up and away from me.
3. Koko's call, ruffling my hitherto unruffled feathers.
4. Adil's nonchalance to point number 3, indicating that he is taking me for granted.

I drink my green lime soda, a concoction created solely to bring on a coronary, surely. But what a way to go.

What do I need to do?

1. I am feeling a lack of self-worth and need to figure out what to do next with my life.

At this, I am quite flummoxed. What am I to do next? Another failed business? Well, that is one option.

Or I could just take a break.

Give myself a chance at recovering from this phase before moving on to the next.

Maybe Koko's invitation is exactly what I need.

Over a plate of jalebi and *rabri*, I make up my mind and firm up my plans. I will take some well-earned rest at Dehradun, revisit Koko and my old haunts and then I will spend a week at Mussoorie, maybe get one of those Airbnbs Sanjay and co. were always taking up for their trips. A charming, Raj-era bungalow with a lush, green lawn. I find myself cheering up at the thought.

I realize it will be my first solo vacation in eighteen years, maybe more. The more I think about it, the better it sounds, like such plans do.

It is rather sad, in a way. Then I order a piece of *ghevar* and eat it all on my own.

Years of mothering have made me efficient in a way that is difficult to explain. I organize things quickly and painlessly. Even this sudden solo trip is so easy to plan. I just have to pretend it is for Sanjay. I brush away quick tears at that.

I cancel my flight back to Mumbai, message Koko that I will be arriving and Adil that I will not. I call the car company and ask them to send a car the next morning. This needs to be a road trip. Delhi to Dehradun. Six hours of thinking time. I review my wardrobe contained in my suitcase and decide that the standard jeans and polo shirts that I have been surviving in all these years will have to do for this trip as well. I bravely decide to text Suggi later, not feeling quite strong enough for one of her cross-examinations. That doesn't deter me from taking a pair of her new trainers, though, bought on some trip abroad from the looks of it and quite expensive.

We are all grown-ups here.

5

The Long Road Home

'B*um bholenath*,' declares the driver as we set off early the next morning.

'Yes, let's go, Somnath ji.' I put on my sunglasses, and we are off.

The roads are bumpy, to begin with. I decide there is a metaphor there. I look at Roadways buses travelling alongside on the same road. How long has it been since I got into one of those? This is turning out to be quite a trip down memory lane already.

Somnath ji is mercifully silent, his earphones plugged in and the car's stereo playing Bollywood songs from an indeterminate era. '*Baharon phool barsao*', it keeps intoning.

Our first stop is nearly two hours later at one of those roadside dhabas next to the highway that are big on sustenance and low on aesthetics. I drink my tea leaning against the car and look at the group of dusty-looking bikes with strings of Buddhist prayer flags draped across the handlebars. Sanjay had gone on a bike trip to Ladakh once and had come back changed in ways even I couldn't grasp. Maybe I should go, too. I drain the *kulhad* of its tea, and we are off yet again, Somnath ji not being the loitering kind.

Ghaziabad, Muradnagar, Modinagar, Meerut, Muzaffarnagar, Saharanpur, Roorkee. Towns of my youth. Pure Vaishno dhabas line the roadside. The road itself hasn't changed much, each bump reminding my spine that I could have taken a flight.

Somnath ji comes out of his reverie every now and then to inform me of the specialties of each town, probably taking me to be some kind of outsider.

'This is called the sugar belt of India; these are all sugarcane fields.'

'If we had taken the other route, we would have crossed Baghpat, which is famous for its kharboojas.*'*

'Shamli is known for its bricks; next time you should take that route.'

And then, every now and then, he does a half-turn and tells me with something resembling pride, '*Flyover-work*.'

'Ji Somnath ji,' I keep mumbling.

It is only when we hit the foothills that I feel deep in my belly what those years had meant to me. It is a spasm I haven't felt in the longest time. All mountains do this to me. The Himalayas do it a thousand times over. There are trees on either side now. Will I spot the *deodars* soon?

'Devbhoomi,' declares Somnath ji as we near Dehradun.

My back hurts but not too much. All the years of *bhujangasana* and *adho mukha shvanasana* – cobra pose and downward dog, if you please – have at least kept the old spine in working order.

We stop at a temple, cross a tunnel, and there we

are. In the town. I try not to blink at the changes, telling myself that destruction is but a natural course, but still, in the eye of my mind, it is so much greener, so much more untouched. A green hill town with wide, tree-lined roads. Isn't this the reason I haven't been back, the reason I avoid going to the hills altogether, because I know I cannot find in my heart the justification for all this awfulness?

At least Mumbai doesn't pretend that she cares.

'Madam, please confirm the address,' Somnath ji turns around and asks me as we weave our way into the city.

I fumble for a reply but cannot for a moment remember where I want to go. This town is a stranger to me, has turned its back on me in the years that I have been away, the trees gone, cars having taken their place, and oh, the noise. I hadn't thought of just how much louder it would have become. I can't place myself in this place. No wonder Koko wants to move. What happened to that one-horse town that we had once called home? I don't want any of this. I want out. I want back.

If I just shut my eyes tight enough and think back hard enough, for a moment I can believe it is 1985 again.

Dehradun, 1985

6

The Very Crabby Mrs Boyce

We had been in Dehradun ever since we were children. Papa worked in the Forest Department in Dehradun. He was a portly man with a kind smile and large, wide-set eyes with thick, curling lashes that both Suggi and I had inherited. We did not get government quarters, needing to move often. Doon was an impossibly fertile little town then, with litchi trees everywhere, full of large houses that had been built during more prosperous times. With mounting expenses and no clear source of income, the landlords were often forced to let parts of their expansive houses out to middle-class tenants like us.

Mrs Boyce was one such landlady, the owner of a sprawling villa off the road that led from Doon to Haridwar. She ran a sewing school for women and was in Suggi's elegantly worded opinion, 'batshit crazy'. Suggi was very nosey even back then, and she had spied on Mrs Boyce long enough to know that she had a collection of greeting cards dating back to 1936 with Navroz wishes scribbled for *'Dearest Jamshet, Mehr and Yasmin'.*

'She spends hours going through them, talks to

herself, too,' Suggi had informed me, calmly eating an apple. I felt a little sorry for the lonely Mrs Boyce but quickly remembered how she had screamed at me for daring to pick just two of her beautiful yellow dahlias for my beloved teacher. How was I to know that the eccentric Mrs Boyce knew exactly how many dahlias were growing at any given moment in that wild, thick, tangled bunch?

For two hours every evening, women of different shapes and sizes trooped into one of the many, many rooms of Mrs Boyce's house, where she would instruct them in the art of collar and cuff making. She informed my mother that she should enrol both her daughters in the class, too, but Suggi threw such a fit at this that the plan was dropped with alacrity and never mentioned again.

Money was tight that year like most years. We rented only two rooms in Mrs Boyce's house - one was the living room where Suggi and I studied in the evenings and camped on the divan at night and the other was our parents' bedroom that also doubled as some sort of a storeroom where my mother kept all the things that she had no use for but could not bear to be parted with - old stone *sil batta*s, piles of *Grihshobha* magazines, cross-stitched tapestries.

One of Mrs Boyce's unending rules was that we couldn't touch or smell or feel any of the many plants in her large garden and elsewhere in the sprawling house. Suggi insisted that she didn't want us to see them either and would make a great show of closing her eyes and stretching her arms out to walk blind in Mrs Boyce's presence. Mrs Boyce, in turn, would give us an earful that would have easily shamed less seasoned truants.

This rule was torture for me, born infatuated with flora and fauna. I would look longingly at the swaying *deodars* and litchi trees, the garden flush with dahlias, roses, asters, gerberas and cosmos, mynahs and *bulbuls* calling from the treetops, even an occasional monkey swinging rapidly past. Mrs Boyce was the giant, and we were the children forever at the periphery of her coveted garden.

'Gaya is the reason we came to this town,' Papa would often say, affectionately patting my head. Mummy had become pregnant with me within a few days of their move to Doon. Since I was a toddler, I liked to walk around amidst the trees. I grew a hedge of sweet peas at eight and adopted my first kitten that same year. 'She couldn't have survived Muradpore,' Mummy would comment with a sigh, though, of course, she wished she was back amongst her extended family in that 'armpit of the armpit of the world' as Suggi put it.

'Uff, what a pain this Mrs Boyce is,' Suggi now complained to Mummy. *'Don't do this, don't go there.* Yesterday, she told me I was not to talk to Inder and gang from over the hedge because it disturbs her creepers. What nerve!'

Mummy mumbled something about not wanting to anger Mrs Boyce if we could help it. Mummy was a great one for stability and normally disliked the unfamiliar. The rent that Mrs Boyce charged was just about affordable and moving would cost a lot. My father was the only one who earned a living, and Dehradun, like most hill towns, was turning out to be more expensive than they had accounted for.

We had been living in this house for just over a year. The year had already brought with it many changes.

For one, Suggi, a grade ahead of me at school, had won a scholarship to Brighton, a very elite institution, and had moved that year, setting us apart for the first time ever. As was Suggi's wont, she had quickly impressed the teachers with her sharpness in class, decided who she wanted to be friends with and had also selected the boys who would be allowed to pursue her in the last two years of school before she trampled on their collective heart and took off for Delhi University. If there ever was a girl with a plan, Suggi was she. Sometimes I feared for her. Was it acceptable to be this confident, this self-assured about one's good fortune? So far, though, Suggi showed no signs of backing down, bulldozing down every last shred of self-doubt with her keen grit and ability to make her mark.

In the meanwhile, I plodded on at our old missionary school, where they had converted old stables into classrooms by covering them with tin sheets. It would get terribly hot in the sunny summer afternoons, but by and large, I liked the school, its quiet pace matching mine. The genial, old headmaster would roam the corridors looking for troublemakers but didn't quite know what to do with them once he caught them. His deputy, Mrs Thapa, though, was a hawk. Her daughter, Nirupama, had been my best friend since we were five. Niru lived in a house near the school, assigned to her mother. We would walk home together; her mother would finish her shift at school a couple of hours later. Her father served in the merchant navy and would bring such exciting gifts for her on his trips home that my insides would twist with envy. Niru said she would trade the gifts to have her father around. I found this unfathomable, given that Papa was always around and had never been away for even a day.

The only reason we had been sent to this mission-run school was because it was close to our home, and given my 'health problem', accessible to my mother if an episode occurred.

My health problem, as it were, was basically an unexplained childhood breathlessness, in which I felt that I would die during an episode but invariably didn't. It wasn't asthma, it wasn't *anything* really, but it did mean that I couldn't participate in any intense sports. This wasn't too bad as, though I was quite tall, I wasn't even remotely athletic and quite slightly built, my skirts often hanging off my frame. I liked to read a lot and lacked Suggi's burning ambition. I was also probably too laid-back to envy my sister. Sometimes, just watching her would tire me out. It was infinitely more pleasurable to dress in my father's faded Madras checked shirts, lean against the old peepul tree, one that had seen it all, stories contained within its rings, and read a dog-eared detective novel through the dappled afternoon, Sahib the cat napping at my feet, my toes rubbing behind its ears.

Suggi, the picture of good health, good looks and good height, wore scandalously short skirts for those times, drove around on our father's scooter, played basketball and was already placed in her new school's relay team. She would cycle to a nearby ground to train most mornings and come home to eat and change before heading to school. In fact, our exit from Mrs Boyce's was triggered on one such morning when I woke to a clatter and Mrs Boyce's screams. I followed Mum as she ran out to check on Suggi, and sure enough, there she was, knees bleeding, white shorts torn, her twisted bicycle looking on innocently at the surroundings and a couple of large planters now in pieces, the smashed plants painting a forlorn picture. Mrs Boyce looked like she was on the verge of a stroke, her face rapidly changing colour.

'See what you have done, see! My poor plants! You always cycle so fast, you stupid girl!'

'No, I don't.' Suggi was shaken and red-faced. 'It was Drippy. She just came out of nowhere and startled me. I crashed trying to save her.' Drippy was Mrs Boyce's beloved bulldog, thus named because of an unfortunate incontinence disorder.

'It's not Drippy's fault. You destroyed my plants. Who will pay for them, huh, who?'

'*Bhabhiji*,' Mummy smoothly entered the conversation. 'I am sure this can wait till we dress Sugandha's wounds.'

Nobody ever called my sister Sugandha. This was serious.

It was clearly an ace move because it shamed Mrs Boyce into silence. Mum took the episode unexpectedly hard. We heard her talking to Papa that night about wanting to move.

'That woman has no *insaaniyat*.'

Suggi and I looked at each other in delight. Having no *insaaniyat* was the greatest insult Mummy could hurl at anyone.

'It was a one-off.' Papa was trying to take a low-key approach to this. 'Suggi is all right. No harm done. Gayatri has board exams this year. Does it make sense to disturb her?'

'No, I don't feel that Mrs Boyce would take care of the girls if the need arose.' Mummy was being uncharacteristically unequivocal about this. A bit of the mama bear in her had been poked. I think even Papa saw that and backed down.

'I think it's going to blow over,' said Suggi, examining her newly acquired bruises, now a multitude of blues and purples.

'Naah, I think Papa will have to look for a new place,' I said, diving deep into the warmth of the *razai*.

7

Arbour House

I was right. Papa started making enquiries about a new place to rent. Every evening he would come home and tell us about the places he had seen and how expensive they all seemed to be. Doon had been a sleepy, out-of-the-way town for the most part, nestled in the foothills of the Shivaliks, marking its place as the gateway to Mussoorie, becoming congested only over the past few decades, reluctantly watching its own rebirth as a bustling, noisy everytown.

'Today I will go and see Arbour House, that place on Morris Road. The broker says there is a small flat they let out in the estate. Must be horribly expensive but no harm in seeing it.'

Arbour House! I hugged myself in delight.

I had seen the place often when I used to take a tonga to school, sharing the ride with two other children and Suggi. The tonga would clip-clop past many beautiful colonial bungalows on the tree-lined Morris Road, rainwater drains running on either side of it. I would always look forward to the turn from where I could catch a glimpse of the house that had intrigued me since I was five. On the face of it, it was like any other estate on that road. And yet, it called to me and the five-year-old imagination housed within my tiny heart.

A hedge separated the estate from the road, and an old, worn-out, rusted gate sat in the centre, a broken lock hanging uselessly from a hook. An old stone address plate was set into the boundary wall.

Arbour House, it said, 17, Morris Road. And then below that – 1915.

The gate opened out onto a long driveway with litchi orchards on one side and what appeared to be a large garden on the other. There was never enough time to see the house clearly, but I knew that in there was a bungalow with a red gabled roof, built to stand the test of time. I would often lean out from the back seat of the tonga, trying to get a longer look, but the Raj-era house would vanish from sight before I could. In the eye of my mind though, I could see everything clearly. The bougainvillea shrubs bursting forth onto the road. The sal and *deodar* trees. The thin barbed wire that separated the litchi orchard from the rest of the estate. The creepers that grew everywhere and could not be contained. The small shrubs of *bela* and *mogra* lining the driveway that wound up to the porch where the vintage cars must stand waiting. A heady floral scent always in the air. The grass shoots and tiny mountain flowers that crept out from between the gaps in the small bricks that lined the driveway. And everywhere you looked, just splashes and splashes of myriad shades of green, just so much shiny green.

I had stopped taking the tonga to school when I turned ten and started cycling instead. But these past two years, I would just walk, taking a narrow alley with man-high hedges on either side that led straight to the road where the mission school stood. Walking was better; it gave me time to run my hands through the leaves, stopping to peer through them to observe the squirrels that sat up and watched me carefully. But it also meant that I hadn't seen Arbour House in a while. I wondered if it had changed, if the wheels of progress had run over it, trampling over its quiet beauty. Too many Enid Blytons had left something of a mark on me, and although I was almost sixteen that year, it took my imagination little effort to romanticize Arbour House such that it became a place of intrigue, holding within its old walls untold stories.

What would it be like to live there? It was too much for my fifteen-year-old heart to hope for. I moved in lower and lower into my *razai* and looked for Suggi for some warmth. I dreamt of Arbour House that night, sitting at the grand piano in the stately drawing room and playing on it, for some reason, my school song.

Within a week of that dream, it turned out that the flat within Arbour House could be rented, the rental only marginally higher than what we paid Mrs Boyce. Rajendra Chachaji, Mummy's uncle, the one who was settled in Nigeria and doing quite well, sometimes used to send her money and chose that very month to do so. Mummy considered this an omen and decided to sign the lease. My joy knew no bounds, though I tried to tell myself to contain my thrill. I probably wouldn't be allowed to explore anything.

'Same rules again,' said Papa, looking at Suggi as he

announced the news, trying to be stern. 'The plants and so on are sacred. The dogs are sacred. The cars are sacred. Stay away. Do not mess around.'

'Man,' said Suggi. 'I need to get rich. I bet I could give orders like landed gentry. Birju *kaka*, *chai lao*. So-and-so, *mere pair dabao*.'

It just seemed pretty incredible to me that they let out parts of their beautiful, ancestral house to tenants.

'If I had a house like that, I couldn't bear to let strangers come traipsing all over it. I am just amazed that they do this,' I said, thinking of the delicate beauty of the place.

'Of course they do,' said Papa. 'I mean, look at the size of the estate. Must cost a bomb for the upkeep, don't you think? The plumbing, the electricity, the water bills. They have sold off and rented out a lot of that estate, except for the main house and the gardens, of course. You will see.'

Mrs Rawat was to be our new landlady. Her husband was Balbir Rawat, whose late stepfather, a Colonel Luthra, had been titled during the British era. I was very impressed by this till I heard Papa mutter something about *deshdrohi*, etc., and the shine came off.

'I've heard they hid British soldiers in the dungeons of Arbour House when the revolutionaries came looking for them.'

'There are dungeons in Arbour House?' I clapped my hands in glee.

'Uff *yaar*, please, Gaya.' Suggi had no patience for my flights of fancy. 'When do we move, Papa?'

'Beginning of next month.'

'What's our new place like? Is it bigger than this one? Do I get my own room?'

Papa sighed.

'It's the back of the house, *beta.* Probably were servant quarters at some point.'

I looked at Papa to check if he was joking but couldn't tell. He didn't seem to mind it at all.

Before we moved, Suggi was made to visit Mrs Boyce with two new planters as parting gifts.

8

Moving In

The day after we moved in was a Sunday. I had always been an early riser, possibly because of the ruckus that Suggi would make getting ready for basketball practice. I got out of bed at about six and put on my tracks and sweatshirt to go for a walk. It was finally time to meet this old friend. I closed the door quietly behind me and stepped out into the cool morning light. I walked right up to the main gate and then turned around, taking everything in through the light mist of the morning. Once upon a time, there had been guards in the sentry boxes at the gates, I was told, but not for many, many years. Everything had a run-down tint to it. I looked at the *mogra* shrubs, stopping to pick up the fallen flowers and taking in their heady fragrance. I knew already that there was an ill-tempered female gardener who hobbled around the estate and hated anyone who was not a Rawat or a Luthra. I stopped to stare into the dark, dark litchi groves, inviting me in. Not a trace of sunlight could enter that thick leaf cover. There must have been thirty, perhaps forty trees in there. Maybe I could steal in when no one was around, see what lay beyond the trees? Once the rains came, the raw green fruit would turn luscious pink. The orchard would be given to a contractor, who would harvest the fruit. Hundreds of houses did that during litchi season and fruit sellers would sit right outside these houses selling their wares in woven baskets. I walked down the driveway, now looking the other way, where the garden stood. There were trees I could name – the Ashoka, mango, massive jackfruit trees, old neem ones. Calendula, roses, *gurhal*, marigold, and for some reason, a number of *Ficus bonsai* plants. I couldn't ever take to the idea of bonsai though. Nature was supposed to run wild, free, abundant. What sense did it make to curtail things? I spotted a *semal* tree; some of the fruit had fallen, burst wide open, forming red bloody splotches on the ground. Such a graceful, five-petalled fruit and dignified even at its end. In time, the tree would send off its seeds in cotton balls. There were mulberry bushes, the *shahtoot* berries a little green still. Bunches and bunches of red ixora and white gardenias hung around the garden. What was that – passionflowers? Tiny pink and red pentas flowers. Chrysanthemums, which Mummy called *guldaudi*. And of course, the ubiquitous *pothos* climbed most of the walls around the garden, not needing much. At some point, I would need to climb those walls to see what lay on the other side. For that is who we are at fifteen, ever curious about what lies on the other side of the wall.

This was not the only garden. There seemed to be another, a kitchen garden perhaps, set towards the back of the house, hedged by a tamer-looking fence, sweet peas growing at the edge.

I closed my eyes for a second, pretending to be not just a quasi-trespasser out to take a quick look but the rightful owner of the beautiful scene stretching out in front of me. In that deeply meditative moment on my first day at Arbour House, the words I heard myself say – *There is nowhere in the world I'd rather be.*

I walked down the driveway towards the house, now smiling to myself. I stood under the porch, wedged between two cars, one of them a half-timbered and rather splendid-looking machine that took up most of the space, the other one a Morris Minor, and now I studied the house. The single-storey building was what the locals called a *'Britisher times ka bangla'*, built on a raised level, some steps leading up to it. A very deep veranda wrapped itself around the structure and was speckled with many plantation chairs with long arms that could be put to good use by resting one's legs on them. Next to them stood a glass-topped coffee table made of cane. Some China palms grew large in terracotta planters. The *chik*s made of woven bamboo that must be pulled down at noon to protect the veranda from the midday sun had been rolled up and tied for now. The walls of the house were covered with glass-paned windows. There was a door that must lead into the central hall. Then a reddish-brown mass, so far hidden behind the cane chairs, got up and lumbered towards me.

'Oh hello, hello,' I breathed and bent down to scratch his large ears. He looked up at me with his drooping eyes and yawned.

'So beautiful, so beautiful. Do you know how

beautiful you are?' I queried of the giant Saint Bernard, stroking his ears and his neck. He heard me out patiently and accepted my compliments, looking at me out of his deep, wise eyes. Then he decided to go back to his spot right behind the chair and get some more sleep. I could see he was ageing; he walked slowly and hesitated slightly before negotiating the three steps that led up to the veranda, possibly a sign of arthritis.

'At least tell me your name,' I whispered. Never mind, it was a matter of time before I would find out. What an utterly gorgeous creature, though. I watched him amble back.

I walked on, hoping that at some point I would be able to see the inside of the house.

It was clear that this house, with its gabled roof, had been a sahib's place of dwelling, not geared for serving the community but clearly meant to lord over the natives. Many columns rose from the veranda to hold up the high ceiling.

Arbour House was set pretty much left of centre of the estate. Parts of it that had been lopped off now held boundaries of other houses. Papa had told us that a part of the estate had been sold off to the Balakrishnan family. They had twins the same age as us and had lived in America till recently. Another piece of land that had been taken off belonged to the large Sandhu clan. There seemed to be many children there, and it seemed like a very promising household, full of raucous sounds and much activity.

I turned homewards, making my way through the lines upon lines of areca palms and gigantic rubber

The Rawats were cordial and distant, and while at the time they appeared positively ancient to me, much like my own parents, they couldn't have been older than in their forties. Nina Rawat was quite dashing but not particularly domesticated from what I could tell. She was the only daughter of a retired ICS officer, a relic of a man who lived with his wife in Darjeeling and was, all told, quite a terror. Nina Rawat had been thoroughly anglicized. She spoke Hindi with a decided accent, and the couple ate what we considered foreign food – boiled soups and baked custards, possibly accounting for their spare frames. Our own parents, though of similar age, looked decidedly run-down by comparison. The two Rawat children went to an elite boarding school, which by an unwritten law, all Rawat youths apparently had to attend. Balbir Uncle and Nina Aunty themselves had apparently graced the institution in their time. Nina Aunty went riding every morning and drove about rashly in her beat-up old Ambassador, one of the three car brands available in India at the time, and never parked with Balbir Uncle's prized old beauties. Sometimes, she would lounge about reading romance novels, the dogs lolling about at her feet but would soon lose patience and call out to Shaili to bring her the car keys and take off for the club to play a game of tennis or bridge. By contrast, Balbir Rawat was a quiet man. His vintage cars were his great love, and he spat and polished them every Sunday with great care. All in all, the Rawats seemed to live in an idyllic cocoon.

'They don't work, do they?' I whispered to Suggi one Sunday morning, a few days after we had moved in, watching Balbir Uncle going at his cars again as I hoisted up the packet of bread and eggs that we had been sent off to get.

'Nah, of course, they don't work. It's all a very princely estate still,' replied Suggi.

We were about to pass Balbir Uncle in awkward silence. He smiled beatifically at us and then suddenly spoke, 'I say, do you girls like books?'

'Yes,' Suggi replied as she always did when it was just the two of us. I nodded along furiously.

'Well, we have a lot of books inside. Koko and Bubbles show no interest, but maybe you will like them. Come and take a look whenever you want. I'll tell Nina.'

Mummy was of course insistent that we needed nobody's *ehsaan*, but Papa was all for this plan to take up permanent residence in the Rawat library.

'Never let an opportunity to read books pass you by.' He offered us another aphorism and looked quite pleased. Both Suggi and I were avid readers. Suggi had a tremendous memory and could retain entire passages in her head. I was likely to read the classics over and over again, uncovering them in layers. 'Yes, you must go. Go today itself.'

At five that evening, we kept our appointment with the library and turned up at the house. Nina Aunty was sitting in the veranda. Guests were often received in this area, and I would sometimes see Nina Aunty presiding over tea when she had company. Mostly, though, their two dogs lounged about on the chairs, pricking up their ears and wagging their shaggy tails as they heard me coming. Soon, they would be devoted to me, like all dogs were. Suggi had many gifts, but this was mine.

Nina Aunty looked distracted when she first saw us but then remembered.

'Come along, come along. I tell you, no one reads these days, do they? I love my books. The romance novels. I like Christie. And James Hadley Chase. Through here.' I had seen some lurid covers of James Hadley Chase novels at the bookstore, very glamourous and racy, and was very impressed that Nina Aunty openly admitted to such forbidden charms.

Here we were now. Finally. A glimpse into the interiors of the stately Arbour House.

We followed Nina Aunty into the large, oak-panelled room, and I breathed in the air. Like old times, I told myself, a mix of pine and cedar. It was a beautiful central hall, complete with a grand piano and a fireplace and rooms that were set off on each side of this hall.

It was double-ceilinged, the oak panels running up the walls, too, I wondered how the grand chandelier would look when switched on. A carpet ran almost the length of the room, threadbare in its beauty. I took in the framed pictures on the walls as we walked through, some of them a little dusty where Shaili's duster had missed them. Who were these stern-faced people in the black-and-white pictures? Had they once walked this hall like I did now? The seating was all stuffed sofas and couches. End tables seemed to hold magazines of some sort, golf perhaps. Someone had put fresh flowers on the side table, an artless arrangement at best, a little lopsided, but it's difficult to take away the beauty of mountain flowers. Heavy curtains covered most of the windows. A walnut-wood sideboard stood to one side, on it some decorative pieces, and on the wall facing us, a fireplace that hadn't been used in half a century at least. I ran a furtive finger on it, the grey dust staining it. Nina Aunty saw me and sighed.

'Yes, well, it's all rather dusty, isn't it? That Shaili needs to get in here. Anyway, so what do you girls like to read? Alistair MacLean? Agatha Christie? P.G. Wodehouse? Oh, yes, yes, they are all in there somewhere. Well, girls, welcome to the library.'

She prattled on as we took in the vast collection of books surrounding us. Thousands of books crammed into shelves that lined the walls. A long table stood in the centre and chairs all around it, sort of like a colonial-era conference room.

'It's not very well-organized.' Mrs Rawat was getting restless. One of her dogs came in – a Golden Retriever – and sneezed. 'Yes, all right, I'll leave you girls to it. This door opens out to the veranda; all rooms in the house open out to the veranda, you know. You can come in from there whenever you like; the latch is broken, so it's always unlocked. Let's go, Flash, stop sneezing! Girls, careful of my xenias as you come in and out; the flower bed is right outside that door.'

'All right then, this could be the beginning of a beautiful friendship,' said Suggi, plonking down on one of the chairs and sending up a cloud of dust.

We started looking through the dusty shelves and found several stashes of detective novels, our favourite kinds, and omnibus after omnibus of Sherlock Holmes and Edgar Allan Poe. For two book-starved teens, this was like finding Aladdin's cave. It was decided that we would haunt the library as much as we possibly could without needing to become Rawats.

After a comprehensive survey of the library, we stepped out of the door that was shown to us and realized that the kitchen was right at the back of the house where the servant quarters were.

'Very upstairs-downstairs,' drawled Suggi upon observing this arrangement.

'The house is beautiful, though,' I breathed.

'Your psyche has been colonized,' Suggi told me comfortably and walked on.

Life at Arbour House soon set into a new routine. I would be at school till one every afternoon. I would walk back on my own after dropping Niru off at her house, taking the narrow, leafy alley with hedges growing on either side, kicking pebbles and stopping to look at the mountain flowers at every opportunity. Suggi's school was farther off; she used to cycle to and fro and got home only by three most days. I would eat lunch and head out to 'mope around the place', as Suggi put it, before she got home. Moping around largely constituted walking around the large *semal* tree, inspecting its fallen fruit, looking at the flowers, trailing the insects, touching and watching the *laajwanti* – touch-me-not – leaves fold or just taking in the drunken fragrance of *bela* and *mogra* that seemed to hang around the estate. I had also taken to the babool tree, a forlorn thorn-laden structure that I felt sorry for, sometimes touching its sticky sap from the bark and wondering if I could use it as glue. Once Suggi came home, we would visit the Rawat library, either bringing books home or reading them there amongst the ghosts of readers past. Shaili would come in sometimes and offer us glasses of lemon squash, which tasted singularly terrible.

One afternoon, as I circled the *raat ki rani* trees, waiting for Suggi to come home, the Sandhu household seemed to be extra noisy. The boundary wall was low enough for me to be able to peer into their garden. Five or six children were running amok, playing *pitthu* with the ardour it deserves. The girls had long hair in braids and the boys were wearing *patka*s. Much jollity was in evidence. Then I observed another older boy sitting behind the steering wheel in a parked Fiat car, his headphones around his ears, a Sony Discman in his lap. He caught me looking at him and waved. I waved back. Then he gestured at me to hop on over. I was no stranger to hopping over walls, though it was best to do it when Mummy wasn't around. Talking to boys was anathema enough; she would have blown a gasket had she seen me leaping across walls to do so. I took a quick look around, hoisted myself and was sitting on the wall in a second, my legs swinging the other side. He was now smiling widely and leaning against the car. He was very tall and would have towered several inches over me.

'What were you doing sitting in the car?' I asked.

'It's so noisy outside. There is never any peace in the house.' He was around my age and had large, kind eyes, which didn't quite match his athletic physique.

'Oh, right.'

'I know you moved recently. I saw you with your sister. You are so alike; she is taller, though.' He talked with the ease of a seasoned raconteur. There was really no need for me to say much.

'I was with my parents till recently,' he carried on, updating me as if he hadn't seen me in a week instead of meeting me for the first time. 'My dad is in the Signals Corps. We moved around a lot. I was in Kota, then Udhampur, Mhow for a bit, then Srinagar and then Dimapur...' He lost his trail of thought, then quizzed me for a few minutes.

'Which school do you go to? No, I haven't heard of it. Is it good? I have only ever studied in Kendriya Vidyalaya. What do your folks do? Oh, okay. This is my grandfather's house. All my uncles live here. My father is the oldest son. *Chai* ji, my grandmother, wanted me to spend time with her. She is not well now, so I have come to stay for a bit. Anyway, Dad doesn't have a family posting these days. He is the commanding office – CO, you know. Anyway...'

He went on and on, telling me about his large extended family, the various places he had lived in, the older brother now at the Indian Military Academy. I didn't realize just how much time had passed; it was so easy to listen to him talk. I suddenly started when the dogs began barking.

'I better go,' I said.

'Cool, off with you then. I'll help you over the wall; it's a bit mossy this side.'

'I'll see you again?'

'You couldn't keep me away.'

I felt a sudden surge of delight at having found him, like a goblin hidden in the grass. I started to climb on his outstretched hands before I remembered something.

'*Arey*, listen, at least tell me your name.'

'Oh, I am Sukhbir, but everyone calls me Sukh.'

9

NIRU

Suggi didn't like the idea of Sukh and then she met him and saw no reason to change her mind. Not used to being dethroned by anyone, she was upset at my having found Sukh and spending time with him. Of course, she wouldn't talk about it but immediately launched the deadliest passive-aggressive attack.

'Why aren't you talking to me?' I asked as she pointedly turned her back to me.

'You go and talk to that Sandhu fellow.' The reply flew out sharp and stinging.

'You've met him, Suggi. He's just so much fun. You can also hang out with us. He is the same age as me.'

'I don't want to talk to you kids.' Suggi put her shapely nose in the air and pretended to focus on her organic chemistry numerical.

'*Hain, hain*, don't fight,' Mummy called out sanctimoniously from the kitchen.

Ironically, the more Suggi resisted, the closer I got to Sukh.

'Suggi doesn't like me,' he observed good-naturedly after being snubbed by her twice in a row. He really didn't mind. Apart from the sizeable army of his younger cousins, his charms had also won over the Balakrishnan twins, and now, Vidhya and Krishna had started emerging from their sequestered existence every evening under Sukh's able guidance. Soon, we could be seen every evening trooping as a group to King Stores, purveyors of all manners of Kwality ice cream, specifically mango bar. Suggi was invited the first couple of times but immediately declined the offer in her brusque manner.

King Stores was manned by a disabled, middle-aged fellow who went by the moniker Gappi Bhaiya. Considering Gappi Bhaiya never parted with any gossip, I'd say he was misnamed, but he did provide a place for us to catch up on the day. Krishna and Vidhya were very studious, and the pressure of grades sat gloomily around their twin beings. Despite attending one of the best schools in Doon, apparently, their only competition was with each other.

'At least there is no spelling bee in India.' Krishna had a gift for satire. Vidhya was quieter; she had beautiful, intelligent eyes, a small *pottu* shining between them. They had an older brother, too, who had done the family proud and had trod the path that was naturally marked out for him and gone off to IIT, hallelujah.

'Then MS from the US, of course,' said Vidhya.

'Of course.' We nodded as if we understood.

'Will you also need to join the army like your father and brother?' I asked Sukh.

'I look like I should, don't I?' he laughed. 'What about you?'

I didn't know. I had never known. The thing is – with a sister like Suggi, all my own edges were blurred. I didn't quite know what to make of myself, what my own shape was. I shrugged as if to say I was too cool to care but saw Sukh look at me intently. I wasn't fooling him.

Krishna and Vidhya had to be home by six sharp, my parents had always allowed ample space for my 'moping around the trees', and Sukh was the proverbial free bird, with only doting aunts in bright lipstick and pretty printed salwar-kameez to call out for him.

I had always grown up as the plus one to Suggi's towering presence. Befriending Sukh was the first tiny act of rebellion that I tried in my bid to grow up a little. Sukh was so self-assured, it was difficult not to have some of it rub off on me, and I was loath to abandon this inchoate friendship.

After a few days of silent treatment, Suggi got tired of it and went back to being her old self, but it was clear that she had not forgiven me for my new friend. She had little time these days, always running from one club to another activity at school. In the meanwhile, I spent time with Niru at school and with Sukh after.

Niru seemed worried. She was an only child, very self-composed and driven, but she seemed preoccupied of late. At first, I put it to the all-enveloping stress of the board exams that awaited us at the end of the year. Niru was not just your average garden-variety nerd; she was an intellectual gladiator, set great store by her grades and rank, competing furiously to get perfect scores in all subjects. This, however, seemed different.

She didn't talk much as we walked back home from school one day. Then we stood outside her gate as she dithered over going in, swinging her school bag from one shoulder to the other, restless and worried.

'You okay, Niru?' I finally asked, getting tired of waiting for her to go in.

'Yes, let's just wait for five minutes.' She looked at me, her neat, shiny bob swinging around her small face, her eyes tired.

I waited some more, looking at the cat cleaning itself in the garden.

'Gaya, it's just that,' Niru looked around and finally spoke in a low voice, 'I think Sharmi is back.'

Gooseflesh appeared on my arms, and I shivered a bit, though it was just April.

'Why do you... what happened?' I asked, my voice coming out in a croak. There was no question of doubting Niru. She had very little imagination.

'I was about to let myself in, and I saw someone within the house from the window, and then I opened it and there was no one there. It... it wasn't a real person, you know, just a shadow of a person. I could tell it was Sharmi.'

I listened in silence. Sharmi hadn't made an appearance for almost three years now. It could be because of Shifty's loss. Shifty, a thoroughly dislikeable Pomeranian who would yap all day long, had been at the centre of Niru's existence for the last ten years. Shifty, arthritic and old, had died the previous year, and since then, Niru has been a latchkey child in the truest sense of the word.

'Have you thought about getting another pup?' I finally asked.

Niru knew what I meant. We had been together since kindergarten.

'It's not that, Gaya.'

I nodded.

'Look, why don't you go inside? I'll come with you. You can't wait outside till Thapa Ma'am gets home.'

I looked at Niru's house as she went in, a typical hill bungalow with a sloping roof, creepers climbing every possible wall and many bay windows that opened out straight on to the garden. The garden wasn't much to look at, neglected as it was. Weeds and moss had overtaken most of it. Niru got in without an incident. I looked inside from the top half of the door that led into the house, made of glass windows. Everything seemed quiet, normal. I waved at Niru to go on inside. She smiled tentatively at me. I looked around uncertainly, then waved at her again, gesturing that I would head home.

I walked home through the familiar green alley, shrubs on either side welcoming me like old friends. The reappearance of Sharmi was bad news. Sharmi was... had been... Niru's aunt, Mrs Thapa's much younger sister. She had lived with them for many years. I had always found Sharmi intriguing and been impressed with her very blue eyeshadow and her very wavy, brown hair. She had finished college and then just hung about the house a lot. She painted a bit, and some of her poems also appeared in the local papers. We also knew she smoked something that did not smell like normal cigarettes and played 'While My Guitar Gently Weeps' on her guitar late into the night. Sharmi had taken violently ill one night, having eaten poisoned mushrooms, and had been rushed to Doon Hospital. She was gone that same night. Niru had been shattered, and Mrs Thapa had walked around with swollen eyes for weeks. Niru's father took a leave of absence from his ship and came home to spend time with them.

I had been saddened at Sharmi's death; I liked her, but nothing could have prepared me for the shock when she reappeared to Niru a year later, reportedly seeming quite unaware of the fact that she had passed on, standing next to where her old guitar hung on the wall. Once Niru had shared this with me, we had, in our collective wisdom, decided to keep it to ourselves. Mrs Thapa put the no in no-nonsense, and her forbidding eyebrows were enough to keep any discussion of ghostly sightings at bay. Sharmi's appearances had been infrequent and brief, but Niru still lost a ton of weight and contracted measles that year for good measure. It all stopped as suddenly as it had started, and we had put it behind us as a tale for bonfire night.

Except that now, Sharmi seemed to be amongst us again. I walked on, thinking of her. She sometimes had college friends come over, but there had been no romantic interest that we knew of. She had, by and large, appeared to be quite content with her art and music. Well, ghosts were supposed to have unfinished business. What did Sharmi need to finish, except the charcoal sketches that still lay in some forgotten drawer in the old house?

10

Sukhbir Sandhu and the Balakrishnans

Sharmi's appearance put a dampener on my mood for the next several days. Niru started to skip meals once again, her cut apples and paratha going back untouched.

'Look, it's not like she harms you in anyway,' I tried to reason with her during recess.

'No, she wouldn't,' said Niru, dark circles now lining her shiny eyes.

'Does she seem aware of you?'

'No, I don't think so.'

'What exactly did you see?'

'Not much. I just feel her presence. Like a shadow.'

I looked at her, sitting on the steps of our school. I knew better than to ask her, but honestly, what did a presence really mean? She caught my look.

'You don't believe me.'

'Of course, I do.'

'I can't tell Mum, Gaya.'

'Yes, her *scientific temperament* would dissuade her.'

Niru almost laughed at this. Mrs Thapa started each academic year with a speech in which *inculcating a scientific temperament* was the chief motif.

Suggi was the last person who could be told about something like this; she would have scoffed at me for days. Sukh was too new, despite his old-shoe feel, to be a confidant in matters involving Niru. So, I hung about 'like a wet dog' in Suggi's words and carried my air of preoccupation and worry like a treasured possession.

'Let's go check on Vidhya and Krishna,' Sukh suggested one evening when the twins hadn't appeared for three days in a row. I was uncertain about this.

'I've never been to their house. Should I go ask Mummy?'

'There is a first time for everything. Come on.'

We walked to the Balakrishnan house, which was built on a piece of land chopped off Arbour House but now could be accessed through New Road, a narrow street that ran parallel to Morris Road. It was a new house, made carefully and expensively, each blade of grass shining in the lawn, the window glass gleaming. I didn't like its freshly manicured feel. Sukh went and rang the doorbell even as I hung back, wishing I could be back home. There was no answer for a few minutes.

'Let's go back.' I pulled at Sukh's sleeve.

'*Arey*, wait *na*, here comes someone,' he said. It was clearly Mr Balakrishnan himself, in a pristine white kurta pyjama, a short man with a receding hairline.

'Good evening, sir.' Sukh was always saying good-evening and good-morning to all the uncles and aunties without sounding pretentious in the least. I, too, folded my hands in a half-hearted namaste.

Mr Balakrishnan stared us down.

'Uh, we are friends of Vidhya and Krishna.' Sukh was

faltering a bit now. 'Came to check on them. Are they free?'

'No,' Mr Balakrishna finally barked at us. 'They are studying.'

'Oh, all right, thank you, Uncle,' said Sukh. We turned around and heard the door slam behind us.

'Why is he so angry?' I whispered to Sukh. He shrugged and was shutting the main gate to the house when something made me glance up to see a pair of large, kajal-rimmed eyes looking at us from a room on the first floor. She moved away but not before I caught a glimpse of long, braided hair and a big bindi. I thought I saw fear in her face. Wasn't that Mrs Balakrishnan?

Then we turned around and walked home.

I brought it up at dinner that night. We never ate together as a family. Mummy made and served hot rotis as Suggi and I sat at our common study table with our plates. Papa would eat after us, and Mummy would eat after she was done with the chores of the day, possibly too tired to taste what she had made. Theirs was the generation that was trying to narrow the gender gap by never trying to domesticate us in anyway. Suggi and I would sometimes half-heartedly chop vegetables or make tea, but we were really no good at housework. Years later, both of us would need to cook and suffer because of our complete lack of kitchen skills.

'I think I saw Sujatha Aunty today,' I disclosed, glad to get it off my chest. 'She seemed nervous.'

'Who asked you to go there, *haan*?' asked Mummy, right off the bat. 'Haven't I told you not to roam around? Focus on your studies; this is your board year.'

Mummy possibly feared that I would forget that this was a 'board year' in the absence of regular reminders.

'This dal is delicious.' I tried to distract her with flattery. Mummy flounced off. In the glorious tradition of siblings everywhere, Suggi was enjoying my discomfiture thoroughly.

'That Sandhu fellow must have asked you to go there.' She liked to blame Sukh for everything. I shook my head at her as Mummy came back, now looking calmer.

'We have just moved here. You should not go poking your nose everywhere,' she now informed me. 'Do you think Niru goes around uninvited to other people's houses?' Niru was idolized and idealized no end by Mummy, being at the top of the class after all. I thought about the uninvited spectral guests at Niru's place and wondered if some of the shine would come off her if I told Mummy about it. Wisely, I kept silent.

There was not much to do after dinner except study and then lie back with our novels, borrowed from the Rawat collection. We had a colour television but weren't allowed to watch too much, the firm parental belief being that good students don't watch TV. We meandered through *Bikram aur Betaal*, *Rajani*, and *Karamchand*, but absolutely adored *Trishna*, which both of us watched faithfully, both Suggi and I nursing a massive crush on the Indianized Mr Darcy.

As we drifted off to sleep, I could hear Mummy saying something about Sujatha Aunty to Papa in the other room. I couldn't catch a clear word and slept off. I dreamt about Sharmi, who had moved to the

Balakrishnan house and was calling out to me from the first-floor window.

'How much you kick around, Gaya? I couldn't get a wink of sleep, I tell you, and my timing suffered during training,' complained Suggi the next morning, kicking off her training shoes as she barged into the room. I was still groggy.

'I had bad dreams,' I said, picking up my towel and bracing to go to the freezing bathroom. Mornings were always cold in Doon, and baths were a miserable affair, there being no geysers and no running hot water. An immersion rod was used to heat bathwater, a contraption that could well electrocute the unfortunate bather in the event of the slightest carelessness.

'Bad dreams every night?' Suggi raised her eyebrows at me. I dived into the bathroom. It was true. Sharmi was becoming a regular feature in my dreams, having replaced the much more pleasant Pierce Brosnan. I shivered through my bath and dressed for school. Suggi, her face warm and flushed from rigorous training, didn't have too bad a time of it, singing loudly as she bathed.

The day started off well. At morning assembly, Mrs Thapa announced that the end-of-the-year bonfire would be scheduled soon after the school fête for the outgoing batch – namely us. The annual bonfire, called Bonfire Night, was one of the big traditions of our school for the top two grades. It was essentially our school's farewell event for the outgoing batch, largely organized by standard nine and supervised by senior staff.

The previous year, I had inhaled too much smoke and had one of my episodes right there on the school grounds, and a doctor had to be called in.

We had P.T. and slogged through the normal range of Julius Caesar soliloquies, refractive index of sundry things and Survey of India map sheets, trying our best to inhale and ingest and somehow make all of this information part of our being. Niru looked slightly better that day. We ate bun-samosa at the school canteen and cheered up considerably. One of the boys from the other section summoned up enough courage to declare his undying love for Niru in someone's slam book. Niru had no intention of getting a boyfriend. Mrs Thapa wasn't above giving her a hiding even at this age. Nevertheless, it was nice to be admired.

After school, we stopped at the shop outside to buy the paan-flavoured sweets that we had been loyal to since kindergarten. Even the stickiest stick jaw from Ellora couldn't touch these. Then we walked home. We had decided that I would wait every day till Niru went inside and said a loud prayer, one we had learnt at school. This was the extent of our expertise in exorcism, and it seemed to be working. Niru hadn't reported a sighting, vague as that term was, in a few days.

All seemed to be well. I started off for home after depositing Niru at hers. School would be out in another week. Six weeks of summer vacation, but there would be extra classes for sure for the unfortunate lot in grade ten. I sighed absently and ran my hands over the wild roses growing in abundance. It was very quiet, even for the always-silent hedged alley, the sounds of my footsteps muffled by the mud path. Occasionally, I would catch sight of a big cat that used to live around there, but today, he was missing, too. I must have reached halfway through the alley when I heard a girl call my name.

Gayatri.

I turned around, expecting to see Niru holding a book that she had taken by mistake, but the alley was empty, not a soul in sight. It was suddenly even quieter, and I stood frozen.

Gayatri.

Once again, the voice called from behind.

I must have stood mesmerized till I heard a leaf crackle that shocked me to my senses. Hoisting my school bag over my shoulder, I sprinted home. Stray branches from the hedges scraped my arms, feeling like Sharmi's nails. I think I was babbling a bit. The winding alley seemed unending, my breath was coming in gasps, but I didn't stop till I reached the end of it, opening out on to a main road, my school shirt and tunic soaked in sweat, heart pounding madly.

That night, I was quite ill. Years later, I would think about this day and wonder if it was a panic attack, but there really was no way to tell. Mummy kept asking me to try to take deep breaths, Papa put a damp towel on my forehead and Suggi kept chewing on her nails.

11

Koko, Then

In all my wisdom, I decided to keep my little interface with 'The Voice Behind The Hedge' to myself. There was no telling how Niru would take it. The first thing I did was to stop taking the alley altogether. This was a loss. The quiet lane had belonged to me, the tall hedges like living walls, close but not too much. I started taking the longer way home, less green, less beauteous but also less likely to be invaded by faceless beings.

Suggi came home fuming one day soon after a jaunt at Rajpur Road.

'These boys, I hate them!' She flung her bag down with a thud.

'What happened, what happened, what happened?' asked Mummy.

'Someone took my Wayfarers!' Suggi was in tears.

'Eh?'

'My sunglasses, Mum, my Wayfarers. The ones I bought from the Tibetan Market.'

'How? Are you okay?'

'Two boys on a bike just coolly rode up to me and took my Wayfarers off. Right off my nose! In broad daylight! And sped off! I was so shocked that I didn't think of following them immediately, and they just disappeared down the road! Oh, I hate them!'

For some reason, I found this very funny, but I knew better than to give in to my instinct to guffaw. Suggi would have pummelled me, and she did have a good twenty pounds over me. I stifled the urge and tried to look serious and concerned.

Mummy declared the whole idea of Rajpur Road a travesty and the concept of Suggi taking Papa's scooter to go gallivanting out there in the wild absolutely abhorrent. Suggi threw a fit and said she wasn't one of those '*ghunghat* types' who could be told what to do. Mummy responded with a wild card and started crying. When Papa came home that evening, everyone had swollen eyes and the house had that nice, wholesome feel that can come only after the most terrific of domestic rows.

I had had enough of the domestic warfare and decided to go out for some fresh air. I sneaked out after dinner and made my way to the Rawat library with the books that we had already finished reading. The air was cool, like it always was in Doon in the evenings. The *raat ki raani* was really out to show off that night, its heady fragrance spread all over the night air. Over the boundary, I saw Sukh lounging on the garden swing. He saw me and jumped off the swing and loped over.

'Gaya, my friend. Where are you off to?'

'Just returning these books. Can you believe this *raat ki raani*? Mummy is convinced it attracts snakes.'

'Snakes with good olfactory sensibilities would

possibly give it a whirl,' said Sukh, looking thoughtful. I laughed and waved him off. I walked across the veranda of the Rawat residence and glanced inside. Nobody seemed to be home. Shaili was singing in the kitchen, her voice carrying from the back of the house. Like in most bungalows of that era, the kitchen was the domain only of domestic servants, not to be approached by the gentry. I had been to the kitchen a few times, and the large refrigerator, specially imported from Britain decades ago, had left quite an impression on me. Years later, I would discover SMEG refrigerators and be reminded of the giant cooling machine at Arbour House. I now made my way to the back of the house and opened the door to the library, noticing that the age-old ceiling fans were not whirring like they often did during the day. A small table lamp was enough to faintly light the library. I hoped Buddy or Flash would hear my footsteps and come to check on me, their coats smelling faintly of some sort of talcum powder that Mrs Rawat was fond of putting on them. I turned to the shelves to put the books back in.

'Gayatri?' said a voice softly from behind me.

I dropped the books, let out a scream loud enough to rouse the Rawat ancestors twice over and made for the door to sprint right back home before Sharmi's spirit could enter my body. I didn't realize that the door had shut behind me when I had entered. I banged right into it, still screaming, struggling to open the door with my sweaty hands. I felt a hand on my shoulder and was very near passing out when the spirit spoke.

'It's okay, it's okay. What happened? Are you all right? Did I startle you?'

I whirled around to see a boy looking very worried. He was quite tall, his hair was cut very short, and he was dressed in pyjamas, still holding the book he must have been reading. He was, well, he was not Sharmi. That much could be established without a doubt. He was now speaking. To wit.

'Mum said Gayatri and Sugandha come over to borrow books. I met Sugandha in the morning, so I figured you must be, well, you. I am so sorry. Here, let me help you with these books.'

I could feel the blood still pounding in my face. I gawped at the boy for a few more seconds, feeling more foolish than I ever had in my life. A comet could come and hit us, and I would just keep up with my vacant stare. At this point, Shaili made a dramatic entry, her hands still covered in flour.

'*Kya hua, kya hua?* Oh, Gayatri didi. Why did you scream? Did a bat fly in? Uff, so many of them around.'

Her chatter started bringing me back to earth, and my teeth stopped chattering. I gulped once or twice and found my voice.

'No, it's okay. I wasn't expecting anyone in here. Normally it's empty. Nina Aunty said you and your sister don't like to read.' This came out as an accusation. *Way to make friends on the first encounter*. He didn't seem to mind, though.

'She's right. I just needed to finish this for school. I am Shivendra.'

'Right, right, of course. You pulled quite a Rhett Butler on me there.' I mopped my brow. He didn't quite get the reference but smiled anyway.

'My apologies. I didn't mean to scare you. We just got home today. Bubbles is around here somewhere.'

'Koko bhaiya,' piped in Shaili. 'Khana is ready.'

'Would you like to join me... us?' asked Koko bhaiya aka Shivendra Kumar Rawat politely.

'No, no, thank you so much. I have eaten,' I said. 'I'll just put these books here.' Both of them waited to see me put the books back. My hands were shaking very slightly. I put them behind my back and turned around to face the duo.

'Right then, I will take your leave,' I offered stiffly. 'Good morning. I mean, good night.' After this debacle, I proceeded to make my way back. Sukh was still outside, now joined on the swing by a couple of his endless younger cousins.

'What did you get?' he called out.

'A solid hit in self-esteem,' I replied and went home.

Suggi was already in bed when I got home.

'Did you get the Christie I asked for?'

'No. I ran into the Rawat son and heir.'

'Oh, Koko. Yes, I met him and Bubbles. They get done with school a week before us.'

'You could have told me. I got the fright of my life seeing him in that dark library.'

'You have been so jumpy of late,' observed Suggi. 'Now please get your own *razai*. You will kick off your own and then try to climb into mine.'

I took a long time getting to sleep.

What is this nuisance? Why did the Rawat offspring need to be here? Granted it's their home, but they could be home without being here, right? And the library should have been off bounds for them. They don't even read. Lurking around in the dark like that, the idiot. Sure, it was not his fault, but I have been having trysts with the paranormal in shaded green lanes, haven't I? Anyone in my place would have screamed. Okay, perhaps I was a little loud. Maybe I have stronger lungs than I get credit for. I hope he doesn't take me to be a complete idiot, though. Not that I care. I probably won't even see him again. Did you notice the accent? Must be a snob. One of those elite 'my school goes back a thousand years'. Old mothball. Anyway, I don't care. I am just glad it wasn't Sharmi.

12

A Party is Planned

Arbour House was the prettiest it had ever been as May rolled around, the garden abloom with roses and geraniums waving about dizzily, the kitchen garden loaded with bottle gourd, radish, corn, beans and cucumbers, doubtless making their way to the Rawat dinner table. The mango trees were now speckled with small green fruit. We had been in grade ten for a month, and now it was time for summer break. School would reopen in July. Niru would take off for Pauri Garhwal to spend the holidays with her grandparents but not till after my birthday. We wouldn't travel for the holidays; we hardly ever did, except to my father's village, which had been such a traumatic experience in the past that neither Suggi nor I were keen to revisit. Our father had traded his past for his family a long time ago and didn't seem to mind going alone. I wouldn't know till much, much later just how heavy a price it would have been for him.

Sightings of Sharmi had dwindled to a bare minimum. Sightings of the Rawat progeny were also infrequent. Since being frightened out of my wits by the younger sibling, I had also made the acquaintance of Bubbles Rawat, who was exceedingly attractive and confident in the way that exceedingly attractive people are. She was statuesque and sported a very trendy haircut that added quite a few inches to her frame and that she constantly kept raking back with her fingers. To my great shock, I found out that Bubbles had failed school quite a few times, and resultantly, she was now in the same grade as Koko. She never showed any signs of being curious about me, reserving a quiet smile for me, although she always came over to chat with Suggi when she spotted her. Both the siblings seemed to be quite sporty and put up a badminton net next to their kitchen garden and also started putting the basketball hoop to good use. They also went for frequent treks. I would catch sight of them loading their car to go to Malsi or Chakrata. I tried to find fault in their clothing, hoping to find ostentatious claims to wealth, but they dressed even more simply than I did.

I don't think it ever struck Suggi to be envious of them; she was just not cut that way, being so full of herself. I, on the other hand, felt a surge of inadequacy any time either of them shot a glance my way. In some ways, Arbour House had been mine till they made an appearance. Nina and Balbir Rawat had been largely absent, and I had had the estate to myself, the trees and the dogs and the house all breathing and responding to me. Now the rightful heirs had made an appearance, and poetically speaking, were roaming the streets that had been mine. So, I largely kept to myself and sulked quietly, spending the evenings with Sukh. One evening, as Sukh and I sat on the swing and shared rum balls kindly bought by Sukh's brother, then a gentleman cadet at the Indian Military Academy, Krishna made an appearance, wearing thicker glasses. We hadn't seen him or his sister since our visit to their place when his father had unceremoniously turned us away.

'Oho, look who's here today. Where were you all this time, bud?'

'All good, all good. We were preparing for a Math Olympiad.'

'Fascinating, the stuff you do for fun.'

Krishna plonked on the swing and sighed.

'Give me some.' He pointed to the confectionary box. '*Bas, yaar*, don't ask. Out there in Madras, all my cousins are racking up achievements. After Ranjan Anna got through IIT, one of my cousins left for America to do her MS. Subbu cleared AIIMS *and* BITS Pilani and a thousand other exams; he is all over the newspapers.'

Sukh patted Krishna's leg in sympathy.

'That's the worst kind of family, champ, but you'll be fine, you are brilliant,' he said.

'I have been forced into brilliance,' said Krishna, leaning back and folding his arms behind his head.

'How is your mum?' I asked suddenly, without even meaning to.

Krishna went silent for a moment and looked at me.

'She is all right.'

'We went to your house the other day,' said Sukh. 'What *yaar*, your father nearly bit our heads off.'

Krishna nodded but didn't say anything. Sukh went on talking, complaining about his own father, then some friend's father who gambled away his new Maruti

800 and then about fathers in general. Sukh just needed a willing audience; there was no stopping him.

'Anyway,' he finally started winding down, 'where is Vidhya?'

'She is at her Bharatanatyam class.'

'But of course.'

'We are a right royal cliché,' said Krishna, the slight drawl he still nursed yet to be dissolved by India.

I thought of something to say to cheer him up.

'It's my birthday next week,' I finally offered.

'Oh, hey, Gaya, that's great. Party!' Sukh immediately got energized by the idea. 'Who all are you inviting?'

'Uh, I don't know yet. We didn't have many friends living close by in our old house. Niru used to come for a small party. And Inder.'

'Now you have us! So, I will be there. And Krishna and Vidhya. Niru will come, you said...' He immediately started plotting and planning with great gusto. I wondered what Mummy would say to so many new faces suddenly appearing at our house for what had always been a quiet celebration, especially *boys*. I could see her eyebrows rising in my mind's eye. Mummy was very confused about the idea of boys when it came to her daughters. Suggi had had no romantic liaisons; she rather enjoyed the idea of seeing people get enamoured by her, in the way of cruel children troubling puppies, but she had plenty of boys in her social groups. Having grown up in Doon, Suggi had little patience for what she considered Mummy's outdated ideas. Mummy was a little bit in awe of her firstborn, who seemed to be getting too large to be contained in her household and its notions. She questioned everything and could not be shut up with a 'because I say so'. To add to Mummy's discomfort, Brighton had a couple of unlikely teachers who encouraged this streak of independence in Suggi.

There were no two ways about it. The birthday party could only be organized with Suggi's help.

Suggi laughed when she saw my guest list.

'Gaya, so many boys, no more a wallflower!'

'Shut up. I was never a wallflower, whatever that means.'

'Do you have to invite that Sandhu fellow?'

'He has a name, and he's my friend.'

'Oh, all right, all right.'

Suggi bulldozed Mummy into agreeing within a couple of days. Mummy adopted a long-suffering expression when she realized that 'all sorts of boys' had been invited to the party and cooked her despicable *tinde ki* sabzi two days in a row. Then the cloud cleared and preparations for the birthday party were kicked off in right earnest. There would be home-cooked food and maybe Citra and Gold Spot for drinks. Mummy would fret over baking the birthday cake, a novelty for her, which would inevitably taste like a heavenly Indian dessert, aromatic with *elaichi* and saffron. Friends would come, we would hang about the house, awkward at first and then becoming ourselves. There would be attempts at games, mismanaged and quite hilarious. Papa would take pictures with his Yashica camera, and later, the picture 'roll' would be developed, the pictures carefully stuck in photo albums with black card paper.

Suggi decided that she would send invitations and

crafted some out of printed floral letter paper. Mummy said she would make custard and jelly, things that were completely out of her repertoire. I suggested puri-aloo would be fine, being my favourite, but she wouldn't listen. There was not much for me to do except hang around and shout suggestions at everyone. Mummy took me to a shop in Astley Hall to buy me my annual set of new clothes. The other set would come on Diwali, if it did. I decided on an oversized T-shirt and denim skirt set that made me look quite like Madonna, I felt. Maybe Suggi could perm my hair to complete the look?

I liked Astley Hall. My beloved Ruskin Bond was supposed to have rented a room there at some point, and that was enough for me to be devoted to the place. We were quite tired walking to and fro the market, but I was quite pleased with my purchase and looked forward to modelling it for Suggi. She was drinking tea from a giant mug when we got in, her physics book in front of her.

'Hey, did you get anything nice?'

'I think so! I'll try it out for you. What news?'

'Nothing much. We didn't have current for a bit. Shaili came looking for *jaaman*. Oh, and I invited Koko and Bubbles to your party. They said they would come.'

Suggi took a large slurp of her tea and went back to doing her homework. Old mothball at my party?

Onwards to sweet sixteen then.

13

Turning Sixteen

What I remember most from my sixteenth birthday is just how gorgeous everybody looked. Mummy wore a beautiful peacock-blue silk sari and her gold ornaments, despite it being a hot summer day. Papa went around beaming at everyone. Suggi outdid herself in a neon shirt and her favourite mini skirt and hair that was supremely voluminous, thanks to some aggressive back-combing, and she turned heads effortlessly. Decades later, I would be invited to a retro-themed eighties party, and I would try to replicate Suggi's look.

There had been complete mayhem in the morning when Mummy had started baking the birthday cake. The current went off midway, so the cake started sinking. Then she had a brainwave and shifted it to the gas tandoor, which was used to make tandoori rotis. The poor cake finally surrendered to these machinations and started to swell up again. Maybe it would have been simpler to get a cake from Ellora Bakers, but it was expensive, and Mummy was of the firm belief that with enough effort anything store-bought could be replicated and would taste much, much better.

I stayed in a state of anxiety about the impending arrival of Koko and Bubbles, trying to see our house through their eyes, cane *moorhas* and steel trunks covered with *gaddis* to create seating for the guests. Suggi had put streamers everywhere, and it looked rather festive, that was true.

Niru was the first to arrive. She hugged me, and I calmed down and started to look forward to the party. Sharmi had been quiet, Niru quietly updated me, but her death anniversary was coming up, so Niru had decided to be extra careful around the time.

Sukh came with some of his cousins, who had insisted on tagging along, and started talking to Papa as if he had known him for years. Papa sidled up to me after Sukh had finally let go of him to eat some chips.

'*Beta*, who is that? I seem to have forgotten him,' he queried.

'Uff, Papa, that's the Sandhu fellow. Always over-familiar,' Suggi explained. Sukh had now discovered the samosas on the table and was chatting to Mummy about a *halwai* shop in Meerut that sold the world's best samosas. Mummy was delighted at having found someone who could reference her beloved Uttar Pradesh thus and started plying him with more food.

Inder, our neighbour from Mrs Boyce's house turned up, his younger brother in tow.

'*Arey*, Inder, *kitta lamba ho gaya*,' Mummy greeted him, making him blush. Inder now towered over me and spoke in a gruff voice, more grown-up all of a sudden, but five minutes later, he felt like the Inder with whom I used to play *pitthu* when we were younger.

Vidhya and Krishna came, looking very freshly washed and shiny. Vidhya wore a small bindi, her hair was open for a change, and she looked like one of those long-lashed girls in the Air India ads, welcoming everyone to this ancient land of wonder. Inder immediately took a shine to her and followed her about like a faithful puppy for the rest of the evening as Krishna watched on in amusement.

People kept filtering in. Suggi's classmates from Brighton came. Some aunties and uncles turned up, and all of a sudden, everything became very loud. Nobody seemed to know exactly who all had been invited. Mummy was offering soft drinks and chips to everyone and trying to keep an eye on the cutlets being fried at the same time. One of our mix tapes played on the stereo – Cyndi Lauper reminding us that *girls just wanna have fun*.

Suggi announced that there would be a treasure hunt before the cake-cutting. This was a complete surprise, even to me. Suggi efficiently divided us into two teams. I would lead Team Duran Duran, and Inder would lead Team MJ. The first clue was presented:

If you learn to climb this
You can feel completely free
The first clue is to be found
Under the big litchi...

Tree! There was a loud cry, and everyone ran out towards the litchi orchard. I turned to Suggi, feeling worried.

'Suggi, we shouldn't be sending everyone into the orchard. Nina Aunty might not like it.'

'Uff, *yaar*, stop worrying. It was Koko's idea to organize a treasure hunt. In fact, here he comes now.'

I turned to see Koko and Bubbles making their way to our house. Koko looked lean in a brown T-shirt that matched his eyes, not that I noticed. Bubbles looked splendid in a powder-blue dress and matching eyeshadow.

'Happy birthday, Gayatri.' Koko grinned at me. 'Sorry we are late.'

Bubbles extended a gift, wrapped in red crinkled paper. Later, much, much later, this book – Agatha Christie's *The Murder of Roger Ackroyd* – would sit on Sanjay's bookshelf, the inscriptions a little faded on the front page.

Dear Gayatri,
Many happy returns of the day.
Fondly,
Bubbles

and lower down, on the same page.

Dear Gayatri,
Like you said, I am not much of a reader, but I am told this is a good one.
Wishing you new adventures in the coming year.
Shivendra (Koko)

I mumbled my thanks, feeling a strange concoction of delight and shyness deep in my belly.

'Well, all right then. Let's begin!' said Suggi. 'Koko in

Gaya's team. Bubbles with Inder. Clues all over Arbour House! Ready, set, go!'

It was the most fun we ever had. Running at top speed till I was breathless and my heart was bumping against my chest. Shouting and laughing so hard that tears started running down my face. Racing against Inder and his troop. Pushing and pulling with all our might. As I snatched a clue up and ran off to the *semal* tree, I knew that my childhood was heading for an end and the beginning of something new was in store. I felt like I could take on what life would throw my way.

In the way that memory had a way of tricking us, the exact details of Koko that day have slipped into some crevice from where it is impossible to retrieve them. What did he say to me? How did he look? Did he exult when we finally won the hunt, smiling such that his eyes crinkled? These are all things I have made up answers to.

Tired and happy, we finally made our way back home. Mummy had already set the cake in place, and Suggi lit the candles when she saw me coming in. The table was laden with food that Mummy had slaved all morning to make, and I felt a swell of love that made me feel like I wanted to cry. *Indian parents, man, they are the best,* I heard someone say and turned to see Koko smiling at me. I smiled back and blew out the candles. Papa captured that moment in a rare, good photograph in which nobody blinked at the wrong moment. In the picture, you can see that everyone is singing. I am smiling straight into the camera, my newly permed curls all around my face, dimples flashing in both cheeks, a bit of something, food possibly, on my nose. Koko is looking at me, an expression I would scrutinize later for hours and hours together. Suggi and Mummy are laughing at something that Papa has said. Sukh is already reaching for the cake. Vidhya and Inder can be seen in the background, sitting on a bench under the window, a paper plate on Vidhya's lap. If we look very carefully, outside that window we can see the reddish-brown hint of that other love of mine – Buddy the St. Bernard, sensing my presence, wanting to be nearer.

I didn't have any way of knowing then what life would bring my way. I didn't expect good fortune to be mine to reach and grab like Suggi did. I didn't feel entitled to success and fame. I possibly wouldn't get too many leg-ups in what I tried to do. The only prescience that I did have on my sixteenth birthday was that I would be loved.

12

Easy Summer Days

When I look back, I realize Koko was the person I possibly talked to the most in my life outside of my family and Niru. The thing was – he felt like family, too, bringing a sense of permanence with him even on the first day he appeared at our doorstep, soon after my birthday, asking me to come play doubles.

'I am not very good at baddy,' I told him, even as I walked with him to the makeshift court.

'That's okay,' he said, and it was. Everything was okay for Koko. Having grown up with Suggi had accustomed me to hard edges, of having to counter big arguments and deep fights to get my own way. With Koko, there was always room. He could make place in his life quickly and effortlessly. There was very little worth fighting for, very little worth entertaining the idea of fighting for. He had an innate generosity and an almost endless capacity for forgiveness. He found the idea of conflict abhorrent. I found my shyness melting away and could speak to him for hours together.

What was my idea of love then? I think I was a fairly typical sixteen-year-old in that I hoped for a Heathcliff from the moors, a complex, brooding, tortured hero who could only claim salvation in the arms of a heroine who understood him, namely me. The idea of toxicity was not even considered by me, a naïve child-girl who drew all her ideas from books alone. I think I was fortunate in that these ideas remained limited to my beloved novels, that these supremely intense men never really crossed over in my life. I was lucky in that despite my own half-baked ideas of being desired obsessively, I met men who treated me as an easy equal.

Sukh and Bubbles. Koko and I. The long badminton games went on even as Arbour House watched on, amused at these young people tossing the shuttle across the net yet again, like many before them had done. All that changed over the years was the clothes, maybe the language, but the young people remained the same – more energy than they knew what to do with, often troubled, knotting up things that did not need to be. Arbour House could have offered a piece of advice. *Slow down, young people, slow down and savour this.*

Koko and I quickly became a unit. I suspected that this was how he ran his life, a laconic easy-come-easy-go approach that allowed effortless entry and a painless exit. He needed partners, he needed company, never quite comfortable with being just by himself.

'I must admit, I thought you would be quite a snob,' I told him one afternoon when we stood under a tree, cooling off after a breathless match with Sukh and Bubbles.

'Oh, but I am.' He laughed and drained his glass of *shikanji*. 'Just not with you.'

Mummy's admonishments intensified with time

– board exams, board exams, board exams. I figured that if I laboured arduously enough through the day, she would start worrying about me by the evening, checking my eyes for dark circles, such that by the time Sukh or Koko rolled along in the evening asking for me, she would be somewhat willing to let me go.

'Playing is good for the heart,' Papa offered by way of support.

'Yes, but she might get an attack,' Mummy fretted. 'It's her board year.'

'Yes, yes, everyone knows, Raji, let it go.'

And so, a little worn out by my day-long tryst with the books, I would finally be free. We would first rush to play badminton. If Suggi was playing, she had to win at all costs, every single time. Koko had no such compunctions, a rare kind of peculiarity in one so athletic. After the match, we would hang about the compound, me talking about the various plants and trees without anyone really paying heed, Flash chasing the squirrels, Buddy lumbering along only under complete duress.

'This tree has been around for ages,' said Koko of the *semal*. 'The trunk is pretty spiky, though.'

'That keeps animals at bay,' I said. 'Mauna says they also call it the red silk-cotton tree. The cotton pods will be floating around soon.'

'I had no idea; we never learnt the names of all these trees,' said Bubbles. 'Even though Mauna used to try to tell us when we were younger. Of course, she was as much a terror back them.'

'I like them,' I said. 'They are beautiful. Everything here is beautiful.'

'Gaya likes this old pile,' observed Koko with a laugh. 'I never can understand why. Look at her all moony-eyed, like it were old Taj Mahal or something.'

'I don't know,' said Bubbles, twirling a twig. 'It would be nice to live in a larger city. There's nothing to do here. I want to go for a grand tour like Amma ji did with her parents. She has often told me about it. You should meet her Gaya, our grandmother; she will be here soon. Very Rajmata, if you know what I mean. She comes for the summer.'

'What about you, Gaya,' said Koko, again, 'where would you want to live?'

There was no question in my mind.

'I hope I get rich enough to buy Arbour House off you,' I said, and everyone laughed, even though I was not joking, not in the least. We walked on and moved almost automatically to the dark litchi grove, the glossy leaves glinting where the sunrays caught them. Sukh quickly climbed one; he was very agile.

'We should go for a picnic. Let's go to Nag Tibba,' he suggested from his perch. Sukh was a year younger to me but all his travels, the constant moving across India's terrains, had given him a confidence with the natural world. He could pitch a tent, knew how to fish, could even collect a bunch of hens if needed, could cook *sarson ka saag* on a makeshift *chulha*, he said. Koko and Bubbles met this suggestion with enthusiasm, Suggi and I didn't know if we would be allowed to go for a picnic. Papa would have to be co-opted.

'Let's ask Vidhya and Krishna, too.' Sukh was unstoppable once he decided to hatch a plan, and all his plans tried to include as many people as possible. His cousin, called Hutch for some reason, appeared at the edge of the litchi grove, shouting that an aunt was visiting and that Sukh needed to show his face immediately.

'I better go.' He clambered down the tree. 'Gaya, will you go over to Vidhya's house and ask for permission to let them come? You know the place!' He winked at me and was gone in a trice. I really didn't want to go to the Balakrishnan residence and definitely not without Sukh. Anyway, there was no time to get into that now as Mummy was marching over determinedly looking for us.

There was a letter waiting for me when we got home. I had penfriends, some of them even in countries abroad. I liked the idea of having friends in interesting places without necessarily having to talk to them. Writing was much easier. This letter, however, was from Niru, who was in Pauri now and getting quite bored from the looks of it. She wrote:

> *I think it is just our house in Doon that is haunted for Sharmi has not appeared to me here. I sometimes almost wish she did, it is so boring here! I want to hear everything about Koko and Bubbles and Sukh and everyone else. Does Inder try to talk to Vidhya? I wish I were there with you all! I am having to study this year, even during the holidays. I carried my books with me...*

Niru's letter rambled on. It warmed my heart, much like Niru herself always did, and I decided I would go over to Vidhya's house after all and try to collect some gossip about Inder and her so that I could write a fat, juicy letter to my friend vegetating up in the mountains.

The next morning, after eating the parathas that Mummy so adroitly produced every morning, I drank some tea – I abhorred milk – and quietly stole out of the house feeling a little guilty. In these last couple of months, I was always stealing out without telling Mummy. I walked slowly over to Vidhya's house, opened the gate and walked in, admiring the persimmon and almond trees that grew in their garden, the grass lush and glossy green, butterflies swarming about. I knew they grew *brahma kamals* also. Mr Balakrishnan was devoted to his garden, always pottering about in some flower bed or the other. I wished he could have been a little more approachable; I could have taken his advice about the dwarf apple tree I was tending to in my little patch, which did not wish to fruit come what may. I rang the doorbell, but there was no sound. Power cut. Again. I knocked a couple of times, but the feeble sounds were hardly enough to beckon anyone. I knew that Vidhya's room opened out to the garden at the back of the house. I could always knock at her door. I walked over the pebbled pathway that ran around the house, and just as I was crossing another glass window, the curtains open, I glanced over and saw Mr and Mrs Balakrishnan in the midst of what seemed to be an argument. They were both standing in the middle of the room, and Mr Balakrishnan was clearly in the throes of rage. I could see the purple veins bulging from his face even at this distance. I stood frozen there for a moment, and then, *thwack*, he hit his wife right across the face. My hand flew to my face in an almost reflexive, protective action, and I think it was the movement that made him look at the window. His bloodshot eyes met mine, making my blood run cold. I instinctively stepped back from the window, and in that split second, decided that it was too much to make my way back to the main gate. I would probably be caught right as I reached the door by the man himself and he would drag me inside and who knew what would become of me. I looked around wildly and decided that I would try to take the nearest brick boundary wall, at least seven feet tall. I had no idea what lay on the other side, but I sprinted the few steps it took to get there, and taking help from the obliging guava tree that grew right next to it, hoisted myself and jumped over. I twisted my ankle just a bit as my leg made contact with the ground, and the pain shot up through my shin. Still, I was a teenager then and could take a lot. I looked around, trying to get my bearings. I seemed to have landed in the compound of an unfamiliar house. My first instinct was to look out for dogs; most houses in the area kept them, but no fierce creature came charging up at me. I seemed to be standing on the gravelly path that led from the gate to the house. The house itself seemed to be a run-down little place, not at all typical of the area. There was a lot of open space in front of the house, but it was running to wild, dried patches of grass everywhere and a distinct air of junk being strewn across the compound, an old tyre here, a broken Dalda tin there. I realized that the house was possibly abandoned and that there was nobody coming to look at this girl who had jumped over the wall. I hobbled out of there as fast as I could, pain radiating up with each step, looking over my shoulder, half expecting to see Mr Balakrishnan giving chase, but at long last, I reached the gate and let myself out.

15

Amma Ji

I never did anything about the slap, and I never spoke about it to anyone either, not till much, much later, but I was unable to shake off the memory, however hard I tried. Sujatha Aunty's stricken face would appear before me at the unlikeliest of times. In university, after a night-long music festival. In a train going through a tunnel under the mountains. On nights after Sanjay was born and I found myself wide awake and bone-tired at 3 a.m. It would come to me in a flash, a sinking feeling deep in my belly. *Coward, coward, coward...* went the litany. And of course, I was a complete coward. That summer, I realized just how little it takes to become a bystander. How quickly I decided to bury that incident deep into my being, to be ignored till it became a festering nightmare in which I was the one hitting and the one being hit.

Koko noticed my reticence, my swollen ankle and my disinterest in the Nag Tibba picnic plans and asked after me several times, but I stayed silent about what I had seen. Suggi knew that something was amiss almost immediately. As always, the stresses of the day emerged in my night-time kicking, an accurate and early dead giveaway of any suffering in my life.

'I know you are in trouble,' she pointed out one morning. Eyes still blurry with sleep, I was about to tell her of my predicament when she continued. 'It has to be that Sandhu fellow. I don't know why you can't stay away from him. He is such an insufferable idiot.'

I swallowed my words with the cup of tea that Mummy had brought in.

We had just another week of summer holidays before classes would resume for our grade. Niru would be back, and I could tell her, I told myself.

That morning as I ventured out, hoping to see Buddy and Flash out and about, I saw an unfamiliar presence sitting on one of the armchairs that lay about on the veranda – an elderly lady with gleaming white hair tied back in a tight bun, a lovely indigo *ikat* cotton sari draped across her ample frame, thick gold-framed spectacles on her nose and an absolutely massive red bindi sitting between her eyes. Two diamonds glinted in the sun from her earlobes. That was a lot of razzmatazz for just one face. She must have been very attractive once; it was clear in the symmetrical lines of her face. She was fair of skin like everyone in the Rawat clan was. Everything in her was now running to fat, the fleshy folds blurring the sharp angles. Buddy and Flash sat adoringly at her feet and offered tail thumps when they saw me but wouldn't get up. Shaili sat on a small stool next to her, rubbing some sort of fragrant Ayurvedic oil into the woman's pale, chubby legs.

'*Haan bhai*, so who is this pretty young lady?' the elderly woman called out as soon as she saw me. 'Come *beta*, have cashews.' She pointed to a big plate in which were placed fat, salted cashews, which she was eating. Some orange segments lay on a silver plate, too, as well as an omelette and toast and coffee. A well-thumbed book lay upside down next to her, the spine coming apart. I glanced at the title. *Surely You're Joking, Mr. Feynman!* What a strange title. I wondered what it was about.

'*Yeh to bas Gayatri didi hain, Amma* ji, *Trivedi* ji *ki beti*,' announced Shaili by way of introduction, indicating that my presence warranted no undue excitement. *Oh, it's just Gayatri.* I offered something between a namaste and a courtesy.

'Come, come, don't be shy,' said Amma ji. By now I had figured this was Koko and Bubbles' grandmother 'What happened to your ankle, huh? Fell from a tree, *nahin*?'

'Something like that,' I said, trying to pull the hem of my pants over my bruise.

She bent forward a little bit, as if to share a secret, bones creaking with the effort.

'It's okay, Gayatri. I used to be the same.'

Then she threw back her head and laughed, an uproarious laugh. I couldn't help smiling.

'And I believe you are the one who has been reading all my books, yes? The library is not that dusty this time.'

I nodded.

'Yes, my sister, too.'

'Very good, very good. What do you like reading?'

She listened keenly as I told her about some of my favourites, suggesting a couple of books that I should look out for. She was the sort of person who immediately elevated those she listened to, interested and warm and paying close attention, a queen putting her subjects at ease. The rare sort of person who genuinely liked people.

Someone opened the door from the main hall to the veranda and stepped out. I turned to see a tall, vulpine man with a thin moustache and a small scar right above his left eyebrow. He was all angles and bones and cut quite a contrast to the corpulent Amma ji.

'Oh, Tejbir, you are up, too. Come, come. This is Gayatri. *Abhi perh se gir kar chuki hain.*'

Tejbir gave me a stiff nod and reached for the newspapers. He turned to Shaili, a strange, condescending look on his face and said, '*Chai yahin le aao.*' Shaili nodded and got up to do his bidding. I also rose to return home.

'Tell your mummy to come see me, *beta*,' said Amma ji and handed me a fistful of salted cashews to take with me. Clearly, she liked to hold a durbar right there on the veranda – a generous, fleshy queen mother, dispenser of nuts, teller of superlative stories.

I spent the day organizing my things for school, which would start the next day. Later that evening, I realized I needed a political map of India and went to the stationery shop next to Gappi Bhaiya's to get it. I ran into Sukh, there with one of his aunts, Pinky Chachi, both drinking fresh sugarcane juice with great gusto. Sukh grinned when he saw me and his chachi ordered another glass of juice for me.

I told Sukh about meeting Koko's grandmother

earlier that morning. As always, Sukh was ahead of the game.

'I know, I know, I know. She's all right but did you meet that old crow – Tejbir Chacha? He is such a villain, no? Straight out of a C-grade movie. Can you imagine him running Arbour House? Will wreck the place. Anyway, do you want ice cream? Pinky Chachi said I could have one. I think I will have chocobar. Same for you, Gaya? *Arey, bol na*!'

My breath was stuck in my throat. I had to cough a few times before I finally found my voice.

'What do you mean – Tejbir Chacha will run Arbour House?'

Pinky Chachi spoke up.

'It's been on the cards for a while. What to do also? Nobody can control what one wants to do with their house. That is why this town has become what it is. But that Tejbir is a slimy old fellow. We have known him for years. He is a sharp one, doesn't speak much, does he? *Khair*, what to say about these people? The house is still in Amma ji's name. She is already touching what, eighty? Should settle things now.' Pinky Chachi took a big gulp of her juice and drained it. She opened her little sequined purse and started paying the shopkeeper. Sukh and I moved out of the shop.

'Sukh,' I voiced my urgent fear, 'what, I mean, do you know what plans he has for Arbour House?'

'Raze it down, I guess.' Sukh was no expert at reading the room. 'No, wait, I think there was some talk of converting it into a private nursing home. They think there will be a market for that soon, all the oldies swarming to Doon and all that. Maybe they need parts of the building for that. Who knows? Anyway, what I was saying was...'

'But what about the trees, Sukh? The old house, the orchards?' I could hear the hysteria in my voice.

'Don't be *pareshan*, *beta*.' Pinky Chachi came up behind me. 'Nothing has been finalized yet. These things take years. You people can comfortably stay there for a long time.'

'But that's why Tejbir has come.' I turned just in time to see Pinky Chachi holding her index finger to her crimson-painted lips at Sukh. Sukh shut up at once and tried to deflect.

'*Chal*, I will buy you ice cream,' he said. Clumsy and affectionate. Dear, dear Sukh. I felt a sudden horrifying urge to cry and shook my head.

'I better go. I have to prepare for a test,' I said and walked back home, thoughts and images buzzing through my mind. *Arbour House was to be razed? What about the* semal*? What about the litchi grove? What about the old* babool *with gooey gum dripping down its bark? The banyan that had been there since before even the house was built? The squirrels, the mynahs, the woodpeckers? What about hunchbacked old Mauna who had grown that garden, planting each sapling with her bony hands? What about Koko and Bubbles? Where would they move to? How did one move from a place like Arbour House? Didn't they mind? Didn't anyone mind? Couldn't we leave it alone – that place of beauty and grace?* I nearly got run over by a Contessa as I absent-mindedly crossed the road.

I went into my room and sat down heavily on the bed. I felt a little bit like when we had received news of *Nani's* death, that sudden punch to the stomach, that horror filled with finality. For the first time in my life, I wanted money more than anything else, enough money such that I could buy Arbour House and never let the likes of Tejbir set foot in it ever again. Enough money to build a wall around it. And a moat all around. Put some deadly crocs in.

Mummy came into the room, carrying a pile of our clothes. She saw me and walked over.

'What happened, Gaya,' she asked with a gentleness that was reserved only for moments of great distress.

'They... they are going to sell Arbour House, Mummy. Sell it off and tear it down.'

Then I hugged my mother and burst into tears.

16

The Day of the Brahma Kamals

'B*ahut sochti hai.*' This was my parents' constant refrain. I sometimes wondered what others did with their minds. Surely everyone is conditioned to think, yes, even to overthink.

Overall, my parents took a practical view of the matter at hand. If Arbour House was to be sold indeed, well, then we would have to look for accommodation once again before too long, and it would be inconvenient and expensive, but it was really not the end of the world.

Suggi, like most siblings do in that intuitive way, knew that I was hurting and was kinder to me those days. She didn't need to argue with me. She made tea for me in the evenings when I studied rather than kicking me repeatedly till I got up to do this little chore as she was otherwise wont to do. She let me play my music cassettes on the little Sony two-in-one that was almost always in a state of disrepair. I listened to 'Money for Nothing' possibly a hundred times over till the cassette gave way and the tape got stuck and twisted. There was no way I could have known that Dire Straits would forever remind me of the heartsickness that overcame me that summer at the thought of Arbour House going down. Money for nothing and chicks for free, indeed.

At least I had school again. Who knew that I would one day be grateful for extra tuition? Niru was back, looking very pink-cheeked and ruddy like she always did when she got back from her grandmother's and brought me the *bal mithai* from her village that I loved. During recess, I ate the *mithai* out of Niru's bulging tiffin box, blinked back my tears and told Niru about the trouble brewing at Arbour House. Niru listened very quietly.

'I feel like I don't even want a room of my own, Niru.' I had discovered Virginia Woolf by then. 'I just want Arbour House. I will never raze it down; I will grow lots and lots of trees in it. Cherry, oak, rhododendron.'

Niru laughed at me but not unkindly. She broke her paratha stuffed with mango pickle in half and gave me one piece. All will be well, that simple gesture seemed to say. And yet, I felt like I would never be happy again.

Soon, June made way for a very rainy July, and it wasn't hot anymore. Somewhere in London, Freddie Mercury was giving the most memorable live performance in the history of my beloved rock music, but I knew nothing about it. All I knew was that everything in Arbour House looked freshly washed and verdant and broke my heart every time I looked at it. The rain put an end to all our outdoor games.

I spent days and days dodging Koko, disappearing behind crumbling brick walls and chicken coops and hedges as soon as I sensed him walking around looking for me, not wanting to risk a conversation, not wanting to launch an attack for being such a perverse capitalist that he could not see what lay at stake here.

Mauna was always in the garden these days, hunchbacked, gnarled and impossibly old, dressed in the same white sari. I would sometimes go and watch her work from a distance. She would talk completely unselfconsciously to the plants, ignoring me completely, letting me potter about on my own and giving me her death stare if I got too close to her flower beds. The drenched geraniums, the roses that seemed to have thrown off the fact that it wasn't summer anymore, the Ranunculus pretending to be roses, honeybees trying to get at the grapes – everything was alive and thriving, oblivious to the threats that hovered above.

One evening, Mauna hobbled over to me.

'*Ay ladki*, you girl,' she barked at me. I was used to being treated like a nobody by Mauna.

'Yes, Mauna?'

'Tonight, the *brahma kamal* will bloom. The fragrance has started. You come. I will show you.' Saying so, she walked off. I gaped at her receding back. Well, this was a surprise. There was always the risk that Mauna was a serial killer and was planning to use my blood to nourish some thirsty other-worldly plants. On the other hand, I had never seen the brahma kamal bloom. I decided it would be best to inform Suggi and take my chances with Mauna.

At 7 p.m., I turned up in the garden, having begged Papa to give me his camera. Mauna was already there, but alongside her stood Amma ji, hands on her mighty hips. I nearly turned back and walked away, but they both saw me at the same time, and Mauna beckoned me. I tiptoed to the flower bed where the stately *brahma kamal* plants grew, guarding their prized flowers under papery brackets, the air already heavy with their fragrance. I peered into the flower bed. Over the last couple of weeks, I had seen the buds burst forth at the edges of the large leaves, seen them grow into beautiful, closed flowers that bowed to the ground. Nothing had prepared me for this, though – this ethereal glow of fireflies within the starry white flowers. I realized I was holding my breath, about to witness something magical. I saw Amma ji look at me and smile to herself.

Over the next two hours, I sat right there, next to the flower bed, and watched the flowers bloom, revealing layers upon layers of white petals, perfect symmetry in each infinitesimal movement.

Like a star taking birth, I thought.

Mauna kept up with her commentary. She rambled first about how these flowers bloomed all over the valley where her tiny mountain village stood. She spoke of the flowers being used in medicines. She spoke of the flower being the seat of Brahma himself.

'Mauna, the girl is not even listening to you,' said Amma ji, now sitting in a garden chair that had been brought out for her, the legs of the chair sinking into the mud. '*Beta* Gayatri, don't you want to take a picture of the flower?'

I remembered the camera that was hanging around my neck, serving only to give me a crick. I shook my head. How could I capture this resplendence in a mere picture?

'*Arey*, why not taking picture? Here, take picture of me,' said Mauna and posed, showing me her toothless smile, right there next to the flowers.

Many years later, I would come across this picture while moving my things from my hostel room at university. In a moment, the hostel room with its one steel almirah, the peeling wall paint, the faded curtain, all melted away, and I was back again in a fragrant, moonlit garden with magical flowers growing all around me. Mauna has tried to straighten herself to full height in the picture, she rests her hand on her walking stick, her head is covered and her smile twinkles in her cataract-infested eyes. You can see that she thinks she considers herself the true creator of the *brahma kamals*. Which she probably was.

'Truly the night queen,' sighed Amma ji as she started to hoist herself from the chair. The flowers had started closing their petals again. 'Aren't you going home, my girl?'

'I'll go in a few minutes,' I said.

'You are going to have some luck,' she told me as she passed by, her eyes shining. 'Now that you've watched these flowers bloom.'

I dwelled over that for a minute. Well, she could give Arbour House to me. That would be a nice, lucky start to things. I stood there waiting for the flowers to close. Ringside seats. One night only. The blooms started bowing to their natural rhythm once again and started to shut against the world. Would they be around to do this again next year? Would I be around to witness this again?

I was sleepy and blurry-eyed the next day.

'Do you want to come inside? Should I make tea for you?' asked Niru when I was walking her home, yawning widely every two steps. 'You look like you are going to crash into something.'

'Na, it's okay. I was up watching the flowers,' I replied, stifling yet another yawn.

'Very exciting,' said Niru, with a laugh. 'Do you have a new admirer that I don't know of?'

'Eh?'

'That boy on the motorbike – he's been following us. Look, he's parked there now.'

I turned around in a studiedly unobvious manner. Yes, indeed, the boy seemed to be staring right at me, but I couldn't recollect having seen him before – quite a rough-looking fellow, too. As we watched, he got down from his bike and started to walk towards us.

'What should we do? What should we do?' Niru could be counted on to panic in every crisis.

'Let's just pretend we don't care,' I offered in all my wisdom and assumed an air of nonchalance.

'He's coming here, he's coming here.' Niru was also an expert at repeating herself under pressure.

The boy stopped a couple of feet away from me and cleared his throat. I prepared for some avowal of adoration.

'Are you Sugandha Trivedi's sister?' he asked.

Niru and I gawped at him. Was he then one of Suggi's devotees?

'Can you do me a favour?' the boy continued. 'Could you return this to her and tell her I said I was sorry.' He thrust something into my hands and walked away.

'So weird.' Niru found her voice first. 'Uff, Gaya, close your mouth and open the packet and see *na*. What is it? Must be a love letter. Do you think we can read it?'

I looked down at my hands and saw the brown paper bag. I opened it and reached inside and drew out a pair of sunglasses.

Suggi's prized Wayfarers, bought at a steep discount at the Tibetan Market.

'How, why?' Niru asked. I had told her about how the ruffians had robbed Suggi of her precious glasses at Rajpur Road, taking them right off her nose.

'I have no idea.'

'We should have asked the boy why he was returning them.'

'Just lucky I guess.'

Lucky. Looked like the *brahma kamals* had turned out lucky after all.

Just not for me.

17

Sharmi, Again

We had a series of rainy days. Mummy got tired of frying pakoras for Papa and us every day, oily diskettes of potato and onion slices steaming at us from shiny steel plates, always served with wet dollops of homemade coriander chutney and cups of sharp ginger tea. Through the dripping windowpane, we could sometimes see Sukh, weighed down by a heavy raincoat, sloshing about determinedly in the rains. Sukh hated being indoors. He would pester me, too, to come out and walk with him, but Mummy thought the rain would bring about another attack of wheezing and forbade it completely, claiming that soaking in the rain lay firmly in the purview of Hindi film heroines, and well, that Sandhu fellow.

The rain had kept away the tenacious Koko, too, but then Suggi slipped on the wet court and took a bad fall at a basketball game one day. I sat by her as she recuperated, her oval face looking worse than the injuries suggested, for all the tincture of iodine that had been dabbed on the scratches and cuts. Her knees were a colourful montage of her battle scars. Koko and Bubbles came to see her, bringing with them a bunch of flowers and a small chocolate cake, badly baked by Nina Aunty herself, a gooey, undercooked mass of exotic cocoa and local sugar. I kept a stiff upper lip and refused to participate in the banter. I declared it a moral victory when Koko kept sliding me confused looks.

'There you are,' I heard as I stood the next day at the edge of the litchi grove, trying to spot the pair of cuckoos I could hear but couldn't see. 'I have been looking for you for days. What happened to you?'

I turned around guiltily and faced Koko.

'School has started,' I said. 'It's my board year, so I have to bore everyone.' My joke sounded weak to my own ears.

'I know. It is for us, too, remember? That's why I thought we should plan that picnic. I asked Sukh what happened to you. He said you are upset about the house.'

'Aren't you?' I asked, hearing the accusation in my voice.

'Gaya,' Koko's voice was surprisingly gentle, and I felt the urge to hit him leak out of me, 'how can I do anything about this? I don't want it any more than Bubbles or Mum or Dad. Or you! The house belongs to Amma ji, it always has. She can do as she pleases with it.'

'But you live here! You and Bubbles and Balbir Uncle and Nina Aunty.'

'It belongs to Amma ji.' Koko's voice was final. 'That's how it is. The oldest son of the oldest son gets Arbour House.'

Something now occurred to me.

'But he is your *chacha*, isn't he? Your father's younger brother?'

Koko sighed and looked away.

'It's complicated. My dad is Amma ji's son from her first marriage. Her husband, the first one, Paramvir Rawat, passed away very young. She moved into Arbour House with her young son when she married Colonel Luthra. Tejbir Chacha is Colonel Luthra's son from his first marriage. Colonel left his first wife to marry the widowed Amma ji. Not that I blame him; everyone falls in love with Amma ji, don't they? So, while technically, Tejbir Chacha is younger, my dad is not really the heir. He just lives here, that's all. I mean, we all do. Arbour House cannot have a Rawat heir.'

I tried to absorb all this new information. No wonder the angular, gaunt Tejbir Chacha bore no resemblance to the resplendent Amma ji. I had assumed he took after his father.

'That's a lot of second marriages for that generation.' I tried to be flippant. Koko smiled.

'There is a lot of that in my family.'

'So, Arbour House then, it belongs to Amma ji?' I couldn't think beyond the house.

'Yes, her husband left it to her, like everything else. It's hers to dispense as she pleases, and she will do no wrong by Tejbir Chacha, see? His own mother is no more. He can burn it to the ground or sell it, she will still leave it to him. I think she feels guilty for what she did to his mother, marrying her husband like she did. Poor woman, she was no match for Amma ji.'

'She could bequeath it to Balbir Uncle,' I said, half-heartedly.

'To her first husband's son? No way! She had

promised to wait till Bubbles and I finished school. Well, then, that's close, isn't it? By the middle of next year, we will be done.'

I nodded miserably.

'Maybe Tejbir Uncle will leave it to you,' I said hopefully. 'If he doesn't do too much damage, you could restore it.'

'Poor Gaya,' said Koko, making me flush.

'I don't know how you can bear to be parted with this.' I waved my hand at the splashes of green all around us, the old oak tree contemplative, a cool breeze portending the rain that would follow any minute. Koko stepped forward and took my hand. This was unexpected and unprecedented, and much as I wanted to act like an elegant main lead in this story of my life, I found myself flushing and squirming.

'Nothing lasts forever,' he said. 'It cannot. Amma ji talks of the Doon from the 1930s and there is nothing that we can recognize from that time. People in turbans. Tongas everywhere. More canals than roads. A jungle where Rajpur Road now stands. It all changed, didn't it? Things always need to change.'

'I'm sure it was better then,' I said, kicking a pebble with more force than I meant.

'You can't be such a Luddite, Gaya.'

That was the first time I had heard the term. I smiled a little at Koko using a serious word, normally found in the books he didn't read.

'I just wish I could do something. I am so helpless. I bet Suggi wouldn't stay back if something she cared about was going down like this. She would kick and scream and fight. But I am me. And I never know what to do.'

Koko sighed.

'That's our tragedy, isn't it? Both of us are too alike. We can't really stand up for much.'

'So, what happens now?' I asked, bending down to pick up a fallen flower. 'To Arbour House, I mean.'

'Tejbir Chacha will try to close the paperwork. He attempts it every summer and Amma ji keeps holding out.'

'Why does she do that? She's getting quite old.'

'Who knows? She is a wily old fox, well, vixen. Maybe she likes keeping everybody on their toes. Or maybe, like you, she just doesn't like the idea of the house going down though she never did want to stay here. She likes Hyderabad; it suits her personality so much more. Waking up at noon. Great food. Parties every night. Uppers and downers.' Koko looked thoughtful for a moment, then his face opened, and he smiled at me again.

'Come on now, should we go for the picnic? Or how about that Buffet Snack Shop? We could get cold coffee with ice cream. Or kulfi at Kumar Sweet Shop? We will all go once Suggi is better.'

'I'll think about it,' I said and turned to walk home, a little pleased at the hurt look on his face. Then I walked back, my oversized Mickey Mouse T-shirt flapping in the wind, a light drizzle beginning to fall on my forearms.

Suggi's wounds healed, and soon, she was out and about, wearing her old Wayfarers once again even though the sun was hardly out, reminding herself just how fortunate she was.

School got tougher and tougher. Niru and I started calling it 'the boulders on our shoulders'. The nightmares where we would be grasping at unfinished answer sheets pulled from our reaching hands would continue for an entire lifetime, long after even our children had written these exams, a stand-in for all the anxiety that was ours to face.

Mrs Chandrahas returned our surprise test results for maths. Shailendra Bisht had got a perfect twenty again. Niru had mistakenly put a *metre* where a *kilometre* should have been and lost half a mark. She was furious. I knew better than to tell her that it didn't matter, for, of course, it did. I myself had an eighteen on the test and thought all my hard work was paying off quite well.

'I need to beat Shailendra, I just have to,' Niru told me, white-knuckled and pale-faced, scowling at the oblivious Mr Bisht. I nodded.

'Let's practise this chapter together,' she continued. 'We can do it after school for a few days.'

Mummy was in favour of this suggestion, eternally optimistic that some of Niru's genius and drive would rub off on me. It was decided that I would stay at Niru's place every day after school till Mrs Thapa got home. Studying with Niru was torturous, to say the least. She was pure, unadulterated selfishness when it came to academics, and one needed to be a subservient pawn in her quest for perfect scores. I had resigned to this way back in middle school, so it did not come as a surprise when she asked me to quiz her on formulae on our first day of collaborative studying. It was tiring me out, this additional effort on an already burdened day, and by the time a rainy Friday rolled along, I was irritable. My period had started that morning and my stomach had been twisting every now and then all day, giving an ominous rumble when it felt like it.

I looked around Niru's house as we took a short break. I had been visiting since I was a small child, and it had remained unchanged. Neither Niru nor her mum had any interest in décor, and the same lace table cover had been adorning the dining table for the last twenty years, when Niru's grandmother had first crocheted it. The floral print on the stuffed sofa was now fading away. The striped curtains looked clean but outdated by about three decades. They had a lady to cook and clean, who would come in the mornings. When Sharmi was still alive, the house had brightened up considerably, her music and art bringing an unusual liveliness to it. Mrs Thapa had not gone out of her way to remove her sister's traces, possibly seeking comfort from her memory, and I could still see pieces of her short life lived in the house. Her paintbox sat on Niru's desk. I touched it tentatively.

Niru came back holding a glass of water for me.

'It's Sharmi's,' said Niru, looking at the box. I took the water from her and took a sip; it tasted warm.

'I know, she used to sit here and paint, looking out of this window. Sort of like "The Last Leaf".' Niru smiled at the memory and picked up the textbook again; this was no time for sentimental reminiscing. She assumed her position on the bed that was tucked away in the corner of her room, sitting with her back against the wall, her knees held up to hold her books. I would always sit at her desk, facing the window and turning sideways to talk to her. We had fallen into a routine and would work steadily till Cheeku, the cat, would jump on the piano with a soft thud to look out at the street, signalling that Mrs Thapa was about to reach home. Then I would collect my books and start my long walk home, still avoiding the hedged alley.

'I can't get this theorem.' I finally pushed the textbook away. 'I am going to leave now.'

'But we are not done,' Niru pointed out, always a firm believer in not stopping when tired but when done.

'I know, but I don't want to kill myself for two extra marks,' I snapped and started collecting my books. Niru didn't reply, and I thought she had gone into a sulk, but when I looked at her, I saw her gaze transfixed at a spot behind me. I knew in an instant what was happening. I could feel my breath slowing down, my body glazed over with a sheen of sweat that seemed to have come out of nowhere. My first instinct was to remember all the gods and goddesses that my mother believed in – and I did, too, fervently, in that instant – and then, my convent education rounded it off in a nice, secular fashion and I uttered the Lord's Prayer, too. Then I slowly turned around to where Niru was staring to finally make acquaintance with Sharmi's ghost.

There was nothing there. Just the wall. I blinked and took another look. Just the room as it always was. My breath started returning to normal.

I looked at Niru. She seemed to be in some sort of a trance, her eyes glazed.

'Niru.' My voice came out in a croak. 'Niru, what is it?'

She didn't hear me. I reached out and touched her arm.

'Niru.' I shook her arm a little. She turned and looked at me with unseeing eyes. Then she snapped out of it.

'Did you... did you see her?' she asked, droplets of sweat above her upper lip.

I shook my head.

'Niru. Listen to me, there was no one there.'

'What do you mean? She was right there!'

'I couldn't see a thing! I looked. Are you feeling all right?'

'Hello! What happened? Who is not feeling all right?' Both of us started and turned around. We hadn't realized that Mrs Thapa had come home. She saw our expressions and immediately knew something was amiss.

'Gayatri, will you please tell me what's going on?' I felt I was back in kindergarten. I looked at Niru helplessly, urging her to take charge of the situation, to say, to do something. Anything.

'Nothing, ma'am. Just something that Niru thought she saw.'

She turned to Niru and raised an eyebrow at her, her crisp, starched sari impeccably in place despite the long hours she had put in at school.

'What did you see, Niru?'

Niru kept looking at her hands. Mrs Thapa turned to me once again.

'You better tell me the truth right now, Gayatri Trivedi.'

My full name had been used. There was not much I could do now.

'Ma'am, Niru thinks she saw Sharmi. Not Sharmi herself, you see, but rather, as a matter of fact, her *spirit*.' I have never felt like a bigger idiot.

Mrs Thapa's arched brow went up a notch higher. She stayed quiet for a moment and seemed to grow taller, till she occupied all the space the room had to offer, shrinking us down to the ground.

'I see, and is this the first time?'

'No, ma'am. It has been happening for a few years. Off and on,' I offered. Niru still wouldn't look up. I suddenly felt angry at her. This was her story to tell, and here I was, holding the narrative in a soliloquy. It was up to me to take the car to the finish line. Mrs Thapa was beginning to get a telltale flush on her cheeks, a sure sign that she was struggling with anger management.

'A few years? And you've known of this all this while, Gayatri?'

I nodded miserably, my stomach knotting further with every passing moment.

'And you, have you also seen this, this *apparition*?'

'Me? No, ma'am. I tried, but she won't appear to me. It wouldn't be a problem if she did though, ma'am. I liked Sharmi.'

Mrs Thapa looked at me for another moment.

'Right. Are you done with your work? Then let's wrap up for now. I need you to go straight home, please.'

I collected my books, eager to get out of there but

also petrified of what would happen to Niru. I stole another look at her, this friend of mine since we were five. She just kept sitting there on the bed with the block-printed bedspread, her strong knees against her chest, still holding the book.

I collected my things and left, shooting an accusing look at Cheeku on my way. Stupid cat, he could have let me know Mrs Thapa had arrived.

What a mess.

18

That Trouble with Niru

Suggi and I were different in many ways but in this one way most of all – she wanted to get away to find herself, impatient for life to begin, *really* begin, to find all the exciting people that would be allowed to play significant roles in her life. I, on the other hand, felt quite certain that *this* was my tribe and my village. I had no way of knowing this then, but I was to spend the rest of my life being homesick for 1985, despite 'that trouble with Niru' that year.

As it happened, Niru got into deeper, hotter water than I had thought possible. First, both Mrs Thapa and Niru disappeared from school for an entire week. In a board year! I heard all sorts of things from the other students, each one making me sick to my stomach. Niru's archnemesis, Bisht, declared that she had joined her father on his ship and would now stay there with him, hobnobbing with the deckhands and giving up on school altogether. I glared at him, and Umesh Uniyal told him to shut up, so that conversation ended quickly, but I was agitated and restless all the time those days.

For one thing, I wouldn't put it past Mrs Thapa to report everything to my parents. Mummy wouldn't get over it, of course, she wouldn't, but it was Papa that I worried about. His daughter, embroiled in such hocus-pocus, would hit him hard. After a few days, I decided that I would confide in Suggi in case she was needed to soften the blow. In any case, it was a matter of time before she heard of it from someone else.

Before I could do that, though, Niru returned to school, looking thinner and withdrawn. I looked at her as she took her seat. Niru hadn't really changed a lot in all the years that I had known her. She just kept getting bigger but kept the same sanguine face, the same shiny hair in a perfect bob, muscular legs that could outrun everyone else in our class. She sat in her usual place but wouldn't look at me through indoor assembly and roll call as it poured outside. Finally, after the first period ended and Mrs Chandrahas left the room, I bounded up to her before the next teacher could come in and quickly slid into the empty seat next to her.

'What happened, Niru? Where did you go? I was so worried. Are you all right?' I blurted, trying to whisper but barely managing to. She looked up at me with her slanting black eyes and nodded slowly.

'Why aren't you talking to me? Are you upset with me? I know I shouldn't have told ma'am about Sharmi, but how couldn't I?'

'My mother is very angry,' said Niru finally, looking more and more miserable with every moment. 'She made me see a psychiatrist.'

'She did? Oh, goodness. What did the doctor say?'

'She said I might have hallucinated.'

I sat in silence at this. Niru seemed to have shrunk. I

squeezed her hand and ran back to my desk, and Mishra Sir waddled in, carrying a pile of our Hindi notebooks. I kept stealing glances at Niru through the lessons, but she stared fixedly at the teachers as they went in and out after each class. Sadness seemed to waft from her. Poor Niru. I wondered if I could have handled Mrs Thapa better on that day, but she did have the talent to stare right into one's soul with that icy gaze of hers. Anyway, a psychiatrist was not such a bad idea. People were known to do exorcisms for such things. At least Mrs Thapa didn't resort to shoe-smelling.

Are you happy now, Sharmi?

But as happens when we are younger, things don't last. It didn't take long for us to fall into our old routine, walking together everywhere, sharing our food, in rhythm as childhood friends invariably are. And yet, this was not the Niru I had first set sights on in kindergarten, when she had told me to not chew on my nails, gliding primly and effortlessly into my life. Something was now gnawing at her, making her look completely lost in unguarded moments.

I had no idea what to do. I kept asking Mummy to make paneer cutlets for tiffin – Niru's favourite food of all time.

For some reason, I even started taking the hedged alley back home once again, the shrubbery welcoming me back and sorry to hear of my recent troubles.

Mauna had taken to me after the *brahma kamals* had bloomed, which is to say she didn't bark at me quite that viciously anymore and wouldn't brandish her lathi at me when she found me loitering in the gardens.

One afternoon, after I dropped the newly taciturn Niru home, I found Inder waiting for me outside the gates of Arbour House, looking suspiciously nonchalant.

'What are you doing here?' I called out to him.

'Nothing much; *bas aise hi.*' He walked up to meet me and then fell in step.

'No, seriously, what are you doing here?'

He took out a packet, neatly wrapped in brown paper. I could see it was a cassette.

'Can you give this to Srividhya?' he asked me.

I stopped in my tracks.

'Srividhya? Our Vidhya?'

'Yes, I have stood outside her house for so many days. She never seems to come out. It's a mix tape.'

I stared blankly at the tape, the memory of Mr Balakrishnan fresh in my mind, and shook my head.

'Listen to me, Inder. I can't, and you should stay away from her. You don't know her family.'

'I know Krishna. Seems like a nice guy.'

'Fool, not Krishna. Her father. He will kill you. He nearly killed me!'

Inder crossed his arms, still holding his beloved cassette, and looked at me with narrowed eyes.

'I am asking you to do something for me. I can't just drop it off at her house. She might get into trouble. Just give it to her when you see her.'

'She doesn't come over anymore, Inder.'

'Well then, go over to her place and slide it over. Ask her if she likes it.'

'Go over to her house? Are you nuts? I can't, Inder! I won't. It's too much. I am dead scared of her dad.'

'Why?'

I thought of the pater of Balakrishnan's hand making contact with his wife's face and winced at the memory. I couldn't look at Inder.

'Her dad, well, he...' I struggled to find the words. How had the Balakrishnan family secret become my personal shame? 'Don't ask too many questions, Inder. I just don't want you sliced in pieces. Which songs are in the tape? Can I see?'

'Fine, Gaya, fine! I will always remember this!' Inder thundered and turned on his heel to storm off in the general direction home, kicking up little dust storms as he went. I called out after him, but he wouldn't turn to even look at me, raising his hand to gesture at me to get lost. I stared helplessly in his direction for a few minutes and then, head hanging, I opened the gate and made my way home. I was really being a fine example of a good friend all around. I shook my head and turned into the gates, feeling quite unsure of myself. I had nearly broken my ankle the last time, fleeing the mercurial Mr Balakrishnan. It was becoming clear to me that I had no real talent for intrigue, the stress of all my secrets weighing me down unbearably.

When I reached the driveway, the Rawats seemed to be headed out. Luggage was being loaded in the boot of their car and some sort of last-minute mayhem seemed evident. Nina Aunty was rushing back and forth, and Balbir Uncle was puffing determinedly at a cigarette like he always did in moments of great significance. Amma ji was perched in her usual cane chair in the veranda, shouting instructions at the staff working in the house and also eating at the same time. Koko came out of the house, carrying umbrellas, just as I was about to cross the driveway to make my way home.

'Bye, Gaya,' he called out.

'Bye? Where are you going?' I asked as he walked up to me, all long limbs and crinkly eyes.

'Back to boarding.' He looked at me. 'Summer holidays are over. Last year at school begins in right earnest!'

Koko would be gone, too. I looked up at him, tall, loping Koko – dangle a cigarette out of that mouth, and he could fit right into a Brit rock band. The Kinks, maybe. Koko of the big heart and the kind voice. Eyes the colour of that chocolate milkshake he liked so much. Hair cut so short, I knew what it would feel like without ever having touched it. Mango juice and badminton games in white sports shorts and matching shoes. Teen Spirit deodorant. White ironed shirts he rolled right up to his elbows. A tiny scar just above his right eye, where he had cut himself on the main door of Arbour House. Later that year, I would smash my hand through the glass pane of the same door and be rewarded with a small lifelong scar on my forearm for my efforts. The door that bound us together. Koko of the slightly crooked teeth and the lopsided grin that made the corners of his eyes dissolve.

'Bye, Gaya,' he said, again, holding out his hand. 'It was just so nice to meet you.'

I snapped out of my reverie, realizing I had been staring.

'Will I see you again?' I asked, my words melting

in an almost hiccupy sob, panicking at the thoughts rushing up to meet me. *There he goes, there he goes, there he goes.*

'Of course, you will. I live here, remember?' He laughed a little before remembering that he may not and sobered.

'I'll see you at Diwali, if you are around. We normally come home,' he said again. Nina Aunty was calling to him, now holding some sort of a wooden case in her hands, a living space for a musical instrument.

'You can write to me.' It was a question.

'Yes, I can tell you all about the trees and the gardens and the chickens,' I said, and he laughed.

And then, he really was gone.

19

Munni Masi with a Side of Mummy

Arbour House had a bereft air about it, moaning and sighing in the evenings when it could not find Koko and Bubbles in its various corners and crevices, watering it with their youthful chatter and their endless plans about picnics and trips. I could sense the shift in the mood of the old house, feeling it mirror my own.

Then our glamorous aunty, Munni Masi, came over for a visit.

Now, Munni Masi wasn't a patch on our pretty mother, I thought then and still stand by it today. She did, however, have that *something, something* that people refer to, helplessly wringing their hands, words failing to articulate the *je ne sais quoi* that elevates some people. She worked for an NGO in Delhi as some sort of a project coordinator and visited us often in Dehradun, where she came for something generically called 'official tours'. She wore her bob with a hairband, pushing it back and then forward to create a sort of 'puff', which really was the epitome of style in our young lives. She was much younger than Mummy, and while Mummy had been 'sold into' a life of domestic burden,

Munni Masi roamed the lands free and wild, living in a working women's hostel in Delhi and spending all her spare time travelling the length and breadth of India, which really was her one true love.

Mummy was always very disapproving of Munni Masi and did not hold back from telling her that. Unfortunately for Mummy, Munni Masi refused to take her seriously and paid no heed to her various instructions and admonitions.

We were all a little bit in love with – and very much in awe of – Munni Masi, who lounged about in black silk pyjamas at home, refused to call our father 'jija ji' and had a whole lot of unusual friends with weird lives that she would often be embroiled with, sending them long, winding letters from wherever she was. Both Suggi and I would bump into people at the most unlikely of places throughout our lives that Munni Masi had somehow influenced, including a steward in an Air Asia flight, but that's really a story for another day.

Munni Masi didn't stay for long that time, but as always, her visit was full of boxes of pineapple pastries that she would buy for us from Ellora's, new identical Madonna-emblazoned blouses for both Suggi and me and evenings full of music and dance.

'Munni Masi, can't you stay longer?' As always, that was our refrain as she packed her bags and got ready to go back. 'You stayed for just three days.'

'Oh, but I will be back soon, *meri jaan*,' said Munni Masi, plonking her stylish scarf around my neck and taking a critical look at my appearance. 'I have a longer stay coming up. Raji will have to put up with me for a few weeks at least.'

As always, Mummy went into a blue funk right after, kneading her disappointments and regrets and making them rise with every passing day.

Soon after Munni Masi's visit, Mummy decided that she wanted to learn how to cycle. She said she had gone through life wanting to do it, and it was now or never. I brought out my trusty old Hero cycle, the colour of a ripe tomato, and Mummy attacked her new project with unprecedented zeal. It was decided that I would be the chief instructor.

'*Arey*, at least wear something comfortable,' Papa interjected on the first day as Mummy tried to assume stance wearing an embroidered, six-yard cotton number. She immediately lost her temper, climbed down from the unfortunate cycle, flinging it to one corner, and stormed off in a cloud of impressive rage. Papa and I looked at each other.

'I'll stay in from tomorrow,' conceded Papa, his shoulders drooping.

The next day, we attempted it again. This time, Suggi came out to help me.

'Very good, Mummy. Now pedal, pedal, pedal!' suggested Suggi once Mummy had perched on the cycle, *pallu* firmly tucked in at the waist.

'Shut up, Suggi, you don't know anything. Pedal, pedal it seems. Be quiet!' snapped Mummy, frowning in concentration. Suggi, not used to being told off by anyone, was about to declare war when I shook my head at her.

'I am going to support you. You won't fall. Let's go,' I said, but what Mummy lacked in balance, she made up for in resolve. She couldn't put both her feet up on the pedals without feeling she would meet the ground headlong. She was terrified of falling. She couldn't make the cycle move half an inch. After forty minutes of this labour, she had had enough and thundered home once again. She refused to attempt it again the next day, despite my exhortations.

'Let it go,' Papa told me in a quiet voice when he saw me wheeling out the cycle yet again. 'Her heart is not in it anymore.'

I shrugged and decided to attack my homework instead. The first thing I noticed as I opened my notebook was my name, written in Niru's clear, cursive calligraphy. I often asked her to write my name on my books, a neat, clean start to a new notebook. I sighed once again.

'Stop sounding like a hissy chimney,' called out Suggi from the corner of the room, where she sat in the only chair in the room, her legs folded up, a crossword on her lap. I got up and went to sit next to her. Suggi could be trusted to help homework get done in half the time if she was in a helpful mood. Just as I was about to beg her to take a look at my notebook, we heard a loud 'Alakh!' from outside. I immediately draped half my body outside the window and looked in both directions, pushing aside the primrose *bel* to do so. Not one, but two sadhus! All pretence of studying was immediately abandoned, and both Suggi and I took off to investigate the duo settling in the garden of Arbour House, not in the least bothered by the cautionary tales about such beings we had been fed since childhood – how they were often crooks pretending to be ascetics and were liable to kidnap children and sell them. In any case, we were older and at least four feet too tall to be put inside any sadhu's *jhola*.

The two sadhus were quite typical in that their hair had not been washed in forever, resulting in impressive dreadlocks. Both wore only saffron dhotis, their upper bodies unclothed except for the *rudraksh mala*s, their ribs outlined under their skin.

'*Hain, hain*,' barked one of them as soon as he saw us approaching. '*Door raho*, stay away. Women are not allowed near Babaji.' I took a keen look at this *chela*. He was a tall fellow, not much older than us surely, a mere boy, but he had probably spent his life in the dark caves of the highest Himalayan ranges, caves that were often buried under snow for the most part of the year, the bearded inmates within surviving on some mystical universal energy. Babaji was older but not grey. He did not appear to be upset to see us, smiling broadly and sitting in an effortless *padmasana* under the mango tree, his dark beard hair shining in the light of the setting sun.

'How did you get in?' asked Suggi of the disciple.

'We don't need to ask anyone. We put our *dera* down when the sun sets,' informed the boy, indignant that she thought that boundaries could hold back mystics headed to enlightenment.

'Very nice,' I said, 'but the owners may not like it. There is no *durbaan* anymore, but people don't just walk in.'

The disciple did not answer and got busy with

preparing Babaji's chillum. We watched the proceedings with great interest, trying to ascertain the exact ingredients that were making up the potent stuff. The boy tried to shoo us away every now and then, but we stayed on.

'Are you a Naga sadhu?' I asked.

'Don't be an idiot,' Suggi immediately offered. 'Naga sadhus don't wear any clothes, only ash, right, Babaji?'

Nobody endorsed Suggi. We found out that the disciple went by the moniker Magananand. Magananand kept working on the chillum, and Babaji went into some sort of a deep, meditative trance, probably to escape our chatter.

'Then what are you, Aghoris?' I tried again.

'Haw, no. Aghoris eat human flesh and they have a skull, too,' Suggi was turning out to be quite a font of knowledge on ascetics. 'Do you have a skull, Magananand ji?'

'Ask Babaji,' I prodded Suggi, seeing that Magananand did not seem very cooperative.

'*Na*, *na*, don't try to talk to Babaji.' Magananand spoke up. 'He hasn't said a word for the last three years. He has taken a *maun vrat*. Very tough penance.'

'I would say so,' said Suggi with a low whistle, who had never remained silent for three minutes at a stretch since she turned one and started blabbering and had no intention of doing so, ever.

'So Magananand ji, how long will you stay here?' I asked, wondering if I would have to relinquish my rights to wandering the garden at all hours of the day. The babas may not take kindly to sharing the property with me.

'Who knows, *bachha*, who knows,' said Magananand, shrugging and looking at the sky. 'Babaji's will is beyond our understanding. The guru will guide, the guru will tell us where to go, and the guru will show the way. Now, go and ask your mother to give us rice and dal. We will now eat.'

Naturally, I was tasked with this by Suggi, who stayed behind to keep an eye on the babas. Mummy was not pleased at this sudden imposition upon her.

'Who Baba, what Baba, I am not giving anything,' she told me, in no mood to get up from the divan, where she had been trying to take a nap.

'Please, Mummy,' I begged, 'Give a little bit. They might get angry. I don't want a *shraap* in my board year.'

'Uff, so superstitious,' said Mummy but sat up anyway, probably agreeing that it was not a good idea to invite a curse for the sake of a nap. I gave Mummy a quick hug and ran back to the garden to resume my entertainment for the day. The group had collected another stooped member, who was now thundering at the sadhus.

'Aye, baba *log*, get up from here.' Mauna had apparently materialized out of thin air and was now establishing rights over the garden. 'I need to plant the bulbs today. You can move to the back of the house.'

'*Hain, hain*.' Magananand tried to scold Mauna, but Mauna was taking no prisoners. She kept up with her tirade till the older sadhu opened his eyes. We waited to see if he would reduce Mauna to ashes with his *brahm-tej* but he only smiled and got up with the help of his stick.

'*Chalo*, *mai*, tell us where to go,' he seemed to tell Mauna with his smile, and the entire party shifted to the backyard, much to our disappointment.

In some time, Mummy came by, holding a pot covered with a steel plate.

'*Arey*, where did you disappear to? I went to the garden to look for you,' she said.

'Venue shift, Mummy,' said Suggi.

Mummy saw the two sadhus, now stationed in the backyard, and feeling the mix of belief and incredulity that is the hallmark of most modern Hindus, nodded at them, offering the pot of food to Magananand, half scared that our Papa, who shared love for the famed scientific temperament with Mrs Thapa, would come by and see this little drama unfold and she would never hear the end of it.

Magananand reached out for the large steel pot with alacrity and took off the lid. The aroma of *kadhi-chawal* wafted through the air. That was that. Both the babas wasted no time in partaking of this *prasad*, licking their fingers and making loud appreciative, smacking sounds. Suggi and I observed the proceedings with interest.

'*Waah, waah, beti, saakshaat annapoorna* you are,' said Magananand, speaking to our mother as if she were a newly-wed, and the older baba nodded along. Annapoorna incarnate blushed a pretty pink at this and held out her hand to take the empty vessel. Like mothers across the length of this great country, she was obsessive about her dabbas, remembering the exact pilferage that had happened in the last twenty-five years, meticulously keeping score.

Your Vasanta Mami, what to say of her, ate all the coconut barfi and didn't return my dabba.

and

I hope Kohli Bhai Sahib pays us another visit soon and remembers to bring back the dabba in which I packed his meal for the train in the September of 1979.

'You have pleased Babaji, Mata ji,' declared Magananand, the mouthpiece. Mummy, just about forty, blanched a little at being addressed thus by this grown man. 'You must ask for something. All wishes will be granted. All!'

Mummy contemplated this sudden boon. Then her eyes lit up.

'You go.' She turned to me and Suggi and sent us packing. Suggi bristled a little at being shooed off but knew Mummy was serious.

'What do you think she is asking for,' I asked Suggi as we made our way back.

'I don't know, another child?' Suggi sniggered, setting off hysterical giggles that lasted for ten minutes.

We never got to know what Mummy asked for, but about a week from that day, I woke up early and couldn't go back to sleep. Then I thought I heard Mummy's voice outside my window. Taking care not to wake Suggi, I got up and looked through the paisley-print curtains at our window, and I saw Mummy, dressed in her customary sari, on my red cycle, riding perfectly, her long hair waving about her flushed face, looking resplendent and very, very young.

20

Niru and Sharmi

The arrival of the two sadhus took away the edge of Koko and Bubbles' absence for a while, but they soon became something of a fixture in the backyard of Arbour House, and our fascination with them slowly wore off. Nina Aunty did not seem to mind them, not too much anyway. Koko wrote to me, small, cheerful notes that spoke about his days at the boarding school, describing fierce inter-school rivalries and Founder's Day preparations. I read each letter many, many times and then saved them in a cardboard Bata shoebox with a red lid. I didn't know it then, but this shoebox would stay with me for the rest of my life, moving with me from city to city and house to house, wearing away like me but never quite getting over those years spent at Arbour House.

Amma ji went away for a short trip to Haridwar.

'Yes, everyone should go for pilgrimages at this age,' observed Mummy piously as Shaili helped her out in shelling large mounds of green peas. Some sort of *matar* festival, I told Suggi under my breath.

'Khee khee,' said Shaili, burying her face in her dupatta, 'there is no pilgrimage. I know what she will do there.' Then she put her thumb and index finger together and mimicked a smoking action, making foo-foo sounds for due effect. Suggi and I immediately started taking a keen interest in the conversation. Mummy noticed our prickling ears and tried to send us out.

'Amma ji takes ganja. I have been with her to Haridwar. Tejbir Sahib has a house there, right next to the Ganga. There is no pooja-wooja. She takes chillum and sleeps. At night, she goes for *aarti*.' Shaili looked around suddenly, belatedly cautious.

'*Chup*, silly girl,' said Mummy half-heartedly, obviously very keen on further details.

'The whole family is like that,' continued the virtuous Shaili, shelling peas at breakneck speed. 'That is why all this wealth won't stay with them. That and the curse of the freedom fighters. Their forefathers supported the British, everyone knows.'

I wondered briefly if the curse would follow Koko, currently immersed in celebrating seventy-five years of his house at his very British school, a strange sort of endorsement for our colonizers.

It was now a real possibility I might really never see Koko again, these letters the last threads holding together a brief friendship. Who knew what plans Tejbir Luthra would hatch? Amma ji might just relent under the powerful effect of ganja that very day and sign it all away. The tenants might be asked to leave, and then, that would be it. The premature end of my story at Arbour House.

I showed Koko's letters to Niru, watching her eyes

sparkle for a moment like they used to. Then she handed them back and looked away. We were sitting on 'our steps' at school, mossy and overridden with weeds, home to ants and bees, right at the back of the school building, from where we could actually see Niru's house. We had hung about these steps for as long as we had been friends, finding them an easy vantage point to keep an eye on everything.

'Nice, he's so sweet,' she said, not bothering to say that she knew exactly what my fears were and they were unfounded, and of course, Koko would come back, and yes, Arbour House would not be razed to the ground and there would be no modern nursing home built where it once stood.

'Oh, Niru, when will you sound like yourself again?' I asked, exasperated once again at her reticence.

'I am all right.'

'Then why don't you speak? All right, have you decided what you will wear for Bonfire Night?'

At this, some of the old Niru came back. As Mrs Thapa's daughter, she had been to many Bonfire Nights. Some of the teachers who had nowhere to leave their young children in the evenings would bring them to the event. Since we were tots, Niru had been talking about the time we would be the stars of Bonfire Night. She had been planning the evening in excruciating detail all this while, how she would wear an absolutely stunning outfit brought from distant shores by her father, her hair swinging about her pretty face, her dimpled left cheek captured forever in the pictures that would be taken that night – hazy, artless pictures that would suffer for the poor flashlights of that era but couldn't dull Niru's loveliness.

As she started describing the blue sequined dress that was sure to capture a hundred hearts this year, I saw a chance.

'Listen to me, Niru,' I said, putting my arm around her shoulder as she paused for a breath. 'What happened that day at your house? What did Ma'am say to you? Why were you gone for a week?'

She stiffened.

'You never told me anything, Niru. I don't want to ask again and again, but I can see it bothers you. You will feel better if you tell me. That's how it works. It's me!'

She shook her head. 'There is nothing to tell. I was made to see a psychiatrist. She said I may have hallucinated.'

'So what? Lots of people have hallucinations. It's good, right? There was no real Sharmi, or her spirit, I mean. Your mind just created it. Let's put it behind us. It's better to not be haunted, isn't it?'

She looked down at her feet and made circles in the dust with her toes.

'You will be angry,' she finally said in a low voice.

'No, I won't. What is it?'

'Gaya, I...' She faltered. I nodded my encouragement furiously, trying to prise it out of her.

'I didn't actually see Sharmi,' she blurted out. 'I... I never did. Oh, Gaya, I am so ashamed.'

I stared at her in silence, things falling into place in my mind. She didn't have to elaborate; I knew what had happened. I felt a little ashamed myself, at just how gullible I had been. I had been fed a story, and I had gobbled it all up, bones and all. I looked at Niru, now crying quite openly, and felt a sudden rage that made me want to slap her. All those years, all those years. Lying to me. Me! Niru was falling fast and deep and becoming more and more human with every passing second. I was not enjoying it at all. My Niru. The ace human.

'I don't even know why I did it. I just made it up, and you believed me, and it was such a strange time for me with Sharmi gone, I couldn't even make sense of it. And it was comforting to have the story.'

I found my throat getting dry. Recess seemed to have ended. We had missed the bell. School was getting quieter, students filing back into classrooms.

'Why again, Niru?' I finally asked. 'I can understand the first time around, all those years ago, but why now? Why again?'

Niru wiped away her tears.

'I don't know. It was nice to imagine that Sharmi was around. Especially when things got rough at school and Daddy was never around. I can't talk to Mum. At first, it was only in my head. I started thinking of what it would be like if Sharmi started coming back from the dead. How would it be? How would she behave? And it was such a comforting thought, and I started to cling to it more and more...'

'And then?' I asked despite myself.

'Then, I have never hidden anything from you, have I? So, I let you in on this story.'

'Except that you didn't tell me that it was a story.'

She shook her head and turned away, my friend of so many years. I hadn't fought with her for more than a day at a time, finding it impossible to lead a normal day without her. I cleared the lump in my throat, urging the hurt away.

'You could have told me, Niru. I would have understood. I don't get everything, but I do get you.' My rage was feeding on itself.

'I know, I know. I am just so sorry. It's been so awful, Gaya. The counsellors my mum took me to, they said they would need to put me under a hypnotic trance, and I would anyway tell them the truth. That's when I had to tell them. They looked at me like I was the biggest liar on this planet. Which I am, I suppose. Mum didn't speak to me for three days. And then Daddy had to come home on a short leave to sort it out. I… I couldn't bear to look at his face. He looked so disappointed in me. I still can't believe it. Everyone thinks I am a model student, and I am just a pathetic little cheat.'

I felt myself bristle at this. Niru, just a liar? Niru, the source of deep disappointment? Put Niru under a hypnotic trance? Niru, the one who had let me in her life with such ease that she had spoilt me for good; no one else would ever match her fierce fellowship. My rage started shifting shape, becoming something else. I was already defending her in my mind.

She didn't mean it, see? Anybody can crumble under pressure. An aunt's death is a powerful thing. People have strange ways of dealing with grief. And Niru is sensitive. I mean, she appears strong, but she takes things to heart...

'And I am so sorry for all that I did to my parents and to Sharmi's memory, but most of all, I am sorry I lied to you.'

'Get up, Niru. Let's go to class. Mishra sir won't scold you, but he might still pull my ears.' I rose and pulled her up. She dusted her skirt and looked around, trying to look as if she hadn't just wept her heart out.

'You aren't very angry, Gaya?' she asked as we started walking back.

I didn't answer for I was now thinking back to that day in the green-hedged alley, where I had been called by my name – *Gayatri* – and scared witless, had fled, not wanting to stay a moment and find out if there really had been a presence. Who was it then? Was someone, some school friend perhaps, calling for me, wanting to walk home together? Playing a prank? Who lurked amongst the shrubs? Even as I glanced at Niru's blotchy face and contemplated telling her about this, I knew I never would. I had already learnt that the most dangerous place we can step into is our minds, and Niru's recent journey down her personal rabbit hole had thrown her out battered and bruised. I bit back my question and finally spoke.

'I didn't even know my anger counted for much. I haven't ever flown into a rage, have I? I am not Suggi.'

'No, you are not,' said Niru and took my hand.

'Thank god,' she added in a whisper.

21

VIDHYA AND INDER

Tejbir Chacha chased the sadhus away, and he did it as soon as he got back after his little trip to Haridwar. Amma ji came back with him, still relaxing, as it were, with the smokables that were a hallmark of the trip. She would sit out on the veranda of Arbour House quite often those days, reading one novel after another, always eating or drinking something, bowls of nuts and biscuits always awaiting her pleasure, glasses of juice being brought in from the kitchen. She loved to share and would often call out to me to come and have a bite.

'Uff, Amma ji gives me so much work,' complained Shaili to my mother as she was once again asked to come and help with making *namakparas*. Shaili had turned out to be the secret supporter who had helped Mummy conquer the bicycle and had since become Mummy's close confidant. Mummy was now thinking of moving on to driving a motorcycle. This was beyond Shaili's ability, but she had offered to get her cousin, Kuldeep, to come down from Sahasradhara, where he worked as a tourist guide, to help Mummy out. Papa had ho-hummed at this.

'Keep rolling the dough,' Mummy instructed Shaili, trying very hard not to openly encourage Shaili, but Shaili needed no encouragement.

'She wakes up at eleven, then she wants to drink Irani tea; *kehti hain* it's because of all those years in Hyderabad. Then she wants to eat *haleem* and biryani and *paaya*. How to cook all that in this cold? She says all these people eat boiled *ghas-phus*, which she cannot stand.'

Shaili contemplated her misfortune for a moment.

'But she is nice,' she continued, remembering something. 'She gave me a real gold chain for Diwali last year! She just needs to stop eating.'

'Has she made up her mind about the house?' I asked, risking Mummy's inevitable ire at my nosiness. Fortunately, she was too busy frying the snacks now.

'Oho, she is a shrewd one, that Amma ji. She won't let Tejbir Sahib get it that easily, but he is getting closer. He keeps plying her with everything she loves, and she loves many things. Whisky. Cigarettes. Food. Travel. Talking. Books. *Waise*, why should I lie to you; he loves her like his own mother,' explained the wise Shaili, before Mummy asked her to put a lid on her stories and take it off the jar to put in the now-ready *namakpara*s.

I walked out, put off by the smell of frying and inhaled the sharp, woody air of Arbour House with relief. Soon, soon, it would all be gone. We would be asked to leave and would move to another house elsewhere in Doon, possibly closer to school. Niru and I would walk home every day. Suggi would play basketball. Papa would groan about rising prices. And soon, I, too, would forget this brief stay at Arbour House, its memory only jolted by the arrival of spring and catching a glimpse of Koko and Bubbles at the popular bakeries at Rajpur Road, where we would meet cordially enough but no longer bound by this lovely house.

I walked over to the boundary wall and looked around for Sukh. There he was, and to my astonishment, Inder, *my* Inder, *my* friend since Mrs Boyce's house, the one I had traded Phantom cigarettes and *The Phantom* comics with, was sitting comfortably with Sukh in that silly cane swing of his. They seemed to have been playing some sort of a board game and were clearly having a good time. Just because I had refused to be his messenger, Inder had clearly shifted loyalties and was now developing a deep relationship with, yes, *that Sandhu fellow*. I didn't know who I was more enraged with by this treachery, but I stormed home without saying much.

Suggi was participating in some inter-school debate competition and was preparing for it with great gusto, gesticulating furiously at herself in the mirror. I, who suffered from intense stage fright, could never really fathom her need to take centre stage in everything and watched her in silence for some time before settling down with my books and then studying late into the night. Suggi went to bed first. We had our usual fight about the lamp.

'Switch it off,' commanded Suggi.

'No, I need to finish this,' I countered.

'Don't pretend to be so studious.'

'I am not! I never tell you to switch it off when you need to study!'

'Stop it, stupid girl!'

'NO, YOU STOP IT, YOU BIG BULLY!'

Papa sauntered in.

'Yes, what's the trouble?' he asked, peering at us from over his half-moon spectacles, holding the bulky tax file that he always seemed to have around his person. Nobody ever knew when tax season came and went because, in Papa's world, it was an evergreen battle that he fought with numbers that never really made any sense to him. Before the deadline finally hit him, he would relent and seek an accountant, but he never, never once in all the years I stayed at home, gave up without a fight.

'Tell this imbecile to go to sleep.'

'Suggi,' Papa was very distressed, 'is this any way to talk about your younger sister? You are older, *beta*; you must take care of her.'

'Humph,' said Suggi eloquently before Papa could bring up my illness. As soon as Papa left, congratulating himself on this swift resolution between warring factions, Suggi turned and smacked my leg, I kicked her once, and thereafter, a truce was declared. About half an hour after Suggi had slept off, I heard a car nearby. Possibly the Rawats returning after a night of partying. I had no idea that it really was the start of the biggest scandal of my short life. We woke up the next morning to absolute mayhem. Shouts and screams in a mix of Tamil and Hindi and Punjabi were flying thick and fast. Suggi jumped out of bed and ran to the window. She reported that nothing much could be seen and that we needed to go out. We grabbed our sweaters to go outside – it had now started becoming quite cold in the mornings – and immediately bumped into Papa, who had been assigned the mission to gather information by Mummy. He had wrapped a muffler around his neck in anticipation of the cold and was now putting on his slippers to venture out. Mummy herself was torn between joining him and preparing morning tea and breakfast. Finally, the need for knowledge won, and despite her exhortations to her daughters to stay home, all four of us ventured outside.

The place of action was the boundary wall between the Balakrishnan house and the Sandhu residence. Nearly everyone on the estate had been brought outside by the row. Balbir and Nina Rawat, bleary-eyed in their respective dressing gowns, Amma ji wearing a flowery tent, which, on closer inspection, turned out to be a nightgown, Tejbir in a tracksuit leaning against the wall and lighting yet another cigarette, Mauna and Shaili who had probably already been awake for a while and at work, Flash barking excitedly at everyone, and Buddy calmly wagging his tail.

Suggi and I tried to make our way to the front. Mr Balakrishnan was one of the prime players in this fight, and he was absolutely livid. He was being held back by Prabhat, the Rawats' errand boy, but he was straining at the leash, trying to attack, of all people, Sukh. Sukh was very well represented though; all his various aunts and uncles and cousins had trooped out and were not taking any insult lying down. Serving in the armed forces was a tradition in Sukh's family, and many of them had the physique and stature to prove it. They were impeccably behaved, but it was clear that if the need arose, Balakrishnan Uncle would be taken down in a fight. We could see Krishna and the elusive Sujatha Aunty looking down at the proceedings from a room on their first floor. It was clear that Sujatha Aunty was crying. Everything seemed to rest on Prabhat's biceps and core strength as of now.

'Is this the way you raise your children? Louts, each and every one of you! I will take you to court! I will see you in hell! You will all rot in jail!' Balakrishnan Uncle was not adding any new information; he was only layering his insults. One of Sukh's uncles replied that he was free to do what he liked and that Sukh was not to be blamed. I tried to catch Sukh's eye to tell him that I was around to offer support, but he looked pale and quite shell-shocked. Pinky Chachi nudged him to make him go inside, but he stayed put, shaking her arm off. I realized Shaili, too, had made her way to our ringside seats.

'What happened?' I whispered to her.

'Vidhya has eloped with some boy. *Arey*, *haan*, isn't he a friend of yours? He had come for your birthday. The silly-looking boy who came with his little brother.'

For a moment there, I smelt oranges, a sure sign that I would faint.

'What, Inder?' said Suggi, possibly more shocked than even I was at this bolt from the blue. 'With that little Vidhya? How is it even possible? Gaya, did you know about this?'

I shook my head and nodded at the same time, thinking of the mix tape and my refusal to carry it to Vidhya.

'Please believe me, I didn't know anything, Uncle,' Sukh now said beseechingly. 'I was only friends with Inder because he used to be Gayatri's neighbour. I first met him at Gaya's party. Ask her; she is standing right there. Tell them, Gaya.'

All eyes turned to me. I wished I had never come to watch the spectacle.

'You! I know you! You were always coming to our house!' Balakrishnan Uncle turned his purple face to me.

'No, no, Uncle,' I stammered. 'I only went once with Sukh to ask for Vidhya. You threw us out!' I could sense Mummy and Papa immediately marching forward at this.

'Bhaisahab,' said Mummy, a little out of breath, 'leave Gayatri out of this. Our daughters are completely innocent. They don't know anything about anything.' Mummy paused for a breath.

'Gayatri knew nothing about Vidhya and Inder.' Papa now spoke up. 'Did you, Gaya?'

The Gaya in question was now wishing the earth could swallow her whole, nightshirt and all. I cleared my throat and gulped a few times.

'Papa, I...' I faltered. Everyone was now intensely focused on me. I was focused on the *raat ki raani* and cursing the day I ever met Inder. Or Vidhya. Or Sukh.

'I sort of knew Inder liked Vidhya,' I finally croaked.

'What? WHAT? I knew she was up to no good!'

'... but I didn't know he would run away with her...'

'And you people claim that your daughter is *doodh mein dhuli*!'

'I was only asked to carry a message which I refused,' I finally petered off.

I don't know who was more enraged – Mummy, Papa, Balakrishnan Uncle or Suggi at being left in the dark. Everyone was expressing themselves freely while I hung my head at this new depth of disappointment I had managed to reach.

A voice spoke up, mercifully drawing attention away from me.

'Listen to me, Balakrishnan ji, you need to go look for your daughter. God knows what sort of trouble these kids would have gotten into. As far as I know, their imagination will take them as far as Mussoorie and no more. Now, Prabhat, go with Balbir Sahib to the bus stand. What's your name, *beta*, you will go with Tejbir to the taxi stand, and you there in the abominable yellow T-shirt will go to...'

Amma ji quickly moved from conscription to organizing the troops. I looked at her gratefully. She smiled at me, and with a nod, indicated that I should vacate the venue, which I did with great alacrity.

I went back home and started getting ready for school, hoping against hope that I would be able to leave before the family could really get their claws into me. That was, of course, too much to ask for. I got an earful before my morning paratha and after and then post school and once again after dinner. Suggi declared that she could just never trust me again, which was acceptable to me as long she would just stop talking for a minute.

It all finally drew to a close when the runaways were

hauled back. I didn't know what had happened to Inder till much later, but Vidhya apparently did not want to return at all. She repeatedly said that it was a matter of a few months before she turned eighteen and would never ever see her father's face again. All this was reported by Prabhat, who had been sent to recover the truants, to Shaili to Suggi to me, so I never really got to know the whole truth and I never did meet Vidhya again. Krishna said that she insisted on staying with her aunt in Mussoorie. She completed the rest of the school year at a school there.

'*Batao*,' said Mummy, 'who does that? Perfectly good child, so good at studies, very pretty also, nice parents, rich household and everything. Why would she want to punish her father like this?'

And I, who had witnessed the slap, held my tongue and said nothing. I wondered if it was safe for me to go and meet Inder, but the family's rage at me kept me away from him.

22

Bubbles in Disgrace

My lack of judgment regarding the Inder episode was forgiven more easily than usual given the ever-threatening board year. September was drawing to a close. We had tests every week. It was very hot and rainy, and Arbour House was lush and leafy and sprouting everywhere. I saw butterflies and birds and started moping about once again thinking about the imminent downfall of Arbour House. Suggi, who never had any patience for my prolonged flights of mopedom, decided to take me to Forest Research Institute (FRI) so that *I could lope around the botanical and zoological museums and stop being such a sentimental wool gatherer for a bit* – her words. As it turned out, like most of Suggi's plans, this was a very good one, and we had a marvellous day, walking through the sprawling, seemingly endless grounds of FRI overlooking the majestic Greco-Roman brick edifice and looking at the shrubbery and trees dotting the land, giggling helplessly for some reason as we saw the collections of animal skins and butterflies in the museum rooms. FRI then was a meditative place, and it was so peaceful that day that even Suggi became quiet as the Mussoorie hills beckoned us through the clouds.

We stopped to eat bun-samosa on our way back, so it was quite late by the time Suggi drove us back home. Amma ji seemed to be on her way out, looking magnificent in yet another splendid sari and rubies in her ears as she waited by the vintage cars. Mummy never really cared much for clothes, and Banarasi brocades, Maheshwaris and Muga silks were not part of our vocabulary, but we were both sensitive enough to understand that this was a masterful work.

'Nice outfit, Amma ji,' Suggi said finally when she parked the scooter. I nodded along furiously.

'Oho, thank you, thank you. Now where will you find this work? Those weavers are gone, those weaves are gone, the sari wearers are also—'

'Gone?' I offered.

She threw back her head and laughed.

'A special occasion?' Even Suggi was tamer in Amma ji's regal presence.

'Oh, well, yes. This Tejbir said we should go to the club to eat. Nina and Balbir are planning to eat cabbage yet again. It's always been like this. Balbir was never one for food. Boarding school kids are perpetually hungry, aren't they? Look at Koko and Bubbles. I always felt only Tejbir and I were the true gourmands! Anyway, I like this new chef at the club; he trained at Cordon Bleu. We shall eat duck confit today!'

We nodded, not knowing duck confit from birthday confetti.

'In fact, you girls should come along!'

Our *sanskari* stomachs, filled to the brim with samosa, rebelled at this, and we cited our lack of appetite for not being able to take her up on this offer.

'Not many options here in Doon,' Amma ji continued. 'You should come visit us in Hyderabad, *beta.* What food, what food.'

'Do you like it there?' I asked. An unnecessary question, to be sure, but it sent Amma ji into raptures.

'Of course! What a regal place. What a way to live. Dehradun was always too dull for me. Couldn't wait to escape. Met Balbir's dad right here, though. He loved this town. Balbir does, too. That is why he stayed on at Arbour House. But Colonel Luthra and I, we couldn't wait to move to Hyderabad ! For me, it is home.'

Tejbir came out, all angles and claws, looking very dapper, like an eagle would were it to unreasonably take to wearing a suit.

Amma ji waved at us, and they drove off.

'Man,' Suggi immediately recovered her powers of speech, 'I hope I can be this full of life when I am pushing eighty!'

'Somehow, I have no doubt that you will.'

'I don't want to become like *Nani*, all satsang and eating once a day and Ekadashi *ka vrat*, you know?'

'I know, I know.'

We made our way back. A little later, Shaili came by to deliver something for Mummy.

'Didi,' she beckoned me as she stopped by our window on her way out, knowing of my keen interest in the subject. 'Amma ji and Tejbir Sahib have gone out to celebrate. She has decided to sign the papers tomorrow. *Mujhe sab pata hai.*' She signed off with a conspiratorial flourish.

This was it, then. The end of Arbour House. It was time to practise stoicism, much discussed that year thanks to *Julius Caesar*, which was part of our syllabus. Amor Fati, and so on. Love what happens.

'For god's sake, Gaya, at least fall in love with a person, not a house!' said Suggi as she saw my shoulders slope. 'Let's sleep. I have early training tomorrow. Anyway, Coach will fix her X-ray eyes on my stomach and scan the contents to find the samosas and make me do extra drills.'

I lay in the dark, bone-tired by all the walking at FRI but unable to sleep, doing mental negotiations with Tejbir.

You can spare the litchi orchard in return for the oaks.

I'll trade you the jackfruit trees for the sals.

The deodars for the jackfruits.

The chakotras for the khubanis.

Growing up as we did, we hadn't been taught to pray. We didn't visit temples. There was no pooja *ghar* in our house, though Mummy did hang the ubiquitous Ganesh-Lakshmi-Saraswati calendar in her kitchen, using it both to keep the gods and the *dhobi ka hisaab* in her thoughts. God, too, was a little bit like that, existing alongside the humdrum and the ordinary, not to be taken out of the everyday.

But that night, I found myself praying to whatever was running the world to spare a moment to delay the annihilation of Arbour House.

The next morning came with the promise of winter. Winter always comes suddenly in the hills. Dusk starts descending earlier and earlier, and the morning nip makes way for a serious bite. Papa had taken to yoga in a big way and had sprained his back in a big way in the process. He was taking the day off and was reading the news aloud to whoever cared to listen to him. Mummy was already making sounds about making me wear my school blazer, given that I was wheezing a bit.

I stepped out into the cool morning, and as always, skipped the back gate, walking longer to the front gate in the hope of seeing Buddy and Flash. Buddy did lumber up to me when I reached the house, his nose cold as he pressed it into my palm, but Flash wagged his tail from the veranda, where someone sat, sipping a cup of tea. She rose as soon as she saw me and hurried out.

'Bubbles!' I ran to meet her. 'How come you are here? I didn't expect to see you till Diwali. Where's Koko?'

Bubbles put her finger on her lips to quieten me down, took my hand and led the way to the gate.

'Everyone has gone to sleep only a couple of hours ago. I am in utter disgrace, man,' she declared when we were out of earshot.

'Really? What happened?'

'Nothing much. I liked my geography master very much, so I wrote a letter asking if he felt the same way. Turns out he did not, and not only that, he reported me to the powers that be! They called home, and my mother threw such a fit, like I had committed a cardinal sin.'

Bubbles relayed the events so nonchalantly that for a moment I struggled with my response. Was it just me, then, who was so utterly shocked? Bubbles had tried to romance, of all people, her geography teacher? That was some commitment to a subject.

'Your, your... master?' I spluttered. 'You mean, like, a teacher?'

'Yes, you should see him, Gaya, he is so handsome. Like Matthew Broderick. I have a picture from our last Sports Day, I'll show you. No fault of mine, I say.'

'Bubbles, gosh, I don't even know what to say.'

'Then don't say anything,' she said and grinned at me, so like Koko in that moment with the sun starting to break on her face. I stammered a little longer, looking for the right words and failing to find them.

'How is everyone at home taking it?' I finally managed.

'Like I said, Mummy blew her fuse at the school. She was very dramatic through it all but couldn't accomplish much. Mother Superior is an absolute tyrant, and none of Mummy's histrionics worked on her. She's taught Mummy, too, you know. Daddy was slightly better, but I think that's because he was drunk. Amma ji is the only one who is being a sport about it, as expected. She said all this is very common and the school should not have overreacted and expelled me.'

'Expelled? I thought you were only suspended! Oh, Bubbles, what are you going to do?'

'Oh, well, they have agreed that I can go back to take the final exams, but I can no longer stay in the hostel or attend classes, so for all practical purposes, I am home for good.'

'So will you take private tuition then?'

Bubbles laughed and put a friendly arm around my shoulder.

'I say, do you think they could get Mr Joshi to be my private tutor? Because that would be perfect!'

I gawped at her. She laughed.

'Koko is right. You do get easily shocked. How are things out here in this old pile?'

'I have school now, Bubs. I'll see you in the evening. How… how did Koko react to everything?'

Bubbles laughed as I got out of the rusted old iron gate; she put one leg on it and swung expertly.

'I met him briefly, but he did say that I was pretty lucky I was getting to go home.'

'You are so brave. Bye!'

'He also said say hi to Gayatri when you bump into her at the library.'

Right then.

23

INDER

'Mummy should be grateful that she has such steady daughters,' announced Suggi. 'Of course, you are liable to go moony-eyed over the silliest of things at times, but by and large, we do well. Look at the others around us; everyone is either romancing their teachers or running away with boys. Changing schools! Mid-year! In their final year! And their parents are letting them live. Oh, yes, sir, Mummy is very lucky indeed.'

'You should let Mummy know about her good fortune,' I suggested, hoping she would wander off and let me get on with my physics numerical. Force wasn't my best topic.

I knew exactly how my life was going to proceed. There would be no mid-year scandal to save me from my board exams. Everything, including death, would have to wait till I was done with them. Niru had upped the ante on prep and had started resembling a human raccoon with all the late nights she was putting in. Mummy had admired this trait from afar and had wished for this diligence in her daughters. Suggi, competitive in every cell in her body, had not taken kindly to this comparison and was now explaining to me why Mummy needed to look at people who were made of morally inferior fibre. Given recent events, there were plenty of these around.

'Suggi, don't yap so much and come help me,' Mummy called from her room. Suggi sighed loudly and went off looking like a martyr making some biblical sacrifice.

Bubbles' recent debacle had created a new dynamic at Arbour House. Bubbles and Nina Rawat fought like angry cats nearly every day. The fights could be heard outside the house. If we had spoken to Mummy in that tone, suffice it to say the passive aggression would have killed us in our sleep. The Rawats were made of sterner stuff though. Nina Aunty called her daughter some choice names in the course of these rows. Bubbles refused to internalize any of the accusations and threw each of them back in her mother's face. Nina Aunty, never adept at the serious business of life, was completely out of her depth. Balbir Uncle was drinking heavily by the looks of it, all swollen eyes and drooping mouth. All in all, it was a distant cry from the idyllic cocoon everyone seemed to have lived in when we had first moved into Arbour House.

That was the bad part.

As it turned out, there was a fire or flood or avalanche (Shaili was unclear on this) at one of Tejbir's plantations or farms, and he had to leave in a rush for the dark, dank corner of the world he shared with other reptiles.

'*Hona hi tha* – it had to happen.' Shaili was proud of her foresight. 'He chased away two holy babas. Curse upon curse!' As was given with Shaili, the incident got darker and darker with each telling, and soon she was claiming that thunder and lightning were striking each of Tejbir's properties down.

The force really does move in mysterious ways, I thought, as I continued to struggle with my physics work. That said, what a narrow escape for Arbour House. Somehow, in my mind, it was only at Arbour House that its fate could be decided. The fact was, Amma ji was free to hand it over anywhere and anytime she wanted to.

Suggi and I ran into Bubbles that evening when we were headed to Niru's house for her birthday party. Bubbles looked less composed than she had when she had first returned in disgrace. Some of the misery of the altercations had rubbed off on her despite her claims that she had done no wrong.

'You don't look good,' Suggi stated matter-of-factly.

'Yes, yes, I know.' Bubbles was hardly one to take offence, having that emotional independence that most boarding-school children seemed to have in my eyes. 'I need to get out of here. These Rawats are driving me nuts.'

'Isn't Amma ji helping you out?'

'Listen, Amma ji's only passion in life is to pursue *la dolce vita*. She is up to here with all the strife and stress when all she wants to do is play bridge in peace. Now, of course, Tejbir Chacha is also gone. I think she will just pack up and leave for her beloved Hyderabad soon. Anyway, where are you both off to looking so clean?'

Niru's birthday party was the same every year.

What Mrs Thapa lacked in imagination she made up in discipline. The menu didn't waver. We ate samosas, wafers and dry sandwiches every year. The décor didn't change. Pink and blue balloons would be hung in the living room. This year was special though because Niru's father was home. Captain Thapa cut an inspiring figure. He was tall and built like a bull but could rock the crankiest of babies to sleep in a minute. We loved him to bits. Niru had told me that he had made an exception to make it for her birthday that year because of the Sharmi incident. Mrs Thapa bustled about as the sound system blared out 'Wake Me Up Before You Go-Go'. Suggi had always been one of Mrs Thapa's favourites when she attended our school, and she now fawned over her, asking about her future plans. I always thought that Mrs Thapa's true persona was that of a school principal, and that is who she was, even as she bought vegetables or went to the doctor or hosted a birthday party. One rather felt like standing to attention in her presence.

We were all out in the garden, Niru wearing a high-necked striped white and black top that, for some reason, I would remember as iconic fashion for the rest of my life. We were joined by other friends from school when I saw a familiar face making his way to the party. It took me a moment to realize it was Inder, but not the Inder I had known since we were small children running amok at Mrs Boyce's house. This was a different person, but I couldn't begin to understand what was different.

'Niru,' I nudged her, 'Inder is here.'

'Oh, yes. I forgot to tell you. I ran into him at Clement Town the other day. It got very awkward. I invited him on the spur of the moment. Didn't think he would come. What has happened to him, though? Doesn't he look strange?'

He did look strange, a little lost but also a little other-worldly. Both of us stared at him in silence.

He came up to us, wished Niru and handed her a present.

'It's a book; you will like it. It's my copy so it's not new.'

'That's okay, Inder. Thank you. Which one is it?'

'*Autobiography of a Yogi*.'

'Oh, all right then, I'll let you know how it goes. Hey, do you want some Citra? I'll get you some.'

Inder finally turned to me and smiled.

'How are you, Gaya?'

This was the first time I was seeing Inder since that day outside Arbour House when he had asked me to carry his mix tape to Vidhya. It had only been a few months, and already, he seemed to have become older. Vidhya and he, how had they planned their tryst? Vidhya came from a fractured family. I knew exactly who her father was, but Inder's parents doted on him. His mum had never given away his baby clothes, she had once told me, laughing all the while as she cleaned her cupboard, but I could see how much they meant to her. What had it taken then for Inder to want to give it all up? Or had he wanted to bring Vidhya back eventually to that home? I had no answers. Wrapped up in my own life, I hadn't been to see him, hadn't bothered sending a letter to check how he was doing after the whole fiasco. I had just sort of assumed that I would run into him soon enough, like I always did. In that early October moment, standing in Niru's slightly muddy garden, I had the opportunity to see just how selfish I could be, and I didn't like it one bit.

'How... how have you been, Inder?' I finally got out some words.

He shrugged and looked at his feet.

'I didn't get to see Vidhya,' I blurted. 'Before she went away, I mean. None of us did. I never see Krishna these days either. Sukh said he takes some extra classes after school.'

He nodded but did not look up.

I wanted to check if Inder kept in touch with Vidhya, but a sudden surge of something resembling pity stopped me just in time.

Suggi came out looking for me and spotted Inder.

'Good heavens, Inder, what happened to you? Have you been unwell? Malaria? Typhoid?' asked my bulldozer of a sister. Inder still wouldn't say anything but kept smiling benevolently at both of us. I wondered if he had lost his mind a little bit. Didn't that happen to people who suffered trauma? And Mr Balakrishnan was trauma all right.

Niru finally got back with a cup of soft drink for him.

'We ran out. I had to get another crate out. Then there was no ice left. Anyway, come, let's play. Daddy is organizing some games.' She rolled her eyes, but it was easy to see how pleased she was at this – her father back to celebrate her birthday.

Inder was quiet through the games and had to leave soon after, telling Mrs Thapa that he needed to leave before it got too dark. Niru was about to cut her cake, so I walked him out instead.

'Why do you have to go so early? Captain Thapa has promised to drop us back home; you can come along. Your home isn't even too far from here,' I said as we stood outside Niru's house, the festivities visible through the open windows, the music louder than ever, laughter wafting outside on the cold air.

'I don't have to go home. I have a meditation session now.'

'A what?' I had no idea what he was talking about. Meditation was for hippies. And the Beatles. And Mahesh Yogi. It was wrapped up in all that the previous decade had meant – drugs and free love and everything that good girls from good families didn't do, as per Mummy.

'I found a guru; he has been teaching me. It's wonderful, Gaya. You should try it out, too.'

Inder and I had no way of knowing it, but meditation and chanting and an aggressive approach to feeling calm would not enter our lives for another twenty years at least and then too in dribs and drabs; so, of course, on that early winter evening in Doon, I almost winced at this suggestion.

'How are your parents reacting to this?'

He laughed and raised his shoulders in a classic what-can-you-do gesture.

'Gaya, can you come? I am going to cut my cake!' Niru hung out from the living room window.

'Go on, Gaya. It was nice seeing you.' Inder turned to leave.

'Inder, I...' I had so much to say to Inder, but I never did. He waved once and then walked into the cold night, onwards to where his life was leading him.

I never saw Inder again.

24

Nag Tibba

Bubbles wasn't able to get her way and was not sent away like she wanted to. Amma ji, too, admirably for her, stuck to Arbour House in this moment of crisis rather than returning to Hyderabad. She hired a young woman of limited means but excellent intellect, an MSc student to teach Bubbles, and we could often see Amma ji sitting and waiting as Miss Alma took Bubbles through her lessons sitting out on the veranda, the dogs lounging at their feet.

It was just Sukh and me all over again. All the friends that we had gathered along the way seemed to have fallen off from our lives. I would come home from school and eat lunch and then read a novel for a while before cursing the big exam and start slogging for it. In the evening, I would seek out Sukh, and we would sit on the boundary wall between the Sandhu property and Arbour House and talk, trying to make sense of all that had happened in the few short months we had known each other, discussing the goings-on at Arbour House.

It was another one of those days. I had just told Sukh about meeting Inder at Niru's party.

'I really thought that madman was going to kill me.' Sukh was recounting his side of the story when it was found that Inder and Vidhya had taken off quite literally for the hills.

'You were pretty fearless for someone who thought he was going to get killed,' I replied.

'Who is killing whom?' We heard a voice and turned around together.

'Koko, my man!' shouted Sukh and jumped on him. I would have liked to do the same but settled on manically grinning in the general direction of the dogs instead, suddenly very shy and flushed.

'What's up? What's up? Give me all the news,' said Koko and leaned against the wall, his shirt sleeve rolled up his brown forearm, not that anybody noticed, Buddy and Flash excitedly running in circles around him, tails wagging furiously, not quite believing that he was back.

'News upon news, Koko boy,' said Sukh and started regaling him with all the recent affairs at Arbour House. 'For one, our good friend Inder tried to do a number with Vidhya, and guess who nearly got done in for that? Me! You should have been here, Koko.'

I, who had just recently met Inder, didn't find the stories about him appetizing and kept quiet, rubbing Buddy's tummy as he lolled at my feet, a little overwhelmed at how happy seeing Koko had made me. Bubbles came looking for him in a few minutes.

'Come on, Your Highness, Shivendra Kumar Rawat ji, a fresh cake has been ordered for you. Their favourite son has finally arrived. I am, of course, the scarlet woman right now. They might throw a few crumbs my way, but we can never really be sure.'

Koko laughed and put an arm around Bubbles and waved at us.

'I better go. Let's make our trek work this time, all right? No excuses. I don't have a long break. And who knows, by the time I come back for the next break, one of you may have run away with someone.'

We offered hollow laughs as the two walked away, the dogs leading the charge.

'Nag Tibba is the best trek,' said Sukh, true to form in his confidence. 'My brother says it's the best one for beginners. It's very easy. We can plan it all out. Ask everyone. Let's all go. Niru can come. And Suggi, too, if she can stand my face. Bubbles and Koko. Will be fun. I'll plan everything.'

'Nag Tibba is a day-long trek, isn't it? We will have to stay overnight. Mummy will never let Suggi and me do it.'

'*Arey aise kaise*? I will speak to Aunty ji. And if she doesn't agree, I will get Pinky Chachi to speak to her. And if that doesn't work, I can always get Daar ji to talk with your father. Don't worry, Gaya. That's your problem – you worry too much.'

To this day, I don't know how Sukh managed to come through on his word and put this whole plan together. He convinced Suggi to come along. He repeatedly nagged Papa till he gave his word, and Papa was, of course, loath to ever go back on his word, even if it meant facing Mummy's wrath at the risk he was putting his two daughters in. Captain Thapa heard about this plan, and being the person he was, insisted that Niru was sorely in need of adventure that was necessary for all-round development and must sacrifice two days of prep time in search of this very adventure. It was decided that Thapliyal Babu, experienced trekker and Daar ji's much-trusted aide, would be sent along this merry troop. Sukh was running around like a drunken bee the whole of those two days, checking on tents and organizing food, his seemingly inexhaustible energy having found a much-needed channel.

Two days later, at 5.30 a.m., bleary-eyed and holding cups of tea handed over by Shaili, we all stood next to a jeep on the patio of Arbour House. The dogs were the only ones who had come to see us off. Mummy had woken up with us but hadn't insisted on staying till we took off. Thapliyal ji, a tall, spare, greying man who looked like a high school PT instructor, was very much in charge, Sukh, grinning widely at his plan finally taking fruition, acted like his trusted lieutenant.

'Okay, *sab log suno*,' Thapliyal ji cleared his throat and began. 'Sukhbir here has decided on Nag Tibba. Not Charbatiya, which is recommended. Anyway. We will now drive from here to Pantwari. That is about ninety kilometres from Doon. The trek itself is nothing much, about ten-twelve kilometres, and it's easy, but fitness helps.' He paused and looked at all of us meaningfully, clearly not very happy with our collective level of fitness. Suggi looked offended, having woken up early to train for basketball since middle school and feeling fit even on unfit days.

'Onwards,' Thapliyal ji commanded. We all clambered into the jeep. Thapliyal ji of course sat in the front with the driver. Sukh, Niru and I sat on one side of the two rear seats, facing Sukh, Bubbles and Koko.

'Finally, eh, finally!' shouted Sukh as the jeep's engine roared to life and we commenced our journey.

'I still cannot believe Mummy let us do this,' said Suggi, huddling against me in the cold.

'And I cannot believe my father made me do this,' said Niru. Koko and Bubbles laughed at this. Sukh looked a little bemused. The jeep gave a lurch and settled down to a steady pace, leaving Dehradun and making its way up the beautiful mountain roads, twisting and turning relentlessly, tempting the driver to take one small snooze if he dared so that we could all go plunging down to our deaths in the deep valleys. Suggi soon fell asleep, being the sort of sleeper who nods off at the very sight of a moving vehicle. The rest of us talked intermittently. Finally, the day started breaking, and we could see the views around us, the famed Himalayan splendour finally beginning to show itself and quietening the most garrulous of travellers with its sheer magnificence. Thapliyal ji allowed our first break at a small roadside village teashop, where we could stretch and feel the bracing morning air against our faces. How young we were then, how much we had to look forward to, our flawless faces turned up against the dappled sunlight as it filtered through the leaves.

Koko was taking pictures with his Minolta camera. Suggi was regaling the others with some tale or the other.

'Cannot waste time.' Thapliyal ji stood at attention and announced this in a final tone. 'Must start immediately. Need to reach base camp today. Not tomorrow. Not day after. When?'

'Today,' we offered meekly.

'Onwards!' And once again, we crowded into the jeep, giggling and tumbling upon each other. Already, we were becoming a unit, against our tyrannical taskmaster. Sukh had carried a lot of *aam papad* it appeared, and Thapliyal ji confiscated all of it, claiming that it would rot our already rotten insides. The jeep made its winding way up, up, up, till a few hours later, we reached a small village where beautiful children with deep, dark eyes ran amok in garish sweaters falling off their spare frames. The village was very poor, as most villages in the hills were at the time, water was scarce, and women had to work twice as hard as their sisters down in the valley, lifting staggering wood weight on their backs, infants strapped to their bellies, just to keep the fires burning. We waited, standing by the roadside, the vales visible down below as Thapliyal ji bustled about organizing our lunch.

'Everyone will eat bread,' he said.

We all stayed silent.

'Answer!' he commanded.

'We hadn't realized it was a question,' said Sukh. '*Haan* ji *haan* ji, everyone will eat bread.'

'Buttered bread,' Thapliyal ji now said.

'Yes, yes, buttered is fine,' replied Sukh.

'That was not a question,' said Thapliyal ji and turned away in utter disgust. We fell over each other, collapsing in mirth, finding everything breathlessly funny as young people do in such situations. I saw Koko sliding over some sticky toffees to the village tots and felt a proprietary joy that I had to shake my head like Buddy to get out of my system.

We now had to do the trekking part of the trek, and as we all started making our way up the rocky path, we realized just how arduous the climb was actually going to be.

'Are you carrying your medicines?' Suggi sidled over to me to check, out of breath already.

I nodded, wondering how we would ever get to the summit, a little ashamed as women twice my age easily overtook me, carrying huge bundles of grass on their heads, finding the energy to spare us a crinkled smile. Sukh was surprisingly the best amongst us, his long, lean legs carrying him somewhat easily up the incline. Bubbles and Koko looked more alike than ever, pink splotches visible in their unlined, fair faces.

'This. Is. Not. Easy,' spluttered Koko.

'Save energy,' commanded Thapliyal ji. 'Up!'

Up indeed. Somehow, I had imagined a neat trail with a slight incline to lead us to Nag Tibba. This rocky, dusty, uneven path had really not been part of that little daydream. Thanks to Thapliyal ji's dictatorial ways, we have but one picture of that day, taken an hour after we started walking from Pantwari village, the motley crew looking a little tired and dishevelled already, Suggi wearing her beloved Wayfarers, all of us in shoes that would today be considered wildly inappropriate for trekking.

'Thapliyal ji,' Niru ventured timidly. 'How much distance have we covered?'

We were certain that we were about to reach the summit.

'Covered? One kilometre in one hour! That's all! Now walk!'

'The journey really is the destination,' muttered Niru as we complied.

'Who said this was a beginner's trek?' Suggi couldn't believe she was struggling to race to the top.

'Of course, it is beginner's trek. Very easy,' snapped Thapliyal ji and led the troop like he was herding particularly stubborn cattle.

Almost an hour after this exchange, sweaty and exhausted, we took a break, stopping at a wayside teashop, not much more than a shed with a grimy stove on which sat a large pot of boiling tea that seemed to have been simmering there since the beginning of time itself. The chai wallah looked like a part of the mountain, his ageless face deeply furrowed and grimy, his toothless smile like a salve. We were given tea with lots of sugar and nowhere near enough milk, which we drank gratefully. The sun was beating down on our heads now.

'Will you eat the noodles?' asked Thapliyal ji.

'I think he means Maggi,' said Bubbles. Some of us nodded.

I had never really taken to Maggi, launched a couple of years ago and finding easy success with the Indian palate, but at this point in time, I would have eaten fistfuls of dirt from the ground and found them nourishing and quite delicious. Thapliyal ji looked like he had just pardoned death row convicts out of the goodness of his soul and tramped about, eager to set forth again as we sat around trying to scarf down as much food in as little time as possible.

Finally, base camp.

I sat down heavily on a boulder, looking at the immense Himalayas spread out all around us and wondering who in their right mind would try to conquer these worship-worthy beasts. Ours was but a meek attempt at a trek when people climbed right up to Auden's Col and Stok Kangri and so many other places. Koko came and sat next to me, too tired to say much, staring at the sun slowly beginning to dip in the distance, colouring the peaks orange as it went down, shaming all clichés. Swargarohini, Bandarpoonch, Kala Nag – Thapliyal ji pointed out views of the Himalayan peaks all around us expertly, his voice warm with devotion to these gods, as clouds rose from beneath us.

We were given dinner and sat around a small bonfire, trying to come up with convincing ghost stories and singing old songs till Thapliyal ji indicated that it was time to call it a day.

I had almost expected Thapliyal ji to make us put up the tents, but fortunately, these were already in place, and all that needed to be done was to fall into a deep, deep sleep.

'At least we can sleep in tomorrow.' Sukh made another attempt at levity.

'Wake up at 4 a.m.,' barked Thapliyal and shut his tent flap.

'I hope tomorrow will be as adventurous,' said Niru with a big yawn as she snuggled down in our tent. Bubbles and Suggi were sharing the other tent.

'Careful what you wish for,' I said and promptly fell asleep. I dreamt heavily through the night, chased relentlessly by some well-known monsters of the past and some new ones added to the fray for good measure. Koko slept in the tent next to ours, and my imagination sat like a ghost next to him through the night.

25

More Nag Tibba

At four the next morning, the sky still dark, cups of hot tea in our cold-jammed hands, we sat around waiting to walk up to the temple. The seemingly inexhaustible Thapliyal ji may have paced up and down the mountain through the night, waiting for the short night rest to end so that he could drive us up the summit; there really was no way to tell but he looked quite untired.

'*Agli baar* we will leave him behind,' Sukh said to me, out of Thapliyal ji's earshot, expansive as that was.

'There may not be an *agli baar*,' I whispered back, pointing to Koko and Bubbles, looking like they were ready to throw Thapliyal ji down the nearest cliff.

Breakfast was sumptuous, relatively speaking, and after partaking of the parathas and aloo-sabzi, we were on our way once again, now holding walking sticks. The cold was now worth complaining about. The idea of thermals was unknown to us then, and we bundled up the best we could and carried on.

The first kilometre or so was easy enough; the trail was still rocky, and each step was a step up, but it went through a fairly dense forest now, glistening sunlight barely slipping through the foliage. Then, however, the mountains started flexing, and we started struggling and kept lagging behind as Thapliyal ji led the charge on the unmarked trail.

Later in life, when I lived in Mumbai, year after year I would see it toss and turn for an entire summer before the monsoon would hit its shores, and then, the tired old city would heave and turn and give itself to the rains, relentless rains that would birth poetry and excite even the most cynical of hearts. The city would raise its brown face up to the sky, the first rain drenching its parched face, filling it with a delight and joy that was just a dream for the rest of the year.

The mountains and its people are like that with snow. It never gets old, and it was no different that day, when seeing the white powder compacted between rocks and boulders, we forgot how tired we were and ran towards it, picking it up in our cold hands, just to see what it felt like.

We reached the Nag Tibba temple and looked almost longingly at the path next to it, the one that would carry others to the very summit. We were now hostages of this mountain, had fallen in love with it, falling under its spell, hoping to go higher just to see what it looked like, forgetting the exhaustion that had set deep into our bones.

The temple itself was a simple enough structure, a small sanctum where the idol sat, the air redolent with the fragrance of *dhoop* and *agarbatti*. We offered our prayers and sat around for a while, resting and looking up at the rhododendron flowers swinging overhead.

'*Burunsh*. Must. Drink. Juice. Good. Health,' said Thapliyal ji, pointing at the red flowers of the trees.

'Next up – snake oil,' said Bubbles, and would later maintain that the incidents of the day were a consequence of this little irreverent remark, uttered right there where the serpent god sat.

Thapliyal ji kept looking up at the sky, and while to me, there seemed to be no sign of rain at all, I knew better than to offer this wisdom to our imperious trek master. Soon enough, he started urging everyone to wrap up and start preparing for the trek back to base camp. Reluctance was heavy in the cold mountain air as we started our long walk back. We could see little puddles of snow, slippery and dangerous. Thapliyal ji told us to be careful before taking the lead with Sukh right behind him. Suggi and Bubbles followed them while Koko, Niru and I brought up the rear.

The twists and turns of the winding mountain path were visible for a great distance down. Not just that, the trek was a bit of a chameleon, changing from dense pine forests to vast clearings to snow in a matter of hours.

Koko, Niru and I saw it happen in slow time. Bubbles was talking about how her shoelace had come loose.

'I won't tie it now, let's wait till—' We never found where, for just then, she slipped on the snow, and instead of falling backwards, she slid down the side of the mountain, her arms flailing to hold on to something, anything, clutching at the branches that peppered the mountainside. Suggi lurched for her hand and almost caught it before she gave way. Koko's scream of horror, my own gasp that seemed to get stuck in my throat, Thapliyal ji and Sukh turning around and the sickening, awful thud as Bubbles landed about twenty-five feet to the path below, branches creaking as it happened – all these I would carry with me in such crystal-clear detail that it would be decades before I would venture on a trek again. I don't remember how we all reached where she lay, but there we were, huddled all around her.

Bubbles lay in a heap, her face badly scratched but mercifully not bleeding too much. Her left arm seemed to be broken. How else would it come to be in that strange, twisted angle? She came to but kept saying that her head hurt. It really was the first real emergency I had ever been in, and in every subsequent crisis that I would face in life, I would find myself channelling Thapliyal ji. He sent Niru, Sukh and Suggi off to base camp to get help, telling them they had to wait for us at base camp as they would slow down the rescuers. The trio started off, and then Suggi remembered something, ran back to whisper something to Thapliyal ji, he looked at me, nodded and then the three started off again. I sat on a boulder by the side, looking at the pale, pale face of Bubbles, her head cradled by Thapliyal ji, who had now covered her in his jacket. Koko looked like he would faint himself as he hovered over his sister, looking more childlike in his panic than ever before, not inspiring any confidence.

I looked around in despair. We had crossed no other trekkers on our way. People of this region had been trekking arduous mountain pilgrimages forever. My own grandmother had bid all of us goodbye before she took off for Kedarnath and Badrinath; she did not expect to return. A death while trying to traverse those holy mountains would guarantee an end to the endless cycle of life and death, she said. When she did, however, return, healthier than ever and quite rosy in the cheek it may be added, it was hailed as a rebirth, and she underwent all the prescribed rituals once again.

Our people were no strangers to climbing mountains.

And yet, the mountain seemed like such a lonely place as I sat there wondering if Bubbles would die right there, my eyes scanning Thapliyal ji's face for any giveaway clues. He sat stolidly, not giving away anything, just waiting. Koko paced up and down, his worry adding to my panic.

Finally, finally, after the most interminable, dark wait, when I was ready to scream, I heard the leaves crackle, and three men came up the path, natives of the village near base camp. They had probably covered the distance in less than half the time it had taken us and with a makeshift stretcher in tow. Thapliyal ji and the men rapidly conferred in Garhwali, and then they shifted Bubbles to the stretcher, her painful, piteous screams echoing in the air. Thapliyal ji, Koko and I followed behind, our tired muscles now completely forgotten.

This is where my memory starts failing. How did we get from base camp back to Pantwari? Suggi would say that there was a doctor in Pantwari, and she helped shift Bubbles to the hospital in an ambulance. All I remember is that Sukh sat next to me on a hospital bench as we waited for the surgeon to set Bubbles' arm. There was a poster on the hospital wall urging the reader to seek medical help for, of all things, indigestion. That hospital green was splashed across the hospital, all the curtains the same colour. Where was this hospital? Dehradun? Beyond Pantwari? Another hill town? I cannot remember now; the little details are all I have.

All told, the worry about Bubbles, the lonely setting in which it happened was more terrible than her actual injuries. There was no concussion, no other fractures other than the broken arm, and as the tired-looking resident doctor cheerfully told us – young people heal fast. For what it could have been, it seemed like Bubbles had gotten away with very little.

When we returned home, there were some solid consequences of this accident. For one, Nina Aunty, having come close to losing her daughter, decided that her transgression at school had been concocted by malicious school-goers and as far as trying to tempt the handsome geography teacher into a life of salacious crime was concerned, Bubbles was, in fact, innocent. Bubbles would roll her eyes when Nina Aunty related this to whoever cared to pay heed, but she, too, kept her silence, her arm in a plaster and a glass of orange juice perpetually on her bedside table those days.

Niru informed Captain Thapa that she had had enough adventure to last her a lifetime and that could he please reserve his desire to catapult her to Himalayan peaks till after her board exams.

Sukh, overcome by guilt as the master of ceremonies, tried to visit Bubbles every day till she got annoyed by this attention and flung a water bottle at him. Post this, he kept his distance and counsel.

Suggi, unfazed and unchanged, decided she would take up trekking in a serious way and would go on to join Trekkers United, a club dedicated to Himalayan expeditions and would, in fact, become its president in a few years.

Everyone in that unfortunate Nag Tibba group thought that a gratitude-filled apology was due to Thapliyal ji, who had really saved the day, not to mention Bubbles' life, but he looked so forbidding as he went about his business in the days following the trek that we abandoned that plan post haste.

And Koko of the brown eyes disappeared almost entirely from my life. His attention and affection, which had been mine for the asking, seemed to be gone for no reason at all. It wasn't even as if he spent time with Bubbles, who hated the idea of any fuss, and in any case, siblings are incapable of smooth affection over long periods. No, Koko cut a solitary figure those days, walking the dogs, walking himself all around Arbour House, till at last, his break ended and he returned to boarding school, and this time, without saying goodbye.

26

Munni Masi Returns

Koko's departure right on the heels of the accident once again plunged the house into misery.

Books being the source of all my imagination, I frequently imagined Arbour House going up in flames like Manderley did before Tejbir Luthra could really get to it, the oaks and pines and litchis all aflame, the dry, old wood of the patio crackling as flames started to lick it, everything crumbling, crumbling, returning to ash even as he watched helplessly, smoke stinging his eyes.

Arbour House seemed to have received a short reprieve, it appeared. With Bubbles in a cast, Amma ji seemed to have forgotten that she needed to close this matter.

'Tejbir Sahib tried to reach her on the phone yesterday, but she had gone to the club,' said the ever-informed Shaili, who seemed to be everywhere at once. 'Nina Memsahib took the call and screamed at him, saying he can wait till Bubbly heals. Who knows, he might come back.'

'Bubbles, not Bubbly,' I corrected her automatically, dreading the day Tejbir made a reappearance.

'Gaya, come inside,' Mummy called reprovingly, knowing fully well that Shaili must be feeding me the Rawat household secrets. '*Kitni baar bataya hai*, don't hobnob with the help, but you just don't listen. Silly girl. Now, clean up your room and empty out one side of your cupboard for Munni.'

'Munni Masi is coming?' I could not keep the excitement out of my voice, making Mummy scowl quite openly at me.

'*Chal bhaag*, do some work,' said Mummy, who would be in the throes of a bad temper now for hours.

I informed Suggi of the good news. Mummy was outside watering the plants with a hose when Papa made his way home.

'Munni is coming tomorrow,' she told him as she started wrapping up the watering hose.

'*Bhai wah*, great news, great news,' said Papa almost absently as he parked his scooter and started taking his things out and was quite stunned when Mummy threw the hose down and flounced inside.

'Cabbage tonight?' he asked us dolefully as he came into our room. We nodded, all three of us joined in silent understanding till it was time for dinner.

Fortunately, Mummy did recover in time for Munni Masi's arrival in a cloud of Chanel No. 5.

'You smell wonderful, Masi,' said Suggi, breathing in her fragrance as she enveloped the two of us in an all-encompassing hug.

'So do you, love, so do you. Like freshly baked bread on a rainy day,' said Munni Masi with a laugh. 'Please don't get any taller, you two. You are dwarfing me out! Tell me, tell me everything!' Munni Masi was always supremely interested in our lives, always probing deeper into them with questions. 'What was this adventure then, huh, and how is your little friend now?' Trying our best to impress her, we told her the tale of our mountain misadventure, trying very hard not to communicate just how frightened we had been.

'Munni, you must tell them that they should stop all this gallivanting. I told them there was no need for this trekking-shrekking business, but nobody listens to me.' Mummy brought in a cup of coffee for Munni Masi, who did not drink tea like the rest of us. Munni Masi winked at us and took a sip of her coffee, completely unaffected by the notion of coffee at bedtime. Mummy fretted and fumed for a bit, but she was tired after the day's labours and went off to sleep soon after. Munni Masi snuggled into the quilts with us, and we talked till late into the night.

Niru came to meet Munni Masi like she always did and was enthralled by the amber necklace she had brought for her. She heard about Niru's plans and preparations for the exams and just how she would be beating Shailendra Bisht at them.

'Why can't our mums be like our aunts?' Niru asked of me when Munni Masi had stepped out, probably thinking of Sharmi, who herself had been quite an aunt.

'Your aunts would be like your mums if they were mums,' said Munni Masi as she overheard Niru.

Munni Masi and I walked to the gate of Arbour House to drop Niru off.

'What a lovely place this is,' she said, wrapping

her pashmina around her as she took in the beautiful silhouette of the house through the mist. I looked at her and wondered if I would ever look like that and if this manner of being could somehow be cultivated and sighed.

'Not for long, Masi. We might not even be here the next time you visit. The house may be gone, too.'

'Yes, Raji did mention something about it. She is not very clear about it, though.'

'Well, it's all up in the air as of—' I suddenly caught a glimpse of a man coming out of the house, lighting up a cigarette as he did so.

'It's Tejbir,' I whispered to Munni Masi, trying to look like I hadn't seen him and trying to rush her home before he could spot us. 'He has returned apparently. He is the vile one who is going to inherit the house, and he will tear it down to make it into, well, not sure what, something awful.'

'Tear this charming house down? Why would he want to do that?'

'I don't know, Masi.'

'Who knows?'

'Only he knows, I suppose.'

'Well then, let's ask him.'

And before I could get another word out, Munni Masi was marching up to Tejbir.

'Hey, Tejbir, over here,' she called out to him while I thought I would need to climb back up on that mountain and fling myself down. 'It's me, Mrinalini; call me Munni. I want to ask you – why do you want to tear this beautiful house down?'

To say Tejbir was startled would be, well, untrue. He stood frozen, staring at the vision that had emerged out of the mist in a green sari to confront him about his sins, real and prospective.

'Um,' he said. 'Um.'

'Can you not smoke? It's not good for me. Or Gaya here. Or you, though, of course, that is your choice.' She pointed at his cigarette case. He handed everything he had over – cigarette pack, lighter, a pen and chewing gum. She expertly put out the cigarette with her heel and smiled at Tejbir.

'Look,' she said, 'we should talk about this, shouldn't we? You must have your reasons. I want to know about them.'

'Munni Masi,' I had unfrozen my own person and had reached her by this time, 'let's go. Mummy must be waiting. Dinner, you know, food.'

'*Arey* wait, Gaya, or you go on ahead. I will speak to Tej and be back in a moment.'

Tej?

The man in question looked quite aghast at this prospect and looked at me quite beseechingly. For a moment, I felt pity for the villainous Tejbir.

I dithered for a moment, but it was Munni Masi – she had decided to talk to Tejbir and talk she would. So, I exercised the only option that was available to me.

I left her to it and went home.

27

Even More Munni Masi

'This Munni,' Mummy was complaining to Papa who looked more and more uncomfortable by the moment, 'badly brought up. That's what she is. How *Bau*ji raised her was very different.'

'*Bilkul, bilkul*,' agreed Papa, looking apologetically at Munni Masi, who looked supremely unconcerned and ate an apple, lounging on our ramshackle sofa with the tiny floral print. She looked so much like Mummy, and yet, completely different, like the same painting rendered by two different artists. Mummy was fair of skin and soft of flesh, even before she had had Suggi and me, squarely blamed for making her corpulent. Munni Masi was sparsely built and almost bony, her dark eyes always flashing in that unforgettable tanned face of hers, fish-shaped gold earrings shining on either side. Both Suggi and I took great pride in being likened to Munni Masi, if it ever happened, and when someone once mistook Niru for her younger sister, Niru went into paroxysms of delight.

'You tell me, what is the need for talking to that Luthra *lafanga*, *hain*?'

'No need, no need.'

'She will have us thrown out before it is time to be thrown out. Now, she doesn't have to live here, does she?'

'No, she doesn't.'

'But nobody listens to me, nobody.'

'Raji,' Munni Masi spoke up, 'our Gaya is heartbroken about the house going down. Shouldn't we find out what's going on and if we can do anything to prevent it?'

'Uff, this Gaya goes around like this place belongs to us. Always hanging around trees and birds and whatnot and crying over stupid things. They can do whatever they like to the house. How does it matter to us?'

'Because it is heartbreaking to see something of beauty die,' said Munni Masi. 'Gaya feels for things; that's a good thing.'

'*Abhi*, in a minute, I will walk over there and make you feel things, Munni.' Mummy's temper was rising, and she was back to being sixteen when Munni Masi was all of six and calling for a slap. Munni Masi shrugged and continued eating.

'And what good will it do anyway?' Mummy now demanded. 'Did that Tejbir tell you anything?'

'You are right,' said Munni Masi thoughtfully. 'He was very quiet. He needs time to think about it, possibly. That's all right. We all need to think over things. We must give Tej another chance. I will have a word with him at length.'

Mummy looked like she was going to have a stroke, looking a bit purple in the face.

'*Bas, bas.*' Papa hastened to diffuse the situation and

got up. '*Chalo*, Munni, we will go for a walk and buy fruit. Oranges. Bananas. Yes.'

Papa herded Munni Masi out of the house and Mummy put Amrutanjan balm on her head and lay down on the divan, telling Suggi to make a cup of tea for her. This was a very familiar dynamic in our family, and we all knew that to steer clear of our mother was the best course to take in this situation. Mummy really had no idea how she could control Munni Masi or even why she needed to do so. All she knew was that her sister's life was playing out very differently from her own and it seemed to be very unfair. She blamed a lot of things for this – her parents, the education system, the changing times and the proliferation of alcohol in Indian society.

I sneaked out to go to the Arbour House library. Amma ji was napping in a plantation chair on the veranda but woke up as I approached.

'Ah, yes, the little lady.' She smiled as she saw me. 'How are your studies going?'

'Yes, all right, Amma ji, all good.'

'That Shaili should make some sandwiches right about now. Do you want some?'

'No, my aunt and father have gone out to buy fruit. Mummy will want us to eat those.'

'Your aunt? Is that the elegant young woman I have seen around?'

I nodded.

Tejbir Luthra stepped out at this point. I think I spoke out in a bid to emulate Munni Masi at this point.

'Tejbir Uncle met her the other day.'

Tejbir flushed a little, nodded and reached for the newspaper. He wasn't much for words, but Amma ji made up for all that.

'*Bhai wah*, everyone seems to have met her but me. Well, call her over. Let's all meet.'

Tejbir looked at Amma ji. She stared back expectantly. I suddenly thought about how Mummy would respond to this invitation that Munni Masi would obviously accept with great alacrity and started to edge towards the library, hoping to distance myself from the scene.

'Yes, uh, let's think about it. I'll check if she is free and so on,' said Tejbir Chacha finally and settled down with the newspaper. Quite a diplomatic answer if you ask me. Clever little slip and slide right there.

'*Arey*, what is there to think? There she comes now,' said Amma ji and waved at my father and Munni Masi, walking back down the driveway with bags of fruit. Munni Masi waved back with the hand holding bananas while Papa looked comically frozen, possibly imitating my expression. Amma ji hoisted herself up, adjusting her sari and shawl.

'I was just saying that we haven't been introduced to Gayatri's lovely aunt.'

'No, no, Amma ji, I would have come by anyway,' said Munni Masi, taking the steps up to the veranda. 'It's just that work has been hectic and then I like to spend as much time as possible with these monkeys of mine. I was, in fact, just buying bananas for them. Would you like one?'

Amma ji, quite charmed and delighted already, laughed and took Munni Masi's arm and guided her to a chair, calling Shaili to bring out the tea and the sandwiches and make pakoras. I looked at Papa, who was doing some sort of a left and right rotatory movement in place, not knowing which way to turn.

'Baldev ji, please come and sit,' said Amma ji. Papa let out a small yelp at this, claiming that he needed to go home immediately. I tried to rescue him.

'I'll help you, Papa.' I tried to look at Munni Masi accusingly, but she was already engrossed in finding out the *raison d'être* of Amma ji's existence, who was flowering even more than usual under all this attention and waxing eloquent about her beloved Hyderabad. Tejbir was openly scowling at Munni Masi now, but she was quite oblivious to this, and it was evident that there was no drawing her away now. I silently took the bananas from her hand and made my way home with Papa.

'Let's keep quiet about this for now, eh?' Papa offered.

'Absolutely,' I agreed fervently.

28

The School Fête

It was already December, and it was the coldest that I had ever seen the valley get. The mornings were absolutely freezing, and bathing with barely lukewarm water was my biggest nightmare.

Our school asked for parent volunteers to help out with the school fête, and as luck would have it, my name was drawn in the lots.

'Munni will be perfect for this,' said Mummy with an air of finality that brooked no arguments. Mummy had lived in dread of this moment for the past several years, feeding her anxiety about her chaste Hindi not being quite adequate for the anglicized environment of the school. No amount of argument could persuade her otherwise. Now with her polished sister in the house, this burden could be transferred easily.

Munni Masi was already quite busy with work, but she took on the responsibility quite cheerfully, wearing one of her trademark saris with matching coats and landing up every evening at the school auditorium where the hundreds of tasks regarding the event would be accomplished. The school fête was open to anybody with an invite and was a very popular event with the parents, who attended it in droves. Students could put up games and food stalls. The fête would close at about 6 p.m. This was as close as we got to a carnival, but even in its simplicity, it had assumed a charming grandeur all its own.

Auditorium was a fancy word for that room with wooden beams and a sloping roof, but it did get a lot done. Parents, representing grades, personalities and social status would come in and help draw informative charts, make lengthy phone calls to vendors and organize food and games stalls. Each year, there would be terrible rows and tearful tantrums and all manners of political coups that could put small countries to shame, but in the end, it would all come together miraculously and our small school with its grassy little playing field and stables-turned-classrooms would emerge as the toast of our town, even getting some press.

And of course, this year, the Parents' Organizing Committee had Munni Masi taking a front-and-centre role. She quickly became the agony aunt, judge, jury and appointed executioner for all the warring factions within the committee and could often be seen listening to their tales of woe with such empathy and indulgence that one felt like drawing up one's own litany of complaints just to get a hearing with her.

The fathers would always be looking for excuses to borrow scissors from her or claiming to be lost with some list or the other, and she could be seen darting from one table to the other, helping everyone out with the kind of energy reserved for toddlers with sugar for blood in their veins. I felt a little bit guilty when people would come up to me and ask, awestruck, if this force of nature really was my mother.

I would go home each day and check the old, dilapidated letter box next to the main gate for letters, hoping against hope that there would be a blue inland envelope from the missing Koko, but he was quiet all of those weeks as the weather turned colder and colder, none of his earlier sunny missives about school now in evidence, my Bata shoebox lying forlorn in a corner.

Niru and I huddled closer together as the exams drew nearer, and even she, champion taker of exams since kindergarten, started worrying if she knew enough.

Suggi went to Mussoorie for a debate competition and was declared the best speaker, returning with a trophy as large as half our bookcase. Papa was so proud that he baked a cake for her, a first for him.

'Guess who I met in Mussoorie?' said Suggi as she unpacked her things that night.

'Who?' I was relieved to take a break from the human circulatory system.

'Vidhya.'

'Our Vidhya?'

'Who else?'

I suddenly realized that once again I had forgotten to check on Inder. In fact, I hadn't seen him since Niru's birthday party and resolved to rectify this as soon as my exams were over.

'What did she say? Did she say anything about Inder?'

'No, she didn't say anything, in fact. I asked her if she was in touch with Inder, and she stared at me blankly.'

'Oh.' I thought about this for a moment. 'Is she doing well?'

'She stood second in the debate and nearly toppled me over from first place, so I would say she is doing very well indeed.'

'But then why wouldn't she talk about Inder?'

Suggi shrugged. I could see she was trying to do it like Munni Masi, an attempt at elegance.

'Maybe she is over the whole thing, which is really not a bad idea.'

I thought about Inder and how he seemed to be coming to me in waves at Niru's party.

'Maybe I should go and see Inder before the exams,' I muttered, suddenly acutely guilty.

'No,' said Suggi. 'You should know by now that poking your nose in these things always lands you in trouble. Focus on the right things.' How easily it came to her, this wisdom, this detachment, this self-preservation against entanglement. Switch on, switch off Sugandha. Munni Masi came in at this point so there was no more talk about this, and soon enough, I forgot about Inder, the upcoming fête taking up all the time I had left over after mugging endlessly.

Niru and I were in charge of a fortune-telling stall. Of course, it was all a giant scam, but we were very committed to it. A crystal ball had been fashioned, a mechanical parrot was obtained from one of Niru's young cousins that was supposed to pick out cards or at least everyone was supposed to pretend that it was picking out cards, and all sorts of fortunes had been scribbled on pieces of paper that could mean anything in the world. To wit.

You will be the change you want to see in others

Ask not what others can do for you, just tell them

Happiness is around the corner, don't take a shortcut

Avoid the colour purple, unless you want to hurtle to trouble

Success, fame, glory – can be quite a gory story

For the privilege of having this drivel shoved down their throats, customers would have to part with one shiny rupee per reading. Quite the business model, if you ask me. We were not very hopeful that anybody would come to our stall, so we had decided to dress up as fortune tellers to drive up the authenticity of our offering.

Munni Masi would be leaving soon after my school fête, she said. She had finished the assignment that her office had sent her for and had taken some leave to extend her stay in Doon. I think back now and the memory of seeing her at my school every day in silk saris and oversized cable-knit sweaters made by Mummy still brings me a thrill.

I had taken to reading Nabokov's *Lolita* surreptitiously at the Rawat library and would often steal out to read as much as I could, sitting in one of the ever-dusty chairs, not daring to bring the book home for fear of Mummy's wrath. I would try to remember as much as I could in order to repeat the chapters to Niru at school, both of us pretending to be more disturbed than we actually were. Years later, I would be cleaning Sanjay's room and his laptop would be open to a fairly graphic pornographic site, and even in that moment of shock, I would be transported to that library at

Arbour House when our imagination had to be more permissive than we ever were, our minds were the only true boundaries to our fantasies and what we didn't know contained almost untold amounts of delight.

'Amma ji has called us all over to the club for New Year's Eve,' announced Munni Masi, as if Mummy was not bound to blow a fuse at this. 'Bubbles' cast is off, so she is coming along. Balbir and Nina will be there. And Tej. I'll take the girls. It will be fun for them!' Mummy looked like she was going to refuse but then retreated into silence. This was pretty common. Confused as she was about Munni Masi, Mummy often oscillated between indulgence and stern castigation, unable to let go of her self-authored rulebook about 'How the Responsible Older Sister Ought to Behave'. A period of trying to rein in Munni Masi at every possible juncture would often be followed by a permissive, well-I-tried-my-best phase where Mummy would give herself a break from all that sanctimony and let Munni Masi, and herself, be.

This party was an unexpected turn of events. School would always be out in the last week of December, right before Christmas break through to the new year, reopening in the first week of January. Ordinarily, we would ring in the new year at home, watching the terrible TV programme on Doordarshan and drinking delicious HPMC apple juice sold in impressively unimaginative packaging by way of celebratory drinks and eating peanuts and oranges.

'This year will be different,' said Suggi, rummaging through her limited wardrobe for something suitable to wear to this unexpected party and creating a small mountain of unsatisfactory garments on our bed. 'God bless Munni Masi.'

Then she sat down and looked straight into my eyes, a sign that she was serious and needed my unwavering attention. I nodded my head up and down a few times to communicate intense interest and complete cooperation.

'Now listen, I am going to try beer at the party. Bubbles said it's easy to smuggle it out of the club bar. You need to watch out, and don't go around telling tales. Don't even tell Koko.'

'What Koko? He is not even here.'

Suggi rolled her eyes and got up. I did not share her fascination for alcohol even at that age, but it was forbidden and therefore covetable. This perhaps was exactly what Mummy was trying to fence us in against.

29

1986

When I look back now, I don't remember the arrival of a new year being a very big deal in those days. Most people stayed indoors thanks to the biting cold. Sukh's family was planning to host their own bonfire, though, the grown-ups were quite toasty, fortified by the whisky procured from that concept of the eighties called the army canteen.

I was given to journaling, called maintaining a diary back then, and I would make flowery declarations out of my resolutions in this diary. Some of them were sweet, but the mention of most makes me squirm today.

I will pray to God every evening at 9 p.m.

I will stop eating six bananas at a go.

I will not think of Koko.

I will not think of Koko at all.

Munni Masi took charge of our appearance that day, and resultantly, we all looked like we had been cut from the same cloth. All three of us very tall and me somewhat gangly still, limbs much ahead of the rest of me. We all wore some shade of green, hair framing our faces. Munni Masi wouldn't wear anything but saris those days, but we were put into jackets and denims and felt very grown-up.

Mummy gave her grudging approval when we came out, ready to leave. Papa was much more vociferous in his praise, his *bahut badhiya* – very good – ringing through the evening air.

When we reached the patio, Bubbles was slouching against one of the vintage cars, wearing a wholly unsuitable black dress for the party. She cheered up when she saw us.

'I say, that Koko should have been here. Stupid one decided to go for a school trip instead. Anyway, so what's the plan? Amma ji will get up to her tricks; she always does. Let my parents finish fighting, and then we can all be on our merry way.'

Nina Aunty came out looking hassled and harried as she always did these days, the dogs trying their best to trip her over. Shaili was running alongside her, carrying several items.

'Ah, yes, where were we? Shaili, don't forget to put the what-do-you-call-it inside the you-know-what. And lock the kitchen door before you leave because that thing gets inside. And, oh, hello, hello, girls, how nice everyone is looking! Where is my mother-in-law? Wait, who is missing...'

She turned right back and walked back into the house, dogs and Shaili following her without missing a step.

'It's a circus,' drawled Bubbles. It was now easy to see Bubbles moving away from Arbour House. She looked uncomfortable and prickly and caged; she had outgrown the house and everyone in it.

Balbir Uncle and Amma ji appeared. Amma ji was

channelling some sort of a queen from a small princely state, all sorts of heirloom jewels glistening at her throat and ears and wrists.

'Beautiful, beautiful,' she exclaimed on seeing us though she had eyes only for Munni Masi. 'It's good to see people taking care of their appearance. *Waise*, this town is too laid-back. What is all this blandness? A colonial hangover if you ask me. Hyderabad, on the other hand, has a—'

'Nawabi hangover?' asked Munni Masi. Amma ji gave her booming laugh, easily amused. Balbir Uncle had dived into a corner for a quick smoke. Now Tejbir Chacha, too, joined him. Nina Aunty came back running, her sari *pallu* floating behind her like a train.

'Oh, where is... there he is... and where is... there she is. Right then, what are we waiting for? Yes, cars. Balbir will drive the oldie-mouldie. Amma ji, come with us? The girls will want to go together. Tejbir can drive them all. Hurry, hurry, I don't want to miss the Housie.'

Housie? Suggi and I exchanged glances. Where forth the debauchery and profligacy?

Tejbir came to the car wearing very upscale clothes and generally looking very well-groomed. Like Pran in the movies, blowing out perfect smoke rings, I thought before I caught myself glowering and decided to follow Munni Masi's example, the very font of empathy and grace. Suggi nudged me in the ribs as he opened the car door for Munni Masi, who was now asking him about his day, his time in the tea gardens of Assam and his favourite colour, all in the same breath.

Bubbles, Suggi and I crowded at the back of the nonoldie-mouldie car and soon fell into the breathless laughing conversations that only teenage girls are capable of, quite blind to the rest of the world.

We made our way to the club somewhere on Rajpur Road. We had attended a couple of weddings at this club, so it was not completely unfamiliar to us. It was a hundred and fifty years old, so, of course, I loved it, a white colonial building standing statuesque in a large, green garden and lit festively this evening in honour of the occasion. Some old British major had established the place, and it still carried his family crest and a portrait of him in a gilded frame. A small crowd had gathered out on the club lawns, drinking and laughing, but most of the guests seemed to be in the main hall of the building, lined with tables with starched white tablecloths and sparkling silver cutlery. Feeling shy as I always did in new environments, I ducked behind Suggi, who was chatting with Bubbles. Nina Aunty led the way to where a game of Housie was in progress and bought tickets for the next round. Balbir Uncle and the rest of our party went to the bar.

Two beautiful legs, one and one, eleven

Mind your son at two and one, twenty-one

I looked around and briefly wondered if this game was played exactly like a hundred years ago in this very room. Nina Aunty was immersed in the game already, holding many tickets and playing on all of them simultaneously, like a grandmaster holding her own at a dozen chessboards in a simultaneous tournament.

Liveried waiters kept bringing delicious morsels to the tables, and I just couldn't stop eating the soufflés and spinach rolls. The game got more and more hilarious. People kept getting more and more drunk. An old, retired brigadier came to our table and asked if he could join us. Then he started regaling us with stories of the ghost of an old commandant who kept an eye on the club, often seen in the rooms, making his way from one to the other. He finished with a laugh, wagging his finger at us and telling us not to venture out alone.

More drinks. More laughter. Some of the guests had gone to the dance floor. Most of the ones outside had been driven indoors by the biting cold. Through the French windows, we could look outside at the mist that had rolled over and covered the garden. It was now almost ten. I was hoping they would serve dinner. The appetizers had really done their work. Munni Masi was being asked for one dance after another by some of the army men, and at some point, someone started singing George Harrison's 'Dehradun'.

Dera-dera-Dun
Dera-Dun-Dun
Dera-dera-Dun
Dera-Dun-Dun

Suggi and Bubbles were now missing from the main hall. Nina Aunty was gossiping with a coterie of women with short hair, crisp saris and an air of professional party people. Balbir Uncle was playing some sort of a drinking game and winning. I got up, needing to go to the bathroom, and afterwards, wandered about in the milling crowds for a minute, smiling at strange faces as I tried to make my way out. The hall was feeling almost warm now. Making my way out of the doors, which some soldier very kindly opened for me, I felt the cool air on my now-flushed face and tried to shake off the air of disorientation that being out and about at this hour had brought upon me.

I made my way to the back of the hall, trying to trace the flowers spreading the almost too-sweet fragrance that seemed to be all over the misty lawns and almost immediately came upon Suggi and Bubbles, holding bottles of beer, a clear plume of smoke rising from a solitary cigarette held between Bubbles' slim fingers.

'Oh, it's just Gaya,' said Bubbles, and both adventurers looked clearly relieved. Happy as I was at not being considered a sneak, it was quite unflattering that I had no credibility for getting anyone but myself into trouble.

'Come on out. Don't stand there and gawp like a clown,' said Suggi. 'Do you want a sip?'

I nodded furiously, intent upon tasting this forbidden liquid at once. Suggi gave me her bottle, and I took a tentative sip. It was absolutely vile and burnt my throat going down. It would be about twenty years before I would attempt to drink beer again. I was about to share this with Suggi and Bubbles in no uncertain terms when I caught sight of a couple kissing under the trees. I put my fingers to my lips and pointed in that direction. All three of us gaped in delight at this sight. Now this would have been exciting enough for a New Year's Eve by itself, but in another moment, all three of us almost simultaneously recognized the man and the woman.

Sure enough. Tejbir and Munni Masi.

Something about the collective gaze of three young ladies upon what was no longer a private, intimate moment made the two break their embrace, and they saw us almost as soon as we saw them.

Beer bottles in hand and cigarette smoke billowing about.

30

The Power Dynamic

'You could have hidden the stuff,' Suggi hissed at me later that night. Munni Masi had decided to sleep in the living room upon return. The whole ride back had been spent in abject silence, Tejbir driving in silence, Munni Masi looking out of the window in silence and the three of us at the back, also, well, silent.

'How about you did not smoke and drink,' I hissed back. Suggi sat back and closed her eyes, clearly worried. This was exactly the sort of thing that Mummy could really take to heart. For the first time, Suggi was worried that Mummy may exercise some of her maternal powers and hold her back in Dehradun for college. To be made to stay back, to not go to Delhi, where college and freedom and success and glory awaited, to have to deviate from The Plan – this was anathema to Suggi.

'Smoking and drinking was not the issue. We shouldn't have been caught.' Suggi was doleful but unrepentant. 'Now what?'

'Who blinks first? Will Munni Masi tell on us? Or will we tell on her?'

'She is a grown-up. She has an inherent advantage.'

'True, true.'

'Bubbles was scared stiff. Her hands were actually shaking. I saw.'

'She has barely got out of the Joshi sir trouble. She can't afford another disgrace.'

'That horrible Tejbir,' I groaned. 'How could he be doing all this... this... stuff with our lovely Munni Masi?'

'Munni Masi did not look too put upon as far as I remember,' said Suggi thoughtfully. 'Let me think.'

I let Suggi think and changed into my pyjamas.

'Here is what we are going to do,' said Suggi, apparently having finished thinking. 'We will do nothing.'

'Wow, what a brainwave.'

'Be quiet. I think Munni Masi won't give us away. It's not like her to tell tales, especially not to Mummy.'

'Yes, but Tejbir might say something to Papa.'

'Unlikely. We will handle that when we come to that bridge. I need to understand the power dynamic.' After impressing me with these words, Suggi turned off the lights and whispered, 'Happy New Year! It's 1986!'

Munni Masi said that she needed to go to Mussoorie the next morning. She was very quiet and subdued and completely unlike herself, quite unlike the bewitching vision in green silk from the night before. We wouldn't look at her and were quite relieved when she, clearly hungover and tired, left for the bus station.

'How was the party?' Mummy asked me, openly suspicious as we headed back after dropping Munni Masi at the main gate.

'It was all right. A lot of fun.' I tried to reply calmly, but my stupid, stupid cheeks were beginning to flush under Mummy's intense frown.

Fortunately, Amma ji spotted us, and in between her booming *naya saal mubarak*s and *come have Karachi Bakery fruit biscuits*, I was able to slip away. A sweaty Sukh was running in circles around his lawn; apparently, his brother was home and was taking Sukh's fitness, or lack thereof, very personally and was now giving him tasks like running every day with his loaded school bag upon his back. I perched upon the boundary wall and watched Sukh sweat it out and felt a little thankful that I was not the only one besieged by strange troubles.

'*Yaar*, when will he go back to Khadakvasla?' Sukh panted as he ran over to me, wiping a reasonable-sized rivulet of perspiration off his face. I patted his shoulder in commiseration and had to wipe my own hand against my jeans.

'Not sure,' he puffed and panted, opening his mouth to gulp in air, 'if I am meant to be a soldier. Can't imagine pushing my sabzi into my roti with a fork, and opening doors for all women, imagine, even you, Gaya, and basically being married to the army! Not sure, man, not sure.'

I hemmed and hawed at this. Sukh continued. 'I am a bit of a poet, you see. Lover, not a fighter. Artistic temperament.'

'Really? What do you do? Draw? Paint? Sculpt? Write?'

He leaned back against the wall and closed his eyes, his breath now settling down.

'All those are minor details. I will figure them out. In the meanwhile, not sure if I want the army.'

'Maybe they won't want you.' I tried to help. Sukh bristled at this, offended at the very thought. His brother came out to check on his progress, and we both immediately straightened up. Afraid that Sandhu senior would try to assess my fitness as well, I quickly made my way back home.

School reopened, and Niru was thrilled to get all the details about the new developments at Arbour House.

'Munni Masi will be back from Mussoorie tomorrow,' I told her, dreading it. 'It's so strange to not look forward to that. Anyway, she will leave right after the fête, she says.'

'You have had too much excitement to even need fêtes and all,' said Niru. 'My New Year's Eve was so tame!'

'All five of us just froze,' I said, recounting the events of that evening. 'Then Tejbir and Munni Masi just sort of looked at each other, turned around and went back inside to the party. No conversation, no explanation to any of us. I hate the silent treatment. I got so panicked, I nearly threw up my dinner.'

'That could have been the beer,' said Niru slyly. I didn't rise to the bait.

'That Tejbir spoils everything. He kept looking at me the whole evening. Evil looks. Possibly wanted to threaten me. Everyone was too drunk to notice, especially Amma ji, who wanted to do the Viennese waltz with a young man. Maybe Tejbir will bump into me in a dark corner at Arbour House soon, wanting to have a quick word, just a friendly chat?'

'There were three of you. Why would he come just for you?'

'Stop being logical, Niru. I am telling you, he is a vile animal.'

'Of course, of course.' Niru hastily corrected her stance and recommitted to our dislike for Tejbir Luthra, cursing his very being.

Niru soon decided that the time was ripe for some trigonometry and so, I had to put my worries aside and focus on the existential angst of triangles instead.

By the time Munni Masi returned from her little tryst, we were feeling a little more like ourselves. Bubbles reported that Tejbir Chacha had also kept to himself and had not referred to the incident at all. It appeared as if this was the grown-up thing to do.

31

The Fortune Tellers

The day of the school fête finally arrived. A hand-drawn chart at our school gate promised:

Live Music!

Coffee and carrot cake!

Games, games, games!

I felt a little sentimental thrill at this. My very last school fête. At this great institution that had nurtured me, looked after my academic development, been a second home, a haven of...

'Gayatri Trivedi, goggle-eyed like a toad as usual.' Mrs Thapa's raspy voice floated into my pleasant little reverie. I looked at her, surrounded as she was by a menagerie of small children.

'No, ma'am,' I said, not sure what the question had been.

'If you have finished daydreaming, can you come inside and take these kindergarten students to their class? Their teacher is having a minor emotional crisis in the staffroom.'

'Yes, ma'am.'

I guided the twenty-odd children to their classroom and had a mini emotional crisis of my own as five of them ran off for the staircase that led to the school terrace; one hit the other with a water bottle, leading to deep and anguished yowls of pain, and two little pig-tailed girls started wailing for their teacher, afraid that I was going to take over her duties.

Nursery teachers. Can't pay them enough.

The dusty little school field looked festive today, with tents put up for the games stalls and a tired-looking merry-go-round parked right in the centre. Some slides were in evidence, too, clearly following the maxim that no colour should be left behind. Balloons and ribbons floated everywhere. Those were simpler times, and fêtes were nowhere near the carnival-like corporate extravaganzas they would grow into, but so many years later, I remember how the very air felt different, replete with the excitement of a few hundred students that day.

I caught sight of Munni Masi, still very much the head of the Parents' Organizing Committee and looking very busy and pretty as she rushed about with a clipboard in her hands, her printed pink sari swishing about her person, the other parents constantly looking to her for guidance, leaving waves of jealousy and admiration in her wake.

Niru and I had been given an out-of-the-way corner for our fortune-telling stall, creatively named Mystical Musings (come, get bewitched!). The kindest thing you could say about it was that it looked unconvincing with its pathetic-looking mechanical parrot and a bunch of forecasting cards. By contrast, the lemonade counter seemed to have been set up by people who went back six generations into lemonade-making and the games stalls made up in garish décor what they lacked in innovation. People had already started flocking to them.

After fixing and straightening up what we could, we went off to get dressed and decided to really make up for our drab stall by way of convincing costumes and exciting make-up. We made our way to our usual corner of the school, deserted as it always was. We started off as mild-mannered gypsies but as we got more familiar with the limited make-up at our disposal, it soon gave way to a look between raging psychopaths and confused brides of Frankenstein.

Finally, Niru, her eyebrows now thrice their normal thickness and shaded a colour between deep plum and vomit yellow, looked at me for approval. I clucked in appreciation.

'Very nice, very fortune-tellerish; that scar you have painted is a masterstroke. Should I add more colour to my mouth?' I asked of my best friend, relying as always on her sound judgment about these things.

Niru appraised my face critically.

'Yes,' she declared. 'And a little more darkness around the eyes. Then you will really look like a raccoon.'

'Thanks.'

'Welcome.'

Finally, we emerged from our little hideaways, our transformation now complete. We bumped into our PT instructor as we were coming out, a tall man with a proclivity for hand-rolled bidis. For some reason, he gave a start and then went away, muttering under his breath.

'Why did PT sir go away in such a hurry?' asked Niru, disappointed. 'I wanted to read him his fortune for free.'

'Must have gone away to collect the others. He will be back soon,' I assured Niru as we made our way back to our stall.

'Maybe we should have added some red to our teeth,' I wondered aloud.

'No, no. We should be subtle.'

Niru was right, of course. Subtlety pays off. A couple of middle schoolers made their way to our stall.

I smiled at them, baring my teeth to extend a warm welcome. They paled a bit and hastened off.

Soon enough, parents started making their way to our school. The field started buzzing with laughter and noise. Younger siblings were running around, ice cream cones and popcorn in their hands. Some of the fathers were taking shots at the balloon walls, hopeless aims by the look of it. Mothers were visiting the crafts stalls and admiring the amateur efforts like they were panels from the Sistine Chapel itself. Our stall, too, started getting some visitors, and they were rewarded for their efforts by our passionate fortune-telling. Parents laughed at us, gave us coins and walked away, shaking their heads.

Suggi came by with Mummy and Papa, meeting all her old teachers and school staff, who made much fuss over her.

'Look at them,' I told Niru, 'fawning over her as if she were a little lamb come home to roost.'

'Outstanding mix of metaphors.'

We told Suggi that her fortune depended entirely on whether she would buy us ice cream, at which point she announced she would not be availing of our fortune-divining services. Captain Thapa was away sailing somewhere on the high seas, so we didn't expect anyone to turn up from Niru's family. We wistfully discussed how Sharmi would have turned up, all eyes on her, hair all up in curls, earrings and bangles jangling as she walked about and long, printed Goan skirts whispering around her boots.

I was sweating in my heavy gypsy costume despite the cold, and some of my mascara was now running from the corners of my eyes, creating the sort of pathos on my face that one would only find in the Pietà.

'I don't think you have ever looked this remarkable in all the years I have known you,' said Niru, admiring my improved look.

'Thanks.'

'Welcome.'

Sukh came by with his younger cousins in tow, unexpectedly accompanied by Thapliyal ji, who took one look at me and told me that I immediately needed some fresh mountain air and *burunsh* juice. The raffle results were declared, and Mummy was very disappointed that she did not win the bright red bicycle despite having bought five tickets. Some of Suggi's school friends came by, and Papa took all of them off to have bright pink cotton-candy, poetically called *budhiya ke baal*.

The fortune-telling business was really looking quite weak. We sat around dully, playing with the toy parrot, which had at some point broken down, and now we needed to face the wrath of the five-year-old owner.

'Consumers have lost the ability to discern quality services,' said Niru. 'They are getting attracted by gimmicky marketing instead.'

'Soulless.'

'At least we look great.'

'We look marvellous.'

I was now sitting with my head on the counter, hoping that we could shut our miserable little stall soon and escape to the general revelry that was on the outside. Niru was jangling the few coins that had collected in our jar.

'I say, possible to get my fortune read?' asked a familiar voice, and my heart gave a lurch, a physical lurch, not the poetic one that one reads about in books. It gave a jump and tried to exit via my mouth.

'Koko!' I said and looked up. He jumped back a step and looked really frightened for a moment. I tried to wipe a bit of mascara off my face to communicate that it was indeed me. To Koko's credit, he recovered his composure and his courage quickly.

'Yes, ma'am, in the flesh.' Same old Koko, soft-spoken and always quite sure of his place in the world, dignity born of generations of privilege.

'How? How? How?' I asked, and then, for the sake of safety, 'How?'

'I took leave from school for, well, some stuff, you know. At home, you see. Anyway, so Bubbles said she was going to your fête, and she had an extra pass, so I tagged along. How are you doing, Gaya? Niru?'

Niru described in great and gory detail how she was doing while I silently admired the visage of the young gentleman with the kind of longing allowed only to sixteen-year-old hearts. He certainly seemed browner and bronzer than ever before, his usual white shirt very much in evidence. He spotted one of his friends in the crowd and took off to meet him. Bubbles came by and complimented both of us on our beauty and charm as our makeup tried to run further down our faces.

'Thanks.'

'Welcome.'

Bubbles leaned over my counter and whispered to me, 'We came with Tejbir Chacha. He drove the car and also the agenda to come for your fête. Look at him, will you?'

Tejbir Luthra was indeed very much on the premises, looking quite Machiavellian in a dark, slim-fitting suit, his customary cigarette missing today in deference to our school rules but the overall air of a movie gangster very much in place. How cultured he looked, how smooth, moving about with long, feline movements, charming the teachers and students alike. Who could tell he would bring the stately edifice of my beloved Arbour House down? He caught sight of the three of us staring intently at him and gave a cheerful wave, as if we had not caught him red-handed with our innocent waif of a Munni Masi just a few days ago.

'Oh, no, look, look.' Niru clutched at my arm. 'Munni Masi is making her way to him.' So she was. And not looking very waif-like, if you catch my drift. She looked quite pleased to see him. There they were, making their way to the ever-popular ice cream stall, and there he was, buying two scones of chocolate – oh, the betrayal – chocolate ice cream. Dismayed, we watched them as they laughed and chatted, quite unashamed of their behaviour just a few evenings ago. Our poor Munni Masi, waylaid and misguided by the man in the charcoal grey suit. And now, she reached and wiped what seemed to be ice cream – could have been droplets of pure evil, who can tell – from the corner of his mouth. Something about the intensity of our collective stare seemed to have shifted the air, and the duo turned to look at us. It seemed that anytime the two of them got together, three young women were there to stare them down.

'Quick, quick, look away, they are headed this way,' said Bubbles, assuming an instant and utterly unconvincing air of nonchalance while Niru and I tried to look very busy with our flourishing business of prophesizing.

Munni Masi and her companion walked over to our stall. Koko, too, found his way back, his friend in tow. There was nothing to do but to acknowledge their presence. I gave what I thought was a sophisticated, unbothered nod in their general direction.

'Hello, hello, girls,' said Munni Masi, her usual ebullience flowing out of her person. 'How's tricks?' Niru and I looked offended at this choice of greeting. There was no trickery in our business of divination, thank you.

'How about a fortune, eh?' said Tejbir, smiling in that enigmatic way of his, party to some precious secret. Munni Masi laughed and nodded.

I didn't say anything, Bubbles and Koko and his unnamed friend looked on with interest as Niru tried to crank up our toy parrot to pick up a card. Fortunately, the decrepit old tin toy did not fail us and seemed to pull out one last trick from its tattered innards. Looking relieved, Niru took the card and read it aloud – *If your desires are not extravagant, they will be granted.* She offered the card to them.

'What does that mean,' asked Munni Masi, taking the card with a grin. Niru shrugged and extended her hand for the fee. Tejbir took out some money and gave it to Niru.

'It possibly means exactly what it says,' he said and smiled at me.

32

Arbour House and Tejbir

As it happened, Koko did not stay for long. The beginning of the end was already here, and I still remember how Suggi returned from basketball practice the next morning and woke me up.

'I met Shaili on my way back home. Looks like Koko has been asked to come to witness the transfer of Arbour House to Tejbir this evening. Amma ji insists that all concerned parties be present when she hands the house over. Quite the grand dame, eh?' I stared at Suggi as she started to take her trainers off.

All concerned parties, she had said. Was I a concerned party? Did my yearning for this place of *deodar*s and *sal*s count for anything?

It was all very undramatic from that point on. It is all too far back in the past to embarrass me any longer, but I did have fantasies of playing the rescuer. Right when Amma ji would be handing over the keys to Arbour House to Tejbir's eager claws, I would barge in like a vigilante and demand all proceedings halt. I would be terribly rich in these fantasies, and while I never quite ironed out the details of how I had come upon this fortune, they always ended in Koko begging me to marry him even as I became the mistress of Arbour House.

How quietly and discreetly the power shifted. There was no big ceremony, and apparently, the whole thing was accomplished over dinner that evening. Tejbir did not hang about after he got his way, quickly returning to his plantation. Koko returned, too, to school the next day. Balbir Uncle took to smoking even more than usual and would offer a sad smile when he saw me drifting by in the mornings. Nina Aunty was busy with her bridge club and tennis lessons once again and did not seem to mind anything too much, flitting about like a bee. As was expected, Munni Masi, too had gone back after the grand success of our school fête, and it was just Suggi and me once again, after what felt like a long time.

Balbir Uncle caught hold of Papa one morning.

'Ahem, Trivedi Saab,' he ventured while my absent-minded father stopped and looked at him. 'I needed to tell you. We need to move out, you see. Not just you, ha-ha. All of us. I mean, Arbour House is now Tejbir's property, you see, and he has some, uh, some plans for it. At any rate, I know you cannot move right away. I know Gayatri's exams are coming up but after that, yes? We should give you, and everyone else, sufficient time to plan this out. I wish I had known that it would all happen so soon. Then I would not have asked you to move here.'

Papa nodded and shook Balbir Uncle's hand for a long time, looking at him and nodding like he understood.

Mummy was very upset that we had to move so soon after we had settled down. She and Papa began talking once again of settling down and building a small house of their own, much like they had at other times in their lives. Their dreams, like most middle-class people at the time, hinged on this fictitious house, but somehow, I could not imagine myself in their dream house, wanting instead an indefinite romance with the stately Arbour House, desolate as it looked these days, its wooden beams slumping in defeat. Soon, it would all disappear. Maybe some trees would be allowed to stay on as showpieces.

The big hall got dustier by the day. Nina Aunty seemed to have no energy left to ask anyone to scrub it clean. I went to the library and stood around, gazing at the hundreds of books lining the shelves, most of them untouched and unopened for decades. What would become of them? So many books, so much dust trapped within their pages, dust older than any of us.

'Oh, I don't know. Balbir will probably donate them to the club. They have a library,' said Nina Aunty when she found me in the library one day and I asked her. 'Now where is that brat Shaili? She needs to bring the boxes down.' She had begun packing, she said, and was already making arrangements to move to a large house on Rajpur Road.

'This colonial nonsense can be someone else's headache now,' she said and blinked rapidly before she turned away and went out.

Things were winding down. The drama of my short year at Arbour House was drawing to a close. One of the men who used to help with the orchards had already returned to his village.

Sukh got to know of our imminent departure and turned up one day at my window, an imaginary cricket ball in his hands, by the looks of it.

'What, Gaya, you didn't tell me,' he said and practised his bowling action. Sukh never needed any participation from me to carry on a conversation.

'You will also go. It will be so boring. My cousins are all completely cracked anyway. Can't you not go? Tell your parents.'

He quietened down as Mummy came into the room and frowned at seeing him, hanging outside our window, his face framed by the primrose vine.

'Namaste Aunty ji. Chachi said I should ask you for your *shalgam ka achaar* recipe. Wonderful it is.'

Mummy softened a little, shook her head at him and went back out.

'What plans I had made. We will all watch World Cup together next year. Who knows, we might win again, he-he-he-he.' He cracked up at his own joviality. Sukh loved cricket more than anything in the world.

'Do you have another house yet?'

'No,' I finally got a word in. 'Not yet. Papa is looking. Also depends on where I go to school next.'

'So much you study. You will go to a good school only.' Sukh was always unstinting in his support. 'Uff, Suggi is coming in through the gate, scowling at me. I will come by later.'

Papa did find a house somewhere in the centre of town. Suggi and Mummy even went to take a look and came back looking dejected. Apparently, the plumbing was not what it was made out to be. It was close to some very good schools, though, and if I managed to do well, it could be quite convenient for everyone.

We were now truly and deeply into exam fever. I had taken to waking up early so that I could get an extra hour of cramming done before getting ready for school. This was the first time I had had to do this, and I felt very virtuous as I sat at the table in the chilly room, sipping on hot tea, a thick Bhutia blanket over my knees as I, wheezing slightly, practised maths or revised Shakespeare's sonnets.

I would look out of the window as a cool February day broke over Doon Valley, bathing our beautiful little town with sunlight, and would wonder, very originally as per me, if Koko, too, was witnessing the same daybreak from the tall windows of his boarding school dormitory.

33

The Bonfire

Two weeks later, right before exams were due to start, came the evening that marked the end of our time at the mission school. Bonfire Night was not glitzy by any stretch of the imagination, but it was exciting to us – our final goodbye to our school.

That evening, I looked up into the mirror and found someone who looked like myself, a young girl excited beyond all measure and faced for the first time with the prospect of loss. I would come back to my school as an old girl now. After years of having seen impossibly grown-up girls and boys do this, it would be my turn, looking around at the familiar classrooms and grounds and people and finding that they had carried on without me. I would lose Niru, too, and how would I cope with that? That rock-like presence had been next to me since I was a small child. All that was familiar, and comforting would soon be taken from me, and the chorus demanding for me to grow up would get louder.

I look back now and wonder if I had any idea just how tough it would be, and I realize with terrifying certainty that I did not. I can only see a girl who, while being very happy where she was, also wanted things to well and truly get going, to gain speed and launch her into the future.

It was this girl who was now preening into the mirror, her hair pulled back with a black velvet hairband à la Munni Masi, a trusted hair aid guaranteed to bring out that elusive French chic or at least what we thought passed for it. Mummy was waiting for me in the living room as I stepped out.

'Here, Gaya, wear this,' she said and held out her precious pearl choker, the one that *Nani* gave to her and caused much consternation within the family, especially Munni Masi, who didn't say anything but always felt that she was the deserving candidate for this stunning piece of jewellery.

I looked doubtfully at Mummy even as my arms took on a will of their own and stretched to meet the choker. I put it on and looked in disbelief in the mirror for I had clearly transformed into a magical creature by the power of the choker, now gleaming prettily around my neck, which could be called swan-like without any exaggeration. I decided that the genetic raw material provided was of pretty good quality and with sufficient silks and jewels I, too, could qualify as a rare beauty one day.

'*Bhai wah, bhai wah*,' declared Papa as I glided out into the living room. Mummy pursed her lips but then gave in and teared up a little. Suggi took several rounds around me like a faithful dog trying to ensure that it was, indeed, still me, and having satisfied herself with the enquiry, plopped back on the sofa and gave me a thumbs-up. Papa dropped me at Niru's house, and then the two of us walked to the school feeling very 'fancy' as the term went, tottering slightly, unaccustomed to heels. Niru felt that I should keep Mummy's choker for myself, seeing that my need was clearly greater than hers. She herself was resplendent in the sequined blue dress, as had been planned.

The bonfire had been set up by the time we reached. In the tradition of the school, all the old exam papers and worksheets, finished notebooks and so on all went into the bonfire. Many of our classmates had arrived and were flitting about, looking gorgeous and uncomfortable and a little shy around each other, unaccustomed as we were to seeing each other 'decked up' like we were.

Nearly everyone was carrying autograph books, colourful notebooks with the sole purpose of having everyone write messages and small verses to be remembered by. I, too, had one, with a cartoon bear carrying an umbrella embossed on the cover. I had carefully crafted a message on the first page, to the tune of wanting to treasure my classmates' friendships and memories to my dying day. The other pages were quickly filled with messages from people that would become hazy with the passage of time. I preserved this little book for a long time and went from cringing at the messages ('Friendship is a rose that never turns old') to looking at it as an object of great emotional value. It stayed with me long enough that I had forgotten half the people who signed it. I don't quite know how I finally lost it, but I wish I hadn't.

Students of grade nine were all in school uniform,

looking very busy and important as they flitted about organizing the events of the evening. This had been us, just a year ago, and Niru and I had put up a comic sketch, which had been very popular with the outgoing seniors.

Someone lit a firecracker in the bathroom, and there was mild panic amongst the teachers while everyone tried to figure out who had done it. Once that bit of chaos had settled, the school's music system was set up and music started wafting out of the decrepit but trusty old speakers. Some of the less self-conscious students started dancing. The evening was rapidly falling upon the day, and soon it was dark. There were some cameras in evidence and pictures were taken. I still have one picture of Niru and me on that day, leaning against a wall. I have my arm around her and am smiling so widely my gums can be seen. Niru is petite and shiny-eyed and more restrained.

'Can you believe it, Gaya, this really is our last day at school. We will come back now only as old students.' Niru was now holding two paper cups of fruit punch and looking around the school building that really had been a second home to her all these years.

'Why, we still need to write our exams here, remember?'

'Uff, you know what I mean. I am going to lose a home in this place.'

I sighed at this. 'And I am going to lose two, with Arbour House also gone.'

The proceedings began. The prefect from grade nine gave a rousing speech about how wonderful we had all been. There were performances, a right *mötley crüe* of Bharatanatyam recitals and theatrical sketches. They had all put in a lot of effort, and it was all very touching in hindsight. At that moment, of course, we were too focused on smart-aleck commentary. Niru was declared Miss ICSE, and jealous cats from our class whispered that it was only because she was Mrs Thapa's daughter. I still remember who those girls were and how badly I wanted to slap them.

I still do.

We were served dinner after this. There wasn't too much of a spread, but I remember all of us gorging on a cake that had been baked specially for the evening. This was followed by more dancing around the now-dying bonfire. And soon, too soon, that evening was drawing to a close.

We were hugging the teachers. Everyone was waving at us.

Goodbye, goodbye.

We were making our way out.

All the best.

We were heading out of the school.

Come back and see us.

We were wiping away tears.

Do well, children.

One last look at the school.

Goodbye, goodbye.

34

Exam Week

March was not too cold, but we were still wearing our school blazers that week. Papa had been busy and had made all the plans. We would move out of Arbour House right after my exam. The house with the bad plumbing had been finalized. Apparently, the rent was too attractive to let things like dripping pipes get in the way. For those two weeks, I nearly forgot about this impending move, though, as life became a cycle of waking up early, revising, getting ready, eating breakfast while having no appetite, writing the exam, worrying about it, returning home, worrying about it, taking a short fitful nap, waking up to study and then repeating it the next day. Everywhere I looked in the exam hall, I saw the same expressions of anxiety and terror. Niru, too, looked jittery.

Suggi helped me revise for the exams, sitting on the bed and quizzing me while I paced the length of our room relentlessly and tried to remember all that I had tried to cram through the year. Sukh came to wish me luck as did Nina Aunty. Mauna even brought me a small bouquet of flowers past their prime, and if that wasn't a victory, I don't know what is. Maths, physics,

Hindi – days started clicking by with speed, and I had all the usual thoughts and regrets that young people do during such times.

If only I had studied a little harder.

If only I had taken to waking up a little earlier.

If only I had paid attention in Ms Mathews' class.

'It's taken the mickey out of you, these exams,' said Suggi when I finally returned home after conquering the last one. I glanced at myself in the mirror and had to agree. Dark circles spread out from under my eyes. I looked more drawn and scrawnier than I had ever been. My hair stood about my face in fierce-looking curls.

'I don't remember studying this much for my boards,' she continued.

'Obviously not,' I snapped. 'You are the genius, remember?'

Suggi shrugged at this, not looking in the least moved.

'So, off we go, hmm?' she said, looking around at the room that we had so recently decorated. 'Not that I mind very much. Houses are all the same. This one is pretty, though. Pity Tejbir got it.'

Over the next few days, as we started to pack up once again, I took to visiting various parts of the House to say goodbye, stealing moments with whoever I could. The litchi groves waved back, the *chameli* bushes raised their flowery heads. The orioles, the magpies, the parrots, the owls carried on without a second look at me. The xenias were flowering when Mauna made me sit down and offered me a cup of tea one evening, speaking to me in fluent Pahadi. I didn't understand a word; I don't think she needed me to, but I kept nodding as she pointed to this tree and that, telling their stories, and through them, telling her own. Shaili laughed when she came by to hang the washing and saw this scene, but she didn't interrupt. We were all grieving in ways that came naturally to us.

Some instinct for self-preservation told me not to dwell on what was to become of Arbour House, the beautiful façade smashed to pieces, centuries-old oak trees hacked down, barren where the litchi groves once stood. I only thought of leaving and blanked out what was bound to follow.

Even Suggi quietened down as the days went by, taking long walks by herself or reading in our room. Sukh and I took to sitting on our red brick boundary wall once again in the evenings, talking about everything except our imminent departure. We would laugh about Sukh's brother and his attempts to make a man out of Sukh, who was barely human as it were. We would look over at the Balakrishnan home, now empty as the family had moved out, and talk about all that happened with Vidhya, Krishna and Inder, the highlight of our ordinary lives. We would talk of the days spent playing badminton with Koko and Bubbles. Amma ji, Tejbir, Munni Masi. Everyone and everything seemed to have slipped away so quickly.

Moving day came, and there were obviously no professional movers and packers. Mummy was the packer, and we were the crew that put it all together, wrapping things in bed sheets and sacks and boxes till the house looked as if a serious-minded earthquake had been at it. A small truck was hired to cart it all away. Sukh hung about the truck with a hangdog expression the entire day, not quite coming in and not quite leaving us to it. Finally, the truck was loaded and away it went. All of us looked at it with a collective forlorn expression.

'Right then,' said Mummy with a fake brusqueness. 'Papa and I will leave now and start getting things set up in the new house. Both of you will lock the house and hand over the keys to Nina Aunty when she comes home.'

Sukh, Suggi and I sat on the steps of our house after locking up, tired, not talking, waiting for the absent Nina Aunty. Eventually, Buddy lumbered by and put his head on my lap and licked my hand a couple of times. A chameleon sat on the *raat ki rani* and contemplated us briefly before turning around to sun himself in peace. Sukh got up and bowled a couple of imaginary bouncers with an imaginary ball to imaginary batsmen. Shaili came by and brought us tea.

'Where is Nina Aunty?' Suggi finally lost patience. 'Wasn't she supposed to be here two hours ago?'

'Yes, must be stuck in a poker game or something.' I explained the delay charitably. In my mind, Nina Aunty flitted about from one frivolous pursuit to another with nary a break. Just as I spoke, though, we saw Nina Aunty's car turn into the gate of Arbour House in its customary cloud of dirt, more ambition than horsepower. She drove down the driveway and screeched to a halt right next to us, climbing out of the car even before it had cooled off.

'Girls, girls,' she said, 'Oh, but have your parents left?'

'Yes,' said Suggi coldly, not taking kindly to anyone who kept her waiting and stretched out her hand. 'We were waiting for you. These are the keys. And now we had better get going.'

'Goodbye and thank you,' I piped in, hoping to soften the impact of Suggi's annoyance.

'Oh, but I wish they hadn't left,' said Nina Aunty, now wringing her hands and looking from me to Suggi to Sukh by turns and looking very harried. 'I have so much to tell them. Oh, it's terrible. That lout Tejbir has eloped with Munni.'

Dehradun, 2016

35

Arbour House, Present Day

'Madam, the address, the address,' Somnath ji repeats himself and probably not for the first time. I jolt back to reality and look around sheepishly, like someone who has wakened from a deep sleep. I look around, confused and disorientated, and try to bring myself to the present. I catch Somnath ji looking at me, his face a mix of expectation and annoyance.

'Arbour House, 17, Morris Road,' I clear my throat and reply. He nods at me and climbs down from the car. I look out the window and try to place myself, but it is like being in a surreal dream – I am reaching out and trying to clutch at something that isn't there anymore. Somnath ji has found a couple of old-timers out for a stroll and is asking them for directions. I am not too hopeful. How would anyone know where my childhood home went? I have underestimated Somnath ji's prowess though, for in a few minutes he is back and looking very pleased with himself, his earlier irritation with me forgotten.

'Ha-ha-ha, madam, it's not even called Morris Road anymore; they have named it Bhootnath Marg. That's the thing with our country, madam, we love changing names.'

Bhootnath Marg. How the mighty have fallen indeed.

'Looks like it, Somnath ji. Well then, Bhootnath Marg it is. Let's go.'

After a few false turns, the car turns into a green lane and I know immediately that we are close, like struggling with a maths equation for ages and then stumbling on the solution that had been hiding in plain sight all the while. Arbour House stands where it always has. The car stops with a jolt right outside the old, ramshackle gate. I sit there quietly for a moment, loath to step out and meet my old friend who looks accusingly in my direction. *And where have you been all this time, young lady?* The address plate is the same one that had been put there when the house was first built – not for it the change in street names. Morris Road itself stretches in both directions, looking forlorn, some of the old bungalows hanging on even in the face of progress, some already defeated and making way for modern houses.

'Nobody seems to be there,' says Somnath ji, peering at the house, possibly quite surprised that I have travelled all this way for this blast from the past. He honks once, hoping that someone will emerge from the house and come up to the gate. I stop him.

'Don't honk, Somnath ji, it's okay,' I say and climb out of the car. 'I'll walk. Let me get the gate for you.'

With feet that are not quite steady, I alight and reach for the rusty gate. The lock that didn't work is gone and the gate, too, has come loose. This was where

Bubbles would swing back and forth. Nobody has bothered to repair it, faithfully collecting the dust and grime of Bhootnath Marg for decades. I try to open it, and it gives way but not without screeching in protest. Somnath ji drives past me and to the patio, parking next to the house where the vintage cars once stood, Balbir Uncle scrubbing and polishing them with all his might. The cars seem to be gone now. I walk slowly down the cobbled driveway, looking at the estate. Nobody has paved paradise. Not yet, anyway. The dusty litchi orchard still stands to my left, less green and not lush like in my memories but there all the same, the undergrowth cooling the earth below, the trees watching me silently go by. The whole estate seems to have burst forth in an overgrown tangle, vines and branches and leaves. The pristine, cared-for lawns are gone, the gardens look wild, windblown and neglected, but they are there, in all their unkempt glory. I think about Mauna, tending to each tendril and root in the gardens like her life depended on it. Who has come in her place? The *chameli* shrubs have dried and withered away but the mulberry bushes are still there, the lilies still dotting the overgrown garden. I am almost afraid to look for the *semal* tree and take a deep breath before I catch sight of it. The driveway has shrunk but maybe because nature was claiming it once again on either side. Everything has shrunk, appearing smaller than it did in my mind's eye. I look out to where Mauna, Shaili and the others had stayed in the staff quarters and can't recognize the place; it looks like there are new houses there. Perhaps that piece of land had been sold off, too. I walk on, looking on either side with trepidation, finding everything more or less the same but missing the technicolour glory of my past. It has fallen upon neglectful times, to be sure, but it is all mercifully still there.

I reach the house, *my* Arbour House. It looks at me, and I feel a lump rise in my throat. The ghosts of Buddy and Flash are at my feet; this was the spot where they would come to me, sniffing and begging for the Parle-G biscuits I would surreptitiously feed them. I would have probably burst into tears at this point if not for the slim, tall figure that silently opens the main door and steps on to the veranda, a phone in his hand and a pair of spectacles on his nose. He sees the car before he sees me and looks left and right with a heartbreaking, quizzical look before I step forward from behind the car and call out his name.

'Gaya?' he calls out, his delight evident. 'Oh, Gaya, is that you?'

'In the flesh, Mr Rawat, and at your service,' I call back, trying to be flippant, swallowing the surge of sudden grief that comes rushing up. Now laughing openly, he hurries down the steps, moving quickly for someone closer to fifty than forty to embrace me. There he is, all that had been wonderful and whimsical and magical about the Doon years. Koko Rawat. Or a faded, sepia-tinted version of him, at any rate, the brown eyes behind the glasses crinkling in his obvious joy at seeing the girl from the library emerge from the dusty past and into his house.

'I heard someone drive up. Look at you, Gaya, look at you.'

'Yes, look at me and marvel at the grime,' I say, attempting to laugh but suddenly very self-conscious, tucking my hair behind my ears and unable to meet his gaze. Who am I now? A greying, fading, wrinkling, stooping rendering of my sixteen-year-old self, the one walking around the estate, dreaming of the time it would be hers.

Koko releases my shoulders and laughs again, now taking both my hands and clasping them to his heart. Then he finally notices Somnath ji, still sitting in the car and impatiently waiting for instructions. 'Bring her luggage out,' Koko calls out to him over his shoulder and takes me by the hand to guide me inside. His hair has thinned and greyed but still falls upon his forehead like it always did. He now walks with the slight stoop of the very tall, his shoulders slumping ever so slightly. His clothes flap around him a bit, his frame very spare. I realize that I am in the inconvenient position of someone whose person of interest has aged much better than themselves, even with what is clearly ill-health writ large on his person.

'Come along, come along, Gaya. Oh gosh, I received your message, but I honestly didn't believe you'd come. I still can't believe you are here!'

'I can barely believe it myself, Koko, I feel I am here, and I am also somewhere thirty years ago.' It is true. I am looking around, trying to take everything in but still not able to shake off the disorientation. The veranda where Amma ji had once eaten copious amounts of nuts and fruit is frozen in time. Everything seems to be in its place. The rattan plantation chairs where Tejbir smoked his never-ending cigarettes. The tall rubber plants in gold-coloured planters polished regularly by Mauna. The patterned floor where Shaili would sit and massage oil into Amma ji's legs. The wooden beams overhead that had watched over Bubbles as she was tutored by Miss Alma. Nothing has moved. I had gone away for thirty years, and they had all stood still and waited for me to return. And now here I was. After all the loss and heartbreak and regret. I reach out and touch a round pillar. *Hello, Arbour House, how have you been?*

Somnath ji deposits my luggage on the veranda. He declines a cup of tea and says that he will drive back to Delhi almost immediately. I settle his bill, and he takes off without a backward glance, possibly glad to be back on the road. I watch him leave and then turn to face Koko, now standing next to one of his mother's favourite chairs.

'You look all right, Koko,' I tell him, smiling as I look him up and down, sizing him up. 'What is all this dying business you were talking of? Gave me such a fright.' He laughs it off immediately.

'Just false pretences, Gaya, to bring you here. Nothing wrong with me at all. Come, come, let me take you inside. I must warn you, though, it is all rather dusty. Shaili comes in every evening to cook, and she dusts when she can, but well, it is a tall order for just one person, as you can imagine. She runs a beauty parlour in town, and she's got two kids. Well, come in now, see for yourself this crumbling old thing. A grand tour for the prodigal!'

Koko grabs my solitary suitcase and holds the door to the house open for me. I step past him and into the main hall, dark and cool against the sunlight outside. Everything rushes at me all at once. I squint and look around. The carpets are the same, very frayed and lovely, the edges now coming off in loose threads. Nina Rawat's bouquets of customary fresh flowers are missing. Golden sunlight sneaks in through the heavy curtains that have collected much dust through the years, the tassels now grimy. All the heavy pieces stand where they always had, the sideboards and the backless Louis XV chairs disused now. The house still smells the same, though – a mix of crisp mountain air and wood. Koko watches me as I take it all in.

I turn to look up at the portraits on the walls, dimly lit by a single, dusty, weak lamp and immediately notice the addition – one of Munni Masi and Tejbir, probably taken after their wedding. They look so glamorous, like film stars of yore, their faces smooth, dark, luxuriant hair framing the beautiful faces. Munni Masi's eyebrows look like they'd been drawn with pencil. She is wearing some of the jewels she must have inherited and looks like she is finally coming into a role she had prepared for all her life. Her hair has been curled, her sari *pallu* covers her head slightly. Tejbir looks like he is dressed for a polo match. I feel my breath catch and turn away quickly. Koko takes my hand and tells me to watch my step. Some of the baseboards are coming apart.

Everything in the house is being cleaned, it appears to me, but not very well. We step through the dark rooms, most of them unused, and make our way to the library, my feet moving on their own, my mind in a place left behind a long time ago. The bedrooms seem to be in a similar state of benevolent neglect. I see the bedspread in Nina Aunty's room that had surely been there all those years ago, too. All the furniture seems to have been left as it had once been. The teak four-poster beds, the wooden chest of drawers with the brass pulls, the planter's chairs with the long, flat arms – they are all there still. The oak has taken on the patina of the years.

'I don't even open all the rooms. What's the point?' says Koko by way of an apology. 'It really is massive, this place; needs an army to keep it in shape.'

The library has been left to its own devices, it appears, and thankfully, has held on, has assumed the silence of rooms that have not had a word spoken in them for years together. I try to breathe without disturbing the dust. The books are all there, lined up, patiently waiting to be read. The grand old table and the matching chairs are all gone, though.

'Termites had got the central table,' says Koko, running his finger through a line of dust on the mantle and then blowing on it. 'The pest control people said it might get at the books. So far, they seem to be all right, though.'

'What will you do with all these books, Koko?' I ask, walking around the bookshelves, looking for the dog-eared detective omnibuses that Suggi and I had loved.

'Donate them to the club, I suppose. Their library has place enough. This, right here, Gaya, was where I saw you for the first time.'

I pause and savour that delicious, uncomfortable memory for a moment before stepping out from the door with the broken lock. Koko follows me, still chuckling.

'I see there is no dog in the place,' I say, looking out at the garden, still thinking of Buddy, for what was Arbour House without his lumbering presence?

'Oh,' laughs Koko, 'I have been wandering too much to do that. Can you believe it, Buddy outlived even Flash. He always seemed ready to go, but he just hung on. We buried them both here, out in the garden. You can see the spot.'

I feel a bit light-headed. Koko sees my face and takes me by the arm.

'Now, do you want some tea? I'll make some. Go sit outside on the veranda. All this old dust isn't good for you.' I obey, and once outside, look through a pile of old magazines left by the chairs.

'Shaili will come down to make dinner,' he says as he returns and sets down the tea tray, complete with the tea cloth because, finally, he is Nina Rawat's son. 'In the meanwhile, though, you must make do with this. Or we can go out.'

'No,' I shake my head, 'this is perfect.' And it is. I feel the colour return to my face as the hot tea makes its way down.

'Gosh, Gaya, I can't remember the last time we sat and talked like this. We never know when it's the last time we do anything, do we?'

'Not everything. When I used to bathe Sanjay as a child, I did not know when would be the last time. Or the last time I would feed him. It would be unbearable if we knew.'

'What is Sanjay like? Did he turn out to be a lot like you?'

'Oh, no, thank goodness. He is very practical. Much more than me, at any rate. I was, well, quite floaty, wasn't I?'

'I liked that about you.' Koko's kindness is still a powerful thing. I smile and look at him. We talk about this and that. The sun sets, and the overhead light bulbs give off some feeble light, and yet, Arbour House looks like a faded Dutch oil painting, a Vermeer, perhaps. And sitting in an old cane chair, Koko keeps looking at me as if he can't believe that I am back, all these years later. I catch his look in an unguarded moment, and we both burst out laughing, the significance of the reunion made light by the sound. I look around to break the spell of the moment and remark on how lovely it all is, still.

'I don't think I ever saw anything as perfect as Arbour House in my life.'

'What about now?' he asks me suddenly.

'Now? Well, it is still pretty perfect, just older. Nobody knows what makes something beautiful, do they? It is just how something makes you feel.'

'Gaya, I need to ask something of you,' says Koko, now looking very determined and yet, unsure. 'The real reason I called you here is because I want you to have Arbour House. Take it, Gaya, and make something of it – something lasting and beautiful, something beyond everything that happened here.'

36

Arbour House and Me

To say that the dashing Mr Rawat knocked the wind right out of my sails and sent it soaring to some unknown land would be, well, accurate. He looks remarkably happy and relieved after having parted with this piece of news. I, on the other hand, look like a shocked goldfish, opening and closing my mouth, trying to take it all in.

'Have you been smoking something unusual, Koko?' I finally manage.

'Not at all, not at all. Oh, Gaya, you are perfect for this place, always have been. I have only made a mess of it since it came to me all those years ago.'

'What have you been doing all this while, Koko? I never actually got to know.'

'Do? The men in this family don't do anything. Look at my father; wasted his whole life after that fancy education. Similarly for self,' he cocks a thumb at himself. 'We didn't have any examples of any, how do you say this, workers in our family. Bubbles and I, we were the first generation that was expected to make something of ourselves. And I would have, had things been different. I got my flying license, even worked for Air India for a while – not that it came easy to me. We were no good at deadlines and discipline and jobs, Bubbles and I – no genetic material in that department at all. And then Arbour House came to me after everything that happened with Tejbir Chacha, and I just lost the drive. What's the point, I started to think to myself. I can always sell parts of the estate and live off the money, like so many Rawats before me. Soon enough, I got fired from the flying job for negligence. I never applied again.'

This is obviously painful for Koko to recount. I think of my own series of failures. I didn't have an estate to fall back on, and yet, I haven't made much of my life.

'I tried this and that with Arbour House,' Koko continues, 'as and when I came back here, which was infrequent, with all my travels. I'll show you the bed and breakfast I tried to create out of the house that was let out to your family. Tried giving it out on those B&B websites that are coming up now. It had some takers, but it takes a lot of upkeep. The staff kept running away. I don't have a head for these things. Maybe Bubbles could do a better job of it. I certainly couldn't.'

'I must say, Koko, you have a lot of faith in my abilities without knowing anything about my skills. Or the lack of them.'

'Well then, the other option is to sell the place, Gaya. I remember how heartbroken you were when Tejbir Chacha wanted to bring it down. I had no say in the matter then. I figured this was the proverbial second chance. I had to ask you.'

'What about your parents? Doesn't Balbir Uncle want to spend any time here?'

Koko sighs and places his glass of water on the coffee table.

'Oh, they are right here, in Doon. They moved to that house on Rajpur Road right after leaving Arbour House. That's where they still live. Quite old now but pottering along just fine. Nobody wants to come here now, Gaya. I myself am hardly here. We pay Shaili to keep an eye on things, hire some hands now and then, but nobody wants to move in here.'

I look around the old house, stately once again in the dark, and smell a familiar fragrance – the *raat ki rani* is flowering just like it always had.

'Oh, I don't know about that. At least I am very happy I came,' I say, but I am not too sure of it anymore. Like rifling through an old diary, memories tumbling out of every page. Did Koko really want me to have Arbour House? What was I to do with it? The main gate creaks, and we see a figure hurrying towards the house on the dark driveway.

'Shaili, look who's here,' Koko calls out. The woman in a printed floral sari who laughingly walks up to us is a complete stranger to me. She has become very portly, her cheeks have filled out, making her eyes smaller, and try as I might, I cannot see in her the slim, hard-working girl I had known. She comes and takes my hand and laughs, a little shy.

'So nice to see you, didi, so nice,' she tells me happily. 'You haven't coloured your hair? I can do it for you. I had told Shivendra Saab you would come. Sorry, sorry, I got so late. Many clients at the parlour today, and then, I couldn't find a rickshaw. Did you eat anything? I will get dinner started.'

Still talking, Shaili bustles into the kitchen. Koko sighs and plonks back in his chair.

'One of the remnants of the old era. I don't know what I would do without her. All sorts of things keep happening in a house this size. We sighted a long snake earlier this year, right there in the hall. Shaili went out looking for help and found a snake charmer nearby. Too much of a coincidence, don't you think? Turns out it was the snake charmer himself who had released the snake into the house.' I burst into laughter. Koko shakes his head at the memory, smiling.

We talk some more, Koko filling me in on the old names and faces as Shaili makes dinner and serves it to us right where we are sitting. Apparently, no one ate at the grand old dining table anymore. Shaili keeps plying me with rotis as she lumbers between the kitchen and the table.

'Dadi used to ask after you, didi. After dinner, you can go and meet her under the plum trees,' she tells me nonchalantly while serving me curry. I splutter in my raita at this. Mauna was already pushing ninety when I last saw her.

'Mauna was buried under the plum tree; she wasn't cremated,' Koko explains hastily, seeing my blanched face.

'Yes, she has become the plum tree.' Shaili clasps the *belan* at her chest and sighs in memory.

'Tell me, Koko, what is Bubbles like now? We never saw her again after we moved out.' There is no end to all that I want to know.

'Bubbles? Oh, she is all right. She was a fashion model for a bit after college. She appeared in a music video, too, can you believe it? We teased her mercilessly about that, of course. Then she joined a city magazine, wrote a gossip column, met her husband there. They both moved to Canada soon after. Looked all right for a few years, then suddenly, she said she was getting a divorce. It was pretty awful, the whole thing. She never married again. No children either. She's pretty active in the community, does a lot of volunteer work with her local gurudwara. She's doing all right. A far cry from her rebellious youth.'

'Nina Aunty and Bubbles never saw eye to eye,' I remember with a smile. 'Some of those fights were truly epic.'

Koko laughs.

'Oh, yes, they used to squabble all the time. Bubbles took some perverse pleasure in getting a rise out of Mummy, and of course, Mummy never quite got her. They still don't get along. I don't think Bubbles has visited them in years.'

After dinner, Shaili cleans up and leaves. Koko and I decide to walk around the estate.

'I am dreading showing you your old house,' Koko tells me. 'You will hate it.' I try not to show how right he is. We walk to our old house, my feet remembering the way on their own. We stand at the steps and stare at the little house in silence. It seems to have shrunk. Or maybe I have outgrown it. Some half-hearted attempts had been made to spruce it up and make it more B&B like, a new door frame, new chairs lying outside but it remains the same – our home for a brief moment in time.

'You haven't named it?' I ask, trying to sound casual, my words coming out louder than intended. I almost expect Papa to come out of the house, wearing a hand-knit sweater over his white kurta-pyjama, his constant companion, the tax file, in one hand.

'Oh, it's called Reminiscence. Makes it difficult to locate. And spell.'

'Really? That's very—'

'I couldn't think of this place without you in it, so, yes, a nod to that.' I feel a lump rise in my throat. Koko naming the house while he thought of the gauche young thing that lived there. I can't bear the thought of going inside so I sit down, right there on the steps leading to the house. Koko winces as he takes his place next to me, something hurting, everything hurting. Something in Koko Rawat is broken.

'How strange,' I say, running my hand on the stone steps. 'These are the steps where Sukh, Suggi and I sat when your mum first told us about Munni Masi and Tejbir Chacha.'

'Is that so?'

'Yes, we were waiting for her to hand over the house keys. Sukh was pretending to bowl that way. Remember how he was always doing that? Then your mum came back from the club in that old clunker of hers. She had received a call from Tejbir Chacha saying that he and Munni Masi had run away and gotten married.'

Koko looks at his feet.

'Gaya, I really wish things had turned out different. You were very close to Munni Aunty, I know that.'

'Everyone adored her.'

'That's true. Even Tejbir Chacha, who despised the world.'

37

Munni Masi and Tejbir

We sit quietly, both of us thinking of my exquisite Munni Masi.

'Munni Masi did invite both me and Suggi quite a few times to the house,' I tell Koko, 'but we didn't dare take her up on the offer. You wouldn't know how it was, Mummy would get furious if we even brought her up. She would tear up her letters even before we got a chance to read them. It was just so difficult to think of her in this house. It was all so unexpected. I couldn't believe she married Tejbir Chacha.'

Koko nods a few times.

'It was unexpected. She tried her best, with all of us, with the house.'

'She rescued the house; that was something.' I think back to the time that Arbour House was sentenced to an untimely end, and yet, here it stands just as it always did, and the people who tried to take it down are all long since gone.

'Oh, yes, but this house is an ingrate, Gaya. It just wasn't kind to her. You know, there was a fire the first week she got here. Not in the main structure, mercifully. And then, some mysterious bug got to the litchi trees and nearly took down the orchard. Tejbir Chacha was hardly here; his plantations were in a mess all their own. He was always travelling. Your poor Munni Masi was the only one trying to keep this decrepit thing together. It was all pretty brutal.' I feel my eyes moisten at the thought of my eternally vibrant Munni Masi struggling.

'I didn't know all this. Didn't you people meet her?' I ask. 'Nina Aunty? Didn't she try to help Munni Masi?'

'Oh, you know how scatterbrained Mum is; never a practical word of advice for anyone. She came to see Munni Aunty a few times; hardly a pillar of support. Bubbles and I were back in school, of course. And then, of course, you know how it unfolded from there. Pretty tragic.'

I think of Munni Masi, my beautiful, brilliant aunt in her lovely saris swishing about her person, calling us her little monkeys and *meri jaan*s, all her wonderful gifts through the years, her complete acceptance of us and her unwavering faith in my non-existent abilities. Sanjay would have loved her. I blink back the early tears, trying to maintain my composure, trying to think about something else before I break down completely.

'Munni Aunty kept the entire staff with her, including the tyrannical Mauna,' says Koko. 'She wouldn't hear of anyone leaving. They loved her for that.'

'Sounds like her all right,' I say, trying to see Munni Masi as the lady of the manor and failing. 'I wish I could have met her just once.'

'She missed the two of you a lot. None of you even turned up for the reception they threw after the wedding. A lot of her friends came, but I think she missed the two of you very much. She talked about you incessantly.'

'Papa wanted to attend, but Mummy kept saying that if she didn't go, Munni Masi would change her mind.'

'She didn't, though.'

I nod. 'Suggi was here that entire year at Brighton. She asked Mummy if she should ask Munni Masi to be her local guardian. Mummy blew a gasket and screamed and shouted till she had to be taken to the emergency ward with elevated blood pressure and whatnot. We didn't bring up Munni Masi after that.'

'Mine was not the only unhinged family in the world, then.'

'Oh, not by a long shot. I must say, Koko, I hated Tejbir Chacha from the moment I got to know he planned to bring Arbour House down. When he married Munni Masi, for some time, I had fantasies of discovering that I had misjudged him. I imagined he would turn out to have a heart of gold after all. Turned out I was right all along. He was quite despicable.'

Koko shrugs and nods.

'He was who he was, a complete snake, but she was very gracious to us. She offered to have us back in the house almost immediately after the wedding, but my parents had made up their minds by then. I think they were quite glad to be done with Arbour House. And so, it was just Munni Aunty out here.'

'She deserved better,' I say, thinking about the unhappy snippets I had heard through the years about her union with Tejbir Chacha, about her doomed stay at Arbour House.

'She did,' Koko agrees. 'I was very surprised she agreed to marry someone like him. I still am, to a degree.'

'Yes, well, she did save this place though.' I look around. 'Not one tree has been felled.'

'Absolutely. She refused to let him touch it. She said she'd leave him if he brought it down. It created so much strife. The fights they would have! He would tell my father that she married him just to save the house. Bloody unfair, the whole thing. They lived here till, you know, the accident... at least she did, which wasn't too long. He travelled a lot. We hardly met them, though. Our own lives were beginning to speed up by then. Both Bubbles and I left Doon and moved on.'

I thought of my aunt on the day of our school fête, lovely and capable. Mummy didn't speak to her at all after her wedding, and we were all forced to side with her. Maybe if we had offered to stand by her, things wouldn't have come to the pass they did.

'We didn't know what Mummy's objection to the marriage was. I think it was just the pent-up resentment of all the years that Munni Masi had refused to listen to Mummy. I think the elopement, the suddenness of the marriage, just threw her off.'

'It was such a shock to hear of her... of *their* deaths,' says Koko, rubbing the toe of his shoe in the dust. 'The police said the car was mangled beyond recognition. It fell deep into the valley. It was a blind turn. It's barricaded now, but at that time, you could just miss the turn and drive right off the cliff. They, well, they say she was the one driving, Gaya. They say she might have done it on purpose.'

The news had been relayed to us by phone. Mummy had wailed like her heart was being pulled out. Her only sister. Ten years younger. The one her *bau* ji had wanted her to take care of. How Mummy had failed Munni Masi and how pitilessly she had been punished for it. Mummy blamed Tejbir for Munni Masi's death. He was driving, she would say, he was driving, and he got them both killed.

'The marriage had really brought out the worst in both of them,' says Koko. 'He had always been one for drink anyway, and this seemed like as good a time as any to really hit the bottle. Munni Aunty herself was suddenly without a purpose and a family for the first time in her life. Nobody really spoke about it back then, but I think she was severely depressed. She used to walk in silence all over Arbour House, feeding on her own sorrow.'

'You know, Mummy never said anything about this, but I don't think she forgave herself for what she did to Munni Masi. Estranging Munni Masi was the worst thing my poor mother ever did. She still has a picture of her on the wall of her room. Right next to one of my father.' I swallow a lump that has appeared out of nowhere.

'Amma ji was the only one who thought the marriage was a wonderful idea. She was the only one who loved Tejbir Chacha, and of course, she adored Munni Aunty. She was shattered when the news came. Never recovered from it. She donated all of her jewels – oh, you should have seen some of them Gaya. All of them went to her family temple in Haridwar, kilos and kilos of them. Splendid pieces. Cursed sapphires and ruby necklaces, the works. I believe the Nizam wanted some of those. Bubbles wept and wept for a brilliant *mayur haar*, but even that was given away. And then, of course, Amma ji herself went away, too.'

'What happened to her?' I thought of the regal Amma ji, calling out to me from her favourite spot in the house. *Come here, Gaya, come eat salted pistachios. What are you reading? Come visit me in Hyderabad.*

'We never found out, Gaya. She did put all her things in order beforehand, so maybe she planned it, but no, we don't know what happened. We never recovered her body.'

How suddenly things had shifted back then. Papa had been transferred to a different department, and we left Doon within a month of moving out of Arbour House. Suggi had stayed on as a boarder at Brighton to finish her final year of school, but I had moved to Lucknow, had been homesick for the hills, much as I would be for the rest of my living years. How was I to know that within a year Munni Masi and Tejbir Chacha and Amma ji would be all gone? This time I couldn't blink back my tears; they were too strong.

38

The Ghosts of Arbour House

I wake up early the next morning, confused. Am I a teenager again, trying to find warmth in a *razai* as I watch Suggi get ready for basketball? Then I think of Sanjay and come back to the present. I reach out for my phone to check for his text to say that he has reached. Nothing. The curtains are not closed tight, and weak sunlight is already filtering in, dust particles dancing in it. Koko and I had stayed up till very late, talking.

Koko had offered to put me up in Munni Masi's old room, but I wasn't quite ready for that. I would have liked to sleep in our own flat, just to feel sixteen again, but it was an in-between place now, not knowing whether to be a bed and breakfast or a home. Finally, I had slept in the old guestroom that Shaili had efficiently dusted and cleaned for me.

I slip my feet into my slippers and wrap a shawl around myself and decide to go outside for a short walk. I step out and feel a familiar gush of delight. Arbour House in the mornings. There is a light, cool mist hanging over everything still, filtering the light and lending everything a lovely glow. I walk around the property, trying to look at everything afresh, trying to remember. The soil is so fertile that even the focused intent of time the conqueror has not defeated it. Grass springs from in between the cobbled stones. I can hear the orioles calling. I walk right up to the gate and look out at Morris Road – no signs of any traffic yet, except the milkmen and newspaper boys.

My memory has displaced many things, moved them about. Surely the large frangipani stood right next to the main gate. How had it moved down all the way to the house? Was the pathway always this narrow? I touch everything, the plants and the fences, the shrubs and the dusty fallen flowers, feeling the missing years under my fingers. I take it all in and wonder at how quickly the years have gone by. I must have wandered about for hours till I finally hear the door opening.

'There you are,' calls Koko, holding up a mug with steam rising from it. I wave back and walk back slowly, my right knee hurting as it likes to when I start feeling too youthful.

'I went to your room looking for you, but trust you to go traipsing off in the morning.' He smiles at me, looking like the Koko from the past, in his school blazer, hands in pockets, a relentless gum chewer. 'Did I fatigue you with all my ramblings last night? I went on and on.'

'What rubbish. I came all this way to hear your ramblings. What's that? Tea? You've become very domesticated, Koko.'

'Not enough,' he says. 'Nobody in the Rawat clan can cook. Mum was a terrible cook, you must remember. Your mum was a phenomenal cook, though. Do you remember your sixteenth birthday party? I can't tell you just how many times I've thought about that.'

'Who can forget that? All Suggi's fault!'

'I loved it! That treasure hunt was brilliant. I thought the world of your family. You all were so, well, normal compared to our insanity.'

'I don't know; we were pretty strange in our own way.' I kick a pebble out of the way. It hits a dwarf apple tree that is bearing fruit.

'I still have the book you gave me,' I tell Koko, finishing the last of my tea, thinking of the Christie that still graced Sanjay's bookshelf, Sanjay's life gliding alongside mine, even when he has gone.

'You do?' Koko looks very pleased at the thought. 'Come on, let's get you some breakfast. You should see my skills with eggs.'

'I tried locating you on Facebook and so on, Koko, many years ago, when these things were just starting out and we were still excited about finding old faces,' I say as we walk back. 'You didn't seem to be around.'

'Oh no, not after my first stalker,' he deadpans, making me laugh almost instantly.

Breakfast is a simple affair, not at all like the elaborate ritualistic ones I have become accustomed to eating in Mumbai.

'You are doing well for someone staying on their own,' I remark, looking around the kitchen.

'I have had practice. I spent a lot of time with Bubbles, especially after her divorce, so I was up in Toronto a lot. She doesn't cook, so either I do or we starve.'

'And now, you will move to be with her permanently, I hear.'

He leans back and puts his fork down.

'The doctors say I need to slow down. Take it easy. Bubbles feels it will be easier out there. That is really why I would like to wrap up this Arbour House business, Gaya.'

'What is the matter with you, Koko. Won't you tell me?'

'Oh, you know, it's this autoimmune thing I have picked up. Seems to be in the air.'

He is being flippant, but I can see that it is serious and that he doesn't like to discuss whatever it is that is wrong with him. I accept the joke and let it go.

'Why didn't you marry, Koko? You needn't have stayed alone? Or did you do it and are there a couple of wives hidden somewhere?'

'No chance, Gaya, no chance. I came close a couple of times but dodged the bullet. And now, if you're done,' he asks, glancing at my plate, 'I have planned the day.'

Adil calls just as I am getting ready to go out.

'I must say, Gaya, I am very impressed. Traipsing off on your own like that! Should I come down, too? Make a holiday of it?'

'Absolutely not,' I say, carefully applying lipstick in the oval mirror. 'This is my trip. Down memory lane, if you please.' I think about telling Adil about Koko's offer but decide against it. I don't have the words, not just yet.

'But you might decide to leave me and stay on in that *bhoot bangla* of yours.'

'That is always a risk.'

'Any news from Sanjay? He hasn't called since he left.'

I have been thinking about that. Sanjay had texted

briefly to say he had reached, but there was no excited call to tell us all about his new adventure. Maybe he is settling down.

'No, he hasn't called.'

'All right then. Oh, I told Jo about your impromptu vacation. She asked if you would go see Sukh's old place.'

I have been thinking about this since I arrived the previous day. There is no escaping it. I will have to go see Sukh's house. I don't know when I will be brave enough to do it. Arbour House has become a place of such loss.

Koko tries his best to show me the best of Doon that day. We eat cake rusks at Ellora's and bun-samosas. We visit the club, which has escaped the fate of other older buildings and looks like a well-preserved fossil, the station clock dating back to the 1800s still ticking away merrily in the grand hall.

'And we thought Doon was polluted then,' says Koko as we drive around the town in the car that he has borrowed from a friend, taking in the Vikrams, three-wheelers and buses, spewing smoke, their diesel fumes everywhere. 'Look at this now.' He is coughing a little now, I notice but know better than to comment on it. His shoulder seems to be hurting, too, every time he changes a gear. Whatever it is that is ailing Koko, it is winning.

'They had banned limestone mining that year,' I say, remembering random snippets of the past as events spring around in my mind, even as it tries to shut itself against the awful reality of the present.

'Even then, seeing Doon from Mussoorie had become damn near impossible. I still remember the time we could tell if it had snowed in Mussoorie by just taking a look at the peaks.'

I catch sight of two Buddhist monks walking by the road and suddenly remember something, clutching at Koko's arm in excitement.

'Do you remember the time those sadhus came by at Arbour House?'

'No, I think I was at boarding then. No. In fact, I think of Inder every time I see a sadhu.'

I look askance at Koko. Koko had known Inder only through me.

'Inder? *My* Inder? What do you mean?'

'Don't you know? Someone told me they saw him at Kumbh a few years ago. He has become a sadhu.'

'What... how is that even possible?'

'Why isn't it possible?'

'People like us don't become ascetics.'

Koko laughs even as his breath catches and makes him cough.

'It doesn't work that way, does it? It was because of Vidhya, you know. Hutch told me, you remember him? Sukh's young cousin, Harminder. He is a local cop now – helped out with the missing person case when Inder's parents filed a complaint. I was also interviewed. They found him up in the mountains somewhere, but he said he didn't want to return. Some guru had given *deeksha*.'
I try to make sense of this. Inder... I had not thought about him too much, not even bothered to ask people what became of him, not tried to track him down on the internet. The truth is, I had forgotten about him altogether.

'What about his parents?' I ask, guilt evident in

my voice. Inder's mother fondly preserving his baby clothes.

'What about them?'

'Didn't they try to stop him?'

'Stop him from taking *sanyaas*? How does that work? I don't know. Maybe they tried. Maybe he didn't listen.'

I sit in silence for a long time, thinking back to the last time I saw Inder at Niru's birthday party. He was already fading away then.

'Suggi saw Vidhya that one time in Mussoorie,' I remember. 'What happened to her, Koko, do you know?'

'Oh, yes, one of my boarding school teachers moved jobs and ended up teaching in Vidhya's school in Mussoorie. Apparently, even after that scandal, she still managed to ace everything and won a scholarship to Singapore. She left India soon after. Completely estranged from her parents; never spoke to them again after that whole fiasco with Inder. I have no idea what happened to her after that.'

I think of Inder and how he had wanted me to carry his little love note to Vidhya, which I had refused. Sukh had been a much better friend to him than I had, despite all the years I had on him.

'Did you realize how serious it all was back in the day?' I ask Koko, feeling ashamed of how little I had cared for Inder.

'I didn't know anything, Gaya, that was the problem with me. I was clueless.'

39

Arbour House, Day Two

It is my second day at Arbour House already. I tell Koko that I need to be alone for a while, take a deep breath and walk out of my room and go to do something I have put off long enough.

The red boundary wall, which used to be just bricks, is now cemented and plastered and looks quite forbidding. I reach out and touch it. Then I lean my back against it, push back my elbows and try to haul myself to the top, something I used to do effortlessly. My legs know what I want them to do, but they apologize for their weakness, no more capable of these gymnastics. Then I turn around, face the wall, place my hands on the top and try to lift myself. I can't do that either. Finally, after some ungraceful scrambling and scraping for a few minutes, I am able to haul myself to the top. It is only after I finally sit on the wall and look over at Sukh's old house that I realize I am crying. The house with the many children, the many affectionate aunts and uncles and the wonderful Daar ji is now quiet. Some sort of an annexe has been built where the cars used to be parked. A child's tricycle has been forgotten out on the lawn. A maid comes out to collect the washing and does not even notice me, a grown woman sitting on the boundary wall like the teenager she once was. Daar ji had sold the house soon after Sukh's death.

Foolish, foolish Sukhbir. There is a plaque dedicated to him somewhere in this country. Amar Shaheed Major Sukhbir Singh Sandhu. And his regiment underneath. A martyr's death, *veergati*, for that silly boy sitting right there in that parked Fiat, a Sony Discman on his lap. How did he get that brave? He couldn't even withstand his brother's training; he would complain endlessly about being made to run around this lawn right here. Nobody had been more surprised than he when he cleared the exam for the National Defence Academy. Nobody had been more loved than him in the academy. I know that because nearly everyone came for the funeral, and everyone had a Sukh story to tell.

That Sandhu fellow. How Suggi had scoffed at us, and yet, it had been an enduring tale of shared experiences. Sukh had collected friends to the very end of his days; he was probably the last friend I made. After all that happened with Munni Masi, Sukh was the one who reached out and comforted me in his own way. Our lives took such different turns – he was constantly moving, and I rooted down so quickly. Sukh was always a presence, though. I was the one he told about Jo, the film student from Pune whom he met, the one he couldn't do without. I was a witness at their wedding, hurried as it was for Jo came from a conservative family, which would never agree to the match.

I try to wipe my face without smearing my make-up too much. *You had no business dying that young, Sukh.*

You had no business dying and becoming a voice in my head. How much I have needed you. How much I have needed to talk to you, my friend. What am I supposed to do about Arbour House now?

I clamber down from the wall, no Sukh to hoist me up and down any more, and make my way back to the house. Koko sees my swollen eyes and gives me an awkward hug.

'Want to go and see your old school?' he asks. I nod. Anything to get away for a few hours.

Koko takes me to where my old mission school had once stood, that old, run-down, charming little structure. Stables for classrooms. Tin sheets for roofs. All of that is gone. It has been renamed and rebuilt, a proper high school now. The gulmohar trees have been spared mercifully and still peek out at the road, but there is no way anyone can peer inside.

'It's very well-respected now,' says Koko, looking up at the imposing walls all around. 'I am told the wait list is a mile long.'

'Niru had told me about this,' I say, not daring to go inside the daunting gate and intimidated by the superior-looking guards. 'Mrs Thapa and Captain Thapa still stay nearby in their old house, the one where Sharmi... but you don't know Sharmi. Niru still got to see the school every now and then through the years. Mrs Thapa became the principal after our old headmaster retired and returned to Australia. Niru told me that the school has really grown. And yet, I didn't realize just how different things would seem. I used to cycle down to school down that road, and that particular stretch was awful. Do you see the slope? I would huff and puff all the way up. And see that alley there. There were green hedges in that lane out there, and I met a ghost there once, or least I think I did.'

'That Niru of yours was quite a nerd,' comments Koko, making me laugh and bristle at the same time.

'She was brilliant. She still is. She is a professor of micro-economics.'

'Fascinating, exciting stuff.'

I grin but don't take the bait.

'I remember you used to worry about which school you would join after this one,' says Koko, looking pale and lighting a cigarette. I think about asking him to stop smoking and then decide against it.

'It was a big deal for me. How was I to know that I wouldn't even be in Doon long enough?'

'We can walk all around the school, see if we can spot an opening,' says Koko, and we cover the perimeter of the building, but there is not a single spot from where one can look inside. My quaint old school has become a veritable fortress. Finally, tired and defeated, we make our way back to the car.

'What happened to those beautiful vintage cars of your dad's? He was so attached to them.' I ask as I settle into the sedan, suddenly feeling very tired.

'Oh, yes, he was always spitting and polishing the old clunkers. One of them made it to the vintage car museum, can you believe it?'

'Let's go back to Morris Road,' I say, suddenly longing for the comfort of the sloppy old chairs at Arbour House and their faded cushions.

'Already? What happened to our plans to drive to FRI and Hathibarkala? Survey Road? Come on, we will go gawk at Ruskin Bond's old house. You always liked doing that.'

I shake my head, the fatigue of the journey suddenly catching up with me. Koko keeps trying to tempt me with this and that but finally relents and takes me home. That evening, we sit in the grand old hall as we wait for Shaili to serve dinner, smoking and drinking sweet local wine – a really potent fruity concoction that goes straight to the head – and talk about old times and old folks.

'I can't tell you how many times I have thought of you, Gaya, sitting right there in that chair,' Koko says easily. He hasn't got an ounce of self-consciousness in him still.

'I bet you did.' I try to shrug and feel ashamed at just how pleased this makes me.

'No, really, you were such a presence in this house back in the day.'

'Don't talk rubbish. We had all sorts of giants here, well, giantesses – Suggi and Bubbles and Rajmata Amma ji, and of course, later, Munni Masi. I didn't stand a chance.'

'Ah, yes, a veritable treasure trove of strong female characters, as they say, but no, you were the only one that truly belonged.' Did I truly belong to Arbour House?

I stare out at the garden where I had once seen *brahma kamal*s bloom, Amma ji as resplendent as the flowers sitting next to me. I think of something I have been meaning to ask him for many years.

'What did it feel like, Koko, to be bequeathed with Arbour House? Quite an inheritance to come into.'

'Under the circumstances, it felt like a curse. And it was.' The bitterness is unusual in Koko, startling me. He sees my expression and sighs. 'I am so done with it, Gaya. Take it off my hands, won't you?'

'You could have tried to make something of Arbour House, Koko,' I say. 'A heritage hotel perhaps?'

'Oh gosh! Even the thought is tiring.' He laughs. 'Plus, someone had to do all that drinking. Which I was an absolute ace at, may I add? Still am.'

As it is with old friends, it is easy to talk of what brought us despair. Creaking knees and troublesome hearts and the crisis of the souls.

'I am a fine one to talk; it's not like I did anything much. I had the foresight to know I wouldn't last a day in a regular job, so I decided to go on my own. And of course, I was terrible at that, too. How much money I sank into those non-starters, Koko.' I put my head in my hands at the memory.

Koko laughs.

'A right royal pair of losers. It's a good thing we didn't end up with each other.'

I don't say anything to that.

'You raised Sanjay, though, Gaya. Surely that counts for something.'

'Yes, the only job I could do well, but it's done, and now, I don't know what to do with myself. I spent the last two decades being a mum, and suddenly, I am not needed anymore,' I say, feeling my eyes moisten in self-pity.

'You won't stop being a mum now,' says Koko, looking very thoughtful. 'You will just need to do it in different ways.'

'Yes, but the days need to be filled with purpose, Koko, haven't we been told?'

'Purpose is overrated. I never had any. And when I did try it, I found it to be tiring and quite unnecessary. Anyway, Arbour House can be your purpose now.'

'You are a king amongst men, always were,' I say with a laugh and wipe my eyes with the back of my hands.

'You always make fun of me. Let's go eat, Shaili is cooking mushrooms. She claims to know how to pick the right ones from the garden, but I have a feeling Mauna hasn't taught her well. Who knows, one of these days, she may just put us out of our misery once and for all.' At this, I think of Sharmi, the one who had been taken away by the wild mushrooms.

That evening, Shaili decides to honour me by bringing out the china that has been gathering dust and collecting cobwebs in the sideboards for so long that even Koko doesn't remember the last time they had been brought out.

'What are all these things?' asks Koko, picking up a French gravy boat and examining it. 'Every corner of this house keeps throwing out oddities.'

'That's some fine porcelain. I think Nina Aunty told me it was Limoges. The treasures you hoard, Koko!'

'Yes, but I just want to be done with all the treasure keeping,' he says, wincing as his shoulder gives another twinge. He really is full of aches and pains, I think wistfully. And he won't stop drinking, much after I am done and ready to collapse.

One thing is certain – Arbour House has no more Rawats coming its way. Am I to take over?

I go back to my room and try to sleep. Was Koko as serious about this as he seemed to be? Live in Arbour House. Turn it into a place of splendour and grace. Protect it. I think back to when I was a helpless sixteen-year-old. All I had wanted was this – to be able to save Arbour House from all that was coming its way. Maybe I wished for it too hard. So hard that it took away Munni Masi. What about my life in Mumbai, the one I had daydreamed through, always wishing I could be back here. What about Adil and Jo and Bulbul? I drift off for some time but wake up in a couple of hours. I check my phone. Still no news of Sanjay. I text Bulbul to ask if she has heard from him, but Bulbul won't be up so early.

I think back to the time I was no more than five and hanging out from my tonga as it trotted past Morris Road on its way back from school, trying to steal a glance inside the gates. What adventures awaited inside, what untold stories.

I think back to the time we moved in and the friends I was gifted within the walls of this estate. I think of Sukh, who now lives within me as a pang, who left behind a family for me even as he left. I think of the warmth of Koko and how memory is such a funny thing and how it allows the past to live within us. I think of Inder and how little I had known and how much I had assumed I knew. I knew nothing.

I think of Suggi in the driveway of this house, looking at the gate and cooking up a plan to take Papa's scooter and take off for Jakhan because the weather demanded it. I think of Papa and his kind eyes and his willingness to give everyone a chance. I think of Mummy and the regrets that she lived with all her life. I think of Munni Masi, who probably sat right there on that sit-out and served tea in a Royal Doulton service, her angry husband pacing the floor. How had we all deserted her after having loved her so much?

Arbour House has got along just fine without me. It has aged, accepted the passage of years without demanding anything of them. The weeping willows and the jacarandas have all accepted their destiny. The squirrels that are looking at me from the branches of the oaks with intense concentration suffer no confusion; they know what follows next. They took the unfailing next step, following their cycles.

I think of the feelings of intense homesickness I have lived with all my life, the desire to come back to this. Would I have become the same person had Arbour House not been a part of my life? Would I have found something else to hanker after? Are some of us misfits, just meant to live in a constant urge to go back in time? And should we, with all our best intentions, try to resurrect the past? What was I to do now? Take up Koko's offer? Should I speak to Adil? To Sanjay, who has already forgotten his poor old mum. To Jo, who will probably take a decision in a minute if she needs to and never look back even once? What should I do?

40

Landour and Me

The night of restless thoughts takes its toll on me and I wake up feeling groggy and tired. It is late by my standards. As always, the first thing I do is to check for Sanjay's text. There is nothing. I try calling him despite the difference in time and it goes unanswered. Worry is no stranger to me; I have held it close to my heart ever since I had Sanjay, and now, of course, I seem to have a real reason for it. The house is very quiet, and Koko isn't up. I make some tea and go for a walk and when I get back, the heir and master is still not up.

'Koko, what's up?' I knock at his door. 'Are you doing an Amma ji, planning to wake up at noon?'

'Come in, Gaya,' I hear him say. He is still in bed and doesn't look well, circles under his eyes and his face pale and withdrawn.

'Good heavens, Koko. You look like death.'

'Exactly what I needed to hear.' He laughs and winces at the same time. 'Too much to drink last night. These local wines have quite a kick sometimes. Also, I really overdid it. I really have to stop. Well, looks like I cannot take you out and about today. Not without dying at your pretty feet anyway. What do you want to do today?'

'I will stay with you.'

'There is no need for that. Shaili will be here soon. The parlour is closed today. And I have nothing but a hangover.'

My phone buzzes. It is Bulbul, saying that she hasn't heard from Sanjay either. Then a text flashes. It is Sanjay.

All good, just really busy, will call later.

I let out a breath with a whoosh and feel relief surge over me. He is all right, just very busy. Leave him be, let him grow a bit, Adil would have said. I try to not worry about Sanjay and bring myself to the present.

'Well, if you are certain you can do without my ministrations, then maybe I will take a trip up to Landour,' I tell Koko, on a whim. 'It's really been too long. Spending all this time with you has fortified me. I think I can brave a trip up to the mountains.'

'Look at you. Quite the globetrotter. Landour sounds great. Okay, let me call the taxi service I always use. He will help you get a hotel room in Landour. I wish I could come along.'

'No, stay in bed. Rest. You should not strain your tired old bones.' Leaving the drawn-looking Koko sighing dramatically, I make my way back to my room and pack my things. Shaili arrives at the house and makes a huge fuss over Koko's illness. The taxi arrives just as I am mopping up the last of my paratha, and I leave the two of them to their own devices, a little guilty at leaving Koko to do this but quite confident in Shaili's abilities.

'Madam, you should go to Mussoorie,' informs the young boy who is driving the taxi. 'Much more to see.

What is there in Landour – *chaar dukaan aur chaubees makaan*, he-he-he.'

'No,' I say more firmly than I intended and try to soften my stance. 'I want to go to Landour. Mussoorie is, well, we can go next time. How long will it take?'

'About an hour and a half, if the traffic permits.'

Mercifully, soon the boy-driver, named Raghunath, gets busy with cussing out other cars on the road and the state of the nation and I am able to look outside the window in peace.

As always, my thoughts first drift to Sanjay, wondering how he is faring in his new life. Then I start to wonder about this new curveball that Koko has thrown my way. Do I really have it in me to throw away my carefully constructed life and plunge into something so novel? Soon, though, my worries shift as the car makes its way up the mountain. Every now and then, we have to stop to pay homage to JCB as they do their best to blast the mountains into oblivion and widen the roads. Thinking of the Lorax, I feel my spirit sinking. I know Mussoorie has been reduced to a shadow of its former splendour, defeated by earth-moving equipment but will Landour, Mussoorie's small cantonment town twin with just a church and a school to its name, have suffered the same fate? I had been a regular at Landour through my childhood years. My travel-averse father needed to visit it for work every now and then, and he would bring me along. We would camp in the forest, and I remember waking up one day to see a Himalayan woodpecker pecking away at a tree less than four feet away from my tent.

As the car makes its way up, I start to take heart. So far, everything looks promising, despite the multiple selfie points that Raghunath dutifully slows down at, urging me to get down and grab the moment. I ask for the air conditioning to be switched off and open the windows, and the crisp, pine-scented air rushes in. No wonder it had reminded those homesick Raj-era fellows of their native Wales. Just a thousand feet above Mussoorie, it is a different world, always had been – a magical place of wooden vintage bungalows and unhurried roads that seemed to lead nowhere.

'Madam, *char dukaan* is here,' announces the boy as he expertly leads the car into the lane next to the stately Kellogg Memorial Church. True to its name, a few teashops and cafes greet us, the walls adorned with pictures of famous people who had partaken of tea there. These pictures may have changed over the years, but the shops remain the same, offering the same cups of ginger tea and pancakes they always had. I let out a deep sigh. *Hello, Landour.*

'The *angrez* used to send their *sipahis* here to recover from the heat, no Indians allowed.' The driver now offers some history. 'It was a sanatorium town for TB patients.'

'Yes, that's right,' I say. 'It still is. Look at all this; enough to cure anyone, even the blackest of city lungs.' Raghunath, used to the sky-high *deodars* and the misty trails, is also apparently quite accustomed to the raptures it brings to visitors. *Give me a sign,* I tell the mountains, and they laugh in my face.

I know of a small inn near St. Paul's church, and

following my shaky instructions, Raghunath is able to navigate the car to the place.

'Nothing to see here,' insists Raghunath as he helps me take out my meagre luggage from the boot. 'You can still go to Mussoorie, madam, I will take you. Library Chowk, Gun Hill, George Everest, so many things to see.'

'No, thank you, Raghunath.'

'So should I stay, or should I go?'

'You must go.' I say and then remember the bars of an old song I used to love.

Darling, you got to let me know,
Should I stay or should I go?
If you say that you are mine,
I'll be here 'til the end of time.

Humming under my breath and suddenly feeling very young, I make my way up the stone steps of the inn. There is a garden outside, full of mountain flowers in planters and easy chairs lying around for the guests. I go inside, where a fresh-faced Tibetan girl at the counter is clearly running the place and running it with an iron fist from the looks of it. A small, cross-stitched tapestry hangs behind her, a malnourished-looking sparrow and beneath the bird, some wise words – *If you love something, set it free.* I chat with the girl for a while and ask for a room. She says that the inn has been in her family for three generations so I realize she must be Jigme's kin. We had known Jigme very well back in the day, but the girl looks a little forbidding so I don't probe any further. She assigns me a small room, perfectly adequate for my needs, and leads the way, me following, dragging my suitcase behind. She opens the door to what is to be my quarters and ushers me inside.

'Best view in Landour.' The girl finally smiles as she opens the windows. Breathtaking mountains and rolling mists and soft rainclouds for as far as the eye could see come rushing through the window, taking my breath away. A light drizzle wets my hands that are resting on the windowsill. 'No winter line in these rainy months, though.' I tell her I come from a place that has no winter so I will do with that.

After the nameless manager leaves, I try calling Sanjay again, and being ignored, decide to call Adil to blame him for this.

'It's all your fault,' I tell him. 'We should have never let our poor boy go all that way.'

'But, Gaya, you were the one who devoted paeans to the American education. Sanjay is fine; he is just very busy I feel. Now tell me, how is our favourite explorer doing?'

'Don't try to change the subject. You must call Sanjay and ask him to call. Or return to India if he is in trouble.'

'Isn't it too early for him to be getting into trouble? You need to calm down.' This is, of course, a cardinal sin. Telling an uncalm person to calm down only worries them more, if you catch my drift. After insisting that Adil contemplate his mistakes at length and repent for them, I feel much better.

Raghunath was right, of course; there is not much to do in Landour except to walk and think and walk some more, and that is exactly what I plan to do. And of course, I can worry about Sanjay, that being my primary occupation.

41

More Landour

The next morning comes upon me with a light rain and the promise of drenched *deodars* and a soaked sunrise and no communication from my firstborn. I am almost tempted to stay in bed, order in some tea and read some old, dog-eared novel borrowed from the inn's meagre library. The outdoors knocks at my metaphorical door quite incessantly, though, and I venture out, wearing a thick sweatshirt that Koko had insisted on giving me. There is nobody at the counter, but the inn has some umbrellas that its unprepared guests can borrow and I choose a large yellow one, cheering myself up. Clouds swirl around the hilltops and a light mist is just beginning to clear up. I look down at my shoes, Suggi's shoes to be true, and in just a few days they bear signs of my travels.

Relying on a hazy memory, I slowly make my way towards Lal Tibba, looking around at all the old vintage bungalows with their red, sloping roofs and the new cafés that have sprouted over the years. Some of the names have been hidden away and remained unspoken for so long, they take a while to get used to again, but like old friends, they soon forgive the passage of time.

Pathways go down the mountainside; some of them could take me to Jabar Khet. Not today, though.

Sisters Bazaar, here I come, I mutter under my breath, and looking up at the *deodars* that walk alongside on one side, and the green, mossy mountain wall on the other. I walk through the mist and gulp in the air. A black-faced langur suddenly leaps out of nowhere and swings from a tree, startling me considerably. He settles down calmly on one of the highest branches and observes me with his wise eyes. Catching my breath, I suddenly have a feeling of acute consciousness of the moment and a bizarre thought. *What are you doing here, on this Himalayan mountain? Your home is next to the ocean, in what used to be a tiny Portuguese fishing village. It smells of the sea and fish come evening and has glorious sunsets and incredible cacophony.* I shake my head. Am I really getting homesick for Mumbai? I look down at the valleys from Sisters Bazaar, the mountain peaks hidden today by the *kohra*.

You may not find a Wi-Fi connection, but you will find a connection, declares a sign nailed to a tree. And almost on cue, my phone rings.

'Hello, hello, Sanjay?' I nearly tumble over into the valley in my haste to answer the phone for my one and only child has decided to call me from the land of the free and home of the brave. I can only hear crackling and some strange, broken words. Suddenly, the pine-scented air and the lush trees are not cutting it for me any more. All I want is a crystal-clear signal to hear the boy's voice. His voice crackles a few times, and then, he disconnects. I try calling back, but naturally, the global telecommunication technology has decided that it won't be possible today. I resolve to go back to the inn, which will hopefully have a better signal. I suddenly think of checking my email, wondering if Sanjay has mailed, but of course, it doesn't load.

After a few moments of pacing up and down on the narrow walkway, I take Adil's upsetting advice and calm down. At least Sanjay is safe. Or was he calling me from his kidnapper's phone? He didn't sound very kidnapped, though, not that there is a benchmark for these things. None that I know of, at any rate.

Thus, worrying and feeding my anxiety, I walk on and on till I reached the cafés and Landour's famous bakehouse, the aroma of freshly baked croissants suddenly reminding me that I haven't eaten any breakfast and it is now almost ten. The bakehouse seems uncharacteristically empty, with only a couple of teenage girls performing some sort of a dance step outside for their camera. I had seen Bulbul perform many of these for her sizeable social media followers. A shaggy mountain dog sits close by, observing the girls carefully and giving encouraging yips now and then. I go inside and settle down at a table next to the window and look at the valley plunging below. The only other occupant of the café is a large man, tapping away on a laptop and immersed deeply in what he is doing. Clouds are swirling up, mixing into the mist. The air has taken on a just-washed nip after the rain. How perfectly lovely it all is. *And yet, isn't there a part of you that is already hankering to be jostled around in Hill Road by the hundreds of trendy shoppers looking for easy bargains?* I shake my head like a wet dog to clear my head. What was it that Suggi had once said – that my psyche had been colonized? This time by Mumbai, of all places.

A tired-looking waiter comes to take my order, probably hating this job, hating me, the madam from Mumbai calmly sitting there with her book while his trees are ravaged and his house taken down. He is a lot chattier with the other guest, asking him if he would like a refill of his tea. The man asks for a slice of cake in his booming voice and goes back to work.

I sip my coffee, delicious and creamy. Sanjay's antics had distracted me from the critical matter at hand, Arbour House. What should I do? Was this that famed second chance being flung at me by the powers that run the world? Or am I just being a middle-aged fool running after a silly, youthful dream from so long ago I don't even remember its contours? Since it is the job of a cup of coffee to make things better, after draining the cup, I feel some of the old carpe diem spirit return. I have been away from Mumbai for five days now. Sanjay has flown the nest for five days now. Five days from when Quasi had demanded to know of my plans for the future.

'First time in Landour?' asks the elderly gentleman from across the café. I look his way. He is bearded and much mufflered, a pair of thick-framed spectacles sitting on his nose.

'Not at all. I used to come here as a child. I am returning after a while, though.'

'Very nice, very nice. Come, have chocolate cake

with me.' Something about his manner reminds me of that other person who used to call me to eat this and that, and possibly because of this, I get up from my seat and join him.

He is a writer, he says, and owns one of the bungalows in the glen. This is how he spends his days, writing and walking through the mountain trails. Sometimes he goes to Doon to teach a class or two at a new university that has come up, but largely, he lives a quiet life.

'And you, where do you come from, Gayatri?'

'From Mumbai, sir.' I say automatically.

'Oh, poor you, but not your fault after all,' he booms and laughs. I smile but also feel a bit bad. *It's not that bad. It is also home to Iranian cafés and Portuguese villas and Gothic train stations.* The ageing writer is an easy listener and I find myself warming up to him, telling him about my trip to Dehradun.

'My friend wasn't well,' I say, thinking of the pale Koko, 'and I had to think some things through, so I came up here.'

'Very wise, very wise indeed. Nothing like the mountains to clear up the cobwebs. I myself walk a lot when I get stuck with a character, a plot twist. And you, my dear, have you had any success yet? Arrived at a decision? Solved your problem?'

I look at his kind face and shake my head. *Not yet, not yet.*

'Well, you know what I think? Sometimes, the right choice is neither this one nor that.' He laughs a bit more, and then, collecting his things, he gets up and leaves, leaving me to think about his words. The bakehouse starts getting more people soon, and I, too, decide to leave and make my way to the woods. The rain has now stopped. My footsteps crunch on the trails as I make my way through the trees. *Neither this one nor that.*

I walk all over Landour that day, on the deserted Tehri Road, up to Woodstock School, Landour Community Hospital, back to the bazaar for Landour is a loop. Sometimes, I get so out of breath on a slope that I forget about my worries, about Sanjay and Koko and Arbour House, and focus only on taking in enough air. Walking meditation, I tell myself and carry on.

Finally, exhausted and nowhere near making up my mind, I make my way back to the inn and settle down for the night, wrapping myself in the blankets and quite happy that it is not quite *bukhari* season then, hoping that I will get to speak to my firstborn and only-born the next morning. I fall asleep very quickly, and possibly all that unaccustomed walking brings me the strangest dream that night.

I am walking through a dense, dark litchi orchard. It is dusk and I can hear the sea roaring just outside the orchard. It is very important that I get out of the orchard for my father is waiting for me by the sea, and as happens in dreams, all manners of obstacles lie on my path out of the orchard, the largest in the world by all that it can hold within itself. A house emerges amongst the trees, and Sukh is there in the house. *Sukh, you are alive,* I am crying. *Of course,* he says, and I am filled with the kind of happiness that is only allowed to small children, that threatens to burst out of our hearts and colour the whole world with it. Sukh tells me the way to get out of the trees, and I follow, but it looks like I am too late, because when I finally clear the forest and stand on the shore, my father is already on his way to the lighthouse in a coracle, of all things. Now there is only one way for me to get to him and that is to swim, but in my dream, I don't know how. And yet, and yet, I am stepping into the cold water. In a moment, it is up to my waist, and in another, I am submerged. *This is how it ends,* I think as the water swirls all around me...

I wake up with a lurch, a thin film of sweat covering my chest and face. I have kicked off the blanket at some point during the dream. I had seen a therapist after these dreams had become frequent after Sukh's death. She had taught me how to bring myself back to the present. I take a couple of deep breaths and count my fingers and toes.

Good lord, thank you for making it a dream, I mutter to myself. *I don't want the dead to come back. I don't want to be dragged into their otherworld. I am here and they are wherever they need to be.* I keep mumbling for a few minutes, still half asleep and in the world of the dream. Finally, my breath sounds like my own.

I can't go back to sleep however hard I try. Finally, I give up, and wrapping myself in my dressing gown, I go outside to the small terrace next to the room and sit there on a cold wrought iron chair, watching the sun turn the Himalayas into a thing of splendour and majesty not seen anywhere else in the world. Weak sunlight fills the spaces in the valley, and soon, church bells started ringing in the distance. I get up to get on with my day. I feel a strange sort of calm descend upon me. My mind is made up. There is no more dithering. *Neither this nor that.*

By the time dawn breaks, I am packed and ready to leave. Jigme's granddaughter, whose name I never did ask, is surprised to see me that early in the morning. I ask her if she could call a taxi for me back to Dehradun.

'How was your trip to Landour, ma'am,' she asks by way of filling the awkward silence as I stand by in her reception waiting for the car to pull up.

'This trip was exactly what I needed,' I say and wave goodbye to her.

It is true.

42

FAREWELL

The car makes its way down from Landour in fits and starts. Every now and then, a traffic snarl on the narrow mountain road sets us back by a few minutes. *When will you be back?* asks Landour of me as I prepare to return.

The phone rings. Of all people, Quasi.

'Hello, Aunty. Sanjay asked me to tell you that all is well. He is settling in and will call soon. How is your break going? He said you were up in the mountains somewhere.'

I speak to her briefly, give a polite summary of where I am and what I am doing and then she has to go. After saying goodbye, I click on her profile picture and see that it is one of Sanjay and her in their school uniforms, his arm around her, laughing into the camera, the sun shining on their pretty faces. I put the phone away and look outside the window, mountain daisies on the hillside commiserating with me as I bid goodbye to that part of my life. I sigh but don't feel too bad about this. Sanjay was well on his way, how do they say this, crafting his own life. This time, when the driver asks me if I want to stop at a selfie point, I nod and ask him to take pictures of me, smiling widely as the mountains provide one hell of a backdrop.

It takes me almost three hours to get back to Arbour House. Koko is sitting outside, looking significantly better.

'Ah, the intrepid traveller returns.' He comes out to the porch. 'I can see you can't stay away from my charms for too long.'

'Doesn't look like it.' I laugh and take my single-serve size suitcase out of the car. He helps me inside and looks very happy at my return.

'You were barely gone, and the house felt so deserted,' he says as he puts away the peanut butter and jam bottles that I got for him on the kitchen shelves. 'How was Landour?'

'It is the same, hasn't changed too much. It was pretty much perfect in every way. I walked around a lot, thought about your offer and Sanjay and Adil and well, everything.'

'I can imagine you traipsing up and down those mountains. You were always, how did Suggi put it, moon-eyed around the trees.'

I look at Koko, feel a surge of affection for him. I touch his shoulder, make him turn around to face me and take his hands in mine.

'Koko, listen to me. Thank you for this wonderful break. It was exactly what I needed, *mon ami*. You will never know how much I needed this, standing there that day at the airport, wondering where I was to turn next. It has done me a world of good. Cleared the cobwebs.'

Koko looks at me silently. I think he knows what is coming next.

'Does that mean that you don't want to...?'

'Return to Arbour House? No, Koko. This place has a piece of my heart, but I think I am done being stuck in the past or worrying about the future. I want to go back to Mumbai and take some time to think about things. I have a couple of ideas. The mountains really should think about getting into the therapy space – how they cleared my head!'

'But, Gaya, you said you didn't know what to do with yourself, you said you were at loose ends, that you didn't know where to go next. This is it! Come here.'

'No, Koko. Just because I am done with that part doesn't mean this is right for me. I don't need to return to the past, lovely as it was. I need to make some sort of a new future for myself.'

'Think again, Gaya. I will leave you in peace. Think all you want. Don't rush into things.'

I laugh at that.

'How do you rush into something that you've thought about for thirty years, Koko? No, this is your house, your ancestral home, you must do as you see fit with it. I need to see what the next chapter out there is, the one for me to write. And now, this is my cue for an exit left.'

Koko shakes his head and turns away to look outside the window that overlooks his mother's prized garden. I step closer and hug him from behind, breathing in the familiar fragrance of tobacco and this old town.

'Gayatri Trivedi, is it goodbye once again?'

'It seems so.' He turns around, and I feel his thin arms around me, feel him hold me and let go.

'Gosh, how you make an old man cry.'

'Ah, you are far from old, Koko. You have many hearts to break and many worlds to conquer yet.'

I nearly ask him if he will call the buyer to discuss Arbour House and decide that it isn't my place to do so anymore. I have already played my cards. It is time to return.

'Come on, Koko, get dressed. Captain and Mrs Thapa have called me for dinner, and you are coming along.'

As it turns out, this was a perfect way to round off my hilly sojourn.

The house where Sharmi's memories had tormented my poor Niru has retained its spirit, I think and wince at the pun, despite the many changes that had to be done to make it liveable. Both Captain and Mrs Thapa are waiting outside to meet us and their delight at seeing me is palpable. They knew Koko slightly, but any friend of Gaya's was a friend of theirs, they said and plied him with drink, which he was always willing to accept.

It is a wonderful, memorable evening, full of do-you-remember-when's. We play rummy and drink gin and Captain Thapa regales us with stories of his time at the sea. Mrs Thapa is no more the stately, elegant school principal that I was very much in awe of and has softened and plumped into someone a lot more approachable.

'Gayatri,' says Mrs Thapa as she comes into the room with a tray laden with coffee and rusks and spots me fingering Sharmi's old guitar, hanging on the wall along with Turkish plates and pictures of Niru and her children. 'That whole business with Sharmi, *beta*, what was it all about? I never asked you. Was there really a ghost?'

I sigh and take the cup she is holding out for me.

'I really don't know, ma'am. I suppose ghosts are not much more than memories that refuse to fade out.'

It is late by the time we make our way back to Arbour House. I go to bed, and sleep peacefully, no dreams of being chased and chasing any more. The next thing I know it's morning and it's time to leave. Soon, Somnath ji will be here to pick me up to ferry me to Delhi. I am booked on the evening flight back to Mumbai. I lie in bed, looking up at the high ceiling and its whirring fan. *Who will you become now, Gaya?*

The phone rings just as I am about to get up.

'Ma, it's Sanjay.'

'Hi, Sanjay, all settled in?'

'Sort of. I am sorry I couldn't call earlier.'

'That's all right, love; you must have been tied up. It's no joke to move countries.'

'Ma, is it really you? Or have you been kidnapped, and is this some imposter in your place? Come on, secret password!'

'What rubbish, Sanjay, of course, it is me. Why do you ask?'

'It's not like you to be this nonchalant, Mum, not about me.'

'Oh, love, I am just letting you be, letting you free. How did that song go?'

'Ma, I think someone has snatched your body.'

'Stop it, Sanjay. Are you doing okay?'

'I called Quasi before I could call Dad or you. It was pretty urgent...'

'That too is all right, my darling. Dad and I are not going anywhere.'

'Mum, seriously, what happened? Did you go for some transformative spiritual course you were always threatening us with? You sound so calm somehow.'

I laugh at that, and Sanjay shouts *stranger, danger* a couple of times before hanging up. Then I once again turn to the window and look outside, wondering what the world had to offer me next. This time with hope, not dread.

Shaili and Koko have gone to great lengths to serve me an elaborate breakfast. Shaili has taken leave from her parlour to be with me that morning and packs me lunch for the road despite my protestations. Koko is quiet and gives me the framed picture of Munni Masi, which has been in his bedroom all these years. Forever young, I think as I stare at the picture of my aunt, so full of life that one last time I saw her, and I carefully put it in my bag. The many kindnesses of Koko. I hear a car pull in and know it is Somnath ji once again.

'Too much traffic at the bypass,' he is telling Koko when I step out. 'That's why I got late. Namaste, madam, should I put your luggage in? Are you ready to leave right away?'

You have never been willing to leave but yes, you are ready.

Somnath ji loads the bags as I turn around to hug Shaili and then Koko. All three of us mirror each other's expressions of loss for times gone by. I get into the car. In the distance, dawn is breaking on the Shivaliks. It is the clearest possible day, the sky over the valley a pale, shimmering blue. As the car starts to take me away from Arbour House once again, I turn around to take one last look at it. Koko and Shaili are standing at the gate. Just before I lose sight of them, they raise their hands in farewell. And behind both of them, Arbour House, too, seems to call out its last goodbye to the girl who had loved it like no other.

Epilogue: One Year Later

Dearest Koko,

We have come a long way from the days, mon ami, when I would wait endlessly for your letters and before I had even read yours fully, I would sit down at our old teakwood table, the one with the shaky left leg, to write out lengthy replies to you. I don't remember what I wrote, but I suspect it was similar in spirit to what I write today, what is happening with me, what bothers me, what I dream of.

It's been a fruitful few months, a year almost, since I returned from Arbour House. Adil was quite sure that I had been on some sort of an Ayahuasca trip, that I had found out my purpose on this earth through some, well, 'tantric ritual' he called it, so different did he find me. It was naturally nothing that dramatic; Adil will exaggerate anything, but for the very first time, I did feel I knew the broad direction I wanted to walk in and a wholly unfamiliar confidence in my decisions. The confidence you placed in me, Koko, in that you wanted me to take care of Arbour House, it rubbed off on me, I started trusting my own self more after that.

I joined a small school nearby, and I teach

kindergarteners now. I figured that was one way to remember how lucky I was to have a grown-up boy!

Speaking of whom, he seems to have settled down in his new motherland quite well. Things were rocky with the beautiful Qasima for a while, but I believe a trip to foreign shores, or Maine at any rate, is on the cards. I don't offer too much advice anymore, and I sleep well at night, so there is something to be said about keeping one's counsel unless asked for it. I guess it is better to let go of the umbilical cord before it forms a noose and hangs us. You have been spared this part of life.

I started taking cooking classes. I have treated it as a chore for so long, I thought I might as well delve into the pleasure it seems to bring to so many people. I don't think I will be rushing into hot kitchens in mad delight, apron over my head any time soon, but I am picking up nuances of slow cooking as I go along.

Slow cooking. That's what is happening to me. Simmering on a slow flame. Really brings out the deepest flavours, don't you think?

I have started a balcony garden. All these years, I resisted it, always homesick for that magical Himalayan soil – it was so forgiving, anything would grow out there. How could I replicate those lush gardens and verdant orchards in the six by two feet of space that hangs in the nowhere outside my apartment? Well, I gave it a shot. There are all sorts of callisthenics that one can do with hydroponics, and that really is a sentence I never thought I would use. I will send you pictures once the flowers start blooming; apparently, there is much capacity for joy in this old life still.

I go out in the evenings to the sea, and I think I may be ready to say goodbye to it, too. There is a homestay in Pune that is run by two of Adil's friends. The husband used to be a corporate lawyer, had a massive heart attack at fifty and hung up his boots in the law world. They are quite ready to give up on it now and are looking for successors. Who knows, I might just take them up on the offer. It remains to be seen.

I find myself looking at pictures of puppies online and sometimes get thoughts of bringing one home. As you can see, whatever it is that I am smoking, it brings on momentary lapses into insanity.

Don't tell me what became of Arbour House when you write back, my dearest Koko. Let that secret be another gift you give me.

I hope you smile as you read this and think well of me.

Yours,

Gaya

Acknowledgements

As is customary, it is time now to say my thanks. To the one who never knew I existed but who made me first think of storytelling as a means of travelling to different times and different places – Gaura Pant 'Shivani', you have been my invisible Guru. You mention in your memoirs that the three Brontë sisters held you mesmerized the same way so I know that you would understand.

The people I thank next are the kind souls who helped me not just to bring this book out of wherever it resided within me but did me a much greater service, they bolstered my belief in myself and in my writing. You will never know how much that means to me.

Mahesh, Adi, Raagu for the endless memories and for being mine. My sisters, Manu Didi and Isha for their patience and love. My mother, for taking me to the Delhi Book Fair that one time and letting me buy as many books as my heart desired. It continues to be an enduring memory. My father, who appears in each and every story that I write in some shape or form. This is how I keep you alive, Papa.

Amma and Appa for being the most vociferous supporters of my writing.

Retro, for a thousand reasons, all of which change over the course of a day.

Aneela, the sister of my heart, for being the one that I can call upon for anything, however insurmountable it seems. Kiran, for the faith she showed in me when I had none left. Deepthi, for giving me a chance to make my dream come true.

Anupama Manral and the team at Hachette India for their kindness and encouragement.

Shinie Antony whose warm guidance was beyond invaluable.

The mountain towns of India that call to me every day.

The 80s kids that I have met and befriended in my own life – the ones at the six different schools I attended in the small towns of UP, the girls at Daulat Ram College, the ones I shared a flat with in Mukherjee Nagar, the irrepressible bunch at MICA, friends from work who put up with someone who very clearly didn't belong in the corporate world, the sisterhood of mothers that I found once I had my children, the compassionate readers of my blog and books, you all shaped me and this story in many ways. Thank you.